Of Ravens and Lambs

Chad A. Cain

Publisher's Note:

This is a work of fiction. All names, characters, places, and
events are the work of the author's imagination.

Any resemblance to real persons, places, or events is
coincidental.

Solstice Publishing - www.solsticepublishing.com

Of Ravens and Lambs

By Chad A. Cain

For the countless victims of Jim Crow. May we continue to learn from our mistakes.

Part I

The Good Old Days Weren't Always Good

"Day after day it reappears
Night after night my heartbeat shows the fear
Ghosts appear and fade away"

~Men at Work, "Overkill"

Prologue

November 2, 2015; 2:18 AM; Evansville, Indiana

From the depths of the human heart come both our most unselfish love and our most egregious offenses. With each new day, there is a chance for redemption or condemnation. Mercy or vengeance. Faith or despair. Is forgiveness possible? Can a man like me ever really be saved?

In the still darkness of his bedroom, those were the thoughts that assailed Herman Bowersox as he rolled, cursed, and glared at the invisible ceiling. Such nights as these had plagued him for nearly seventy years.

God, just let me go now. Please. You've already taken Virginia. It's just me here in this cold empty place. I'm used up. I'm tired of everything. Please God, just let me go and see my Virginia again.

Virginia had been his rock, his shelter for almost six decades of marriage. Though he carried on like the true soldier he was, the loss had shattered him. She had given him two children and a lifetime of love and absolution. With her, he felt it was possible to be redeemed for the terrible crimes he had committed. In her absence, he increasingly felt like an inmate on death row. But now he welcomed the noose in spite of the fact that he was quite certain hell was waiting on the other side.

Jesus, I know you died for me. I know that's supposed to cover all my sins. But you know what I've done. I can't take it back. How can I possibly end up in heaven? I'm a monster.

Herman Bowersox jerked the covers and rolled onto his left side, intent on achieving sleep by daybreak. He knew that things always look different in the morning light. But in the darkness, when the ghosts appear and swirl through his mind in an infinite loop, there is no salvation. No rock to cling to. There is only regret, and guilt, and loathing.

But Virginia knows what I've done. There's no hiding anything from her now. She sees everything. She sees me as I really am. How can I ever face her if I do get to heaven? I'd rather go to hell than have to look her in the eyes and see the shame.

No sleep tonight. But it seemed a small penance for his deeds. He would likely live to see the light, though his ninety-three year old body felt like it could simply crumble to dust. His mind, however, was sharp. Sharp enough to fill the nights with anguish, because every memory was vivid. Every face, every scream, every blow was encased in his mind as if in a museum. They were on display each night, as an exhibit for an audience of one.

"I love you, Virginia. I hope you still love me," Herman whispered to the unoccupied right side of the bed. He rolled over again and closed his eyes. The night was just beginning.

Chapter One

March 7, 2016

From the *Evansville Courier-Press*

Herman Robert Bowersox, 94, passed away on Saturday, March 5th, at his home. He left behind a large family that loved him very much.

Herman's life was a testament to his faith in God and love for his family. He served honorably in World War II as a paratrooper, earning a Purple Heart on D-Day. After the war, Herman worked as a millwright at the Whirlpool plant for thirty-five years before retiring and becoming a car salesman. His co-workers always enjoyed his upbeat spirit and great sense of humor.

Herman also was very active in his faith. He served as a deacon at Grace Southern Baptist Church for many years, while also regularly teaching Sunday School to both kids and adults. He never hesitated to tell others about the saving grace of Jesus Christ.

Herman was preceded in death by his wife of sixty years, Virginia. Surviving are his daughters, Ellen Howard and Maggie Bowersox, his grandchildren, Henry and Lacey Bowersox, and one great-grandchild, David.

Services will be held at Grace Southern Baptist Church on Tuesday, March 8th at 4 pm with visitation from 1 to 3 pm at Dexter Funeral Home. Donations to the church will be accepted in lieu of flowers.

***

Henry stared unbelieving at the folded newspaper, reading the summation of a great man's life. At age thirty-five, he felt blessed to have had so many years with his grandfather. With no real father to speak of, Henry had naturally gravitated to his Grandpa Herman and looked to him as his role model and sage.

The loss, though he'd known it was coming for weeks, was crushing. The man loomed heavily over everything Henry had accomplished. The realization was slow and agonizing: no more games of Rook and low rummy, no more sitting on the porch listening to the Cardinals play on humid summer nights, and no more measured advice on any subject Henry cared to ask him about.

He began to well up again, but then regained control and tossed the paper onto the kitchen bar inside Herman's house. Losing Grandma Virginia, the soft-spoken Rosie the Riveter whose Sunday afternoon home-cooked meals were legendary, had been searing. This was worse, harder to accept somehow. The only true source of stability and wisdom in Henry's life was now only a memory.

The sixty-year-old house, whose musty smell repulsed his wife but was so dear to Henry, bustled with activity. His sister was in the kitchen orchestrating a hectic effort at creating a late lunch for the family. His mother sat at the dining room table alongside two of her aunts. She stoically sifted through stacks of black and white photos that had been stored in an old DeJong's department store box, putting aside those she wished to take home.

Carrie, Henry's wife, stood near him and chatted with a nameless cousin. After her husband's relative wandered away, muttering about needing to eat so he could take a pill, Carrie stepped toward Henry and slid an arm around his waist.

"Nice to see so much family here. I haven't seen this many Bowersoxes since our wedding," she said as he surveyed the small parade of relatives roaming around in the living room.

"Yeah. It says a lot about Grandpa. He was everyone's favorite. I still can't believe how long that line was at his viewing."

"You need me for anything? If not, I'm going to try to rescue Lacey in the kitchen."

Henry grinned and began to realize that they had been waiting nearly two hours for the promised quick lunch.

"I'm fine. Just not in the mood to talk to everyone. I may slip down to the basement for a bit." He kissed Carrie softly on the top of her head. She gave him a squeeze and then proceeded toward the kitchen. Henry followed closely behind her before ducking around the corner and down the stairs.

He knew these thirteen steps as well as any place on Earth. In his younger days, he spent his summers sprinting up and down them, alternating between playing army or eight-ball in the basement, to shooting baskets on the patio, to eating hot dogs at the kitchen bar, to playing Rook with Grandma Virginia and Grandpa Herman at the dining room table. He made a slow descent, taking time to relish the echo of each footfall. He ran his fingers along the scuffed wood paneling, and then tapped the low hanging ceiling with both hands as he reached the bottom.

The remnants of a thousand good days still lingered within these walls. The musty odor was much more pronounced down here. No other place in God's creation smelled quite like this. In the stillness of the moment, Henry noted the muffled voices and continual creaking from the well-traveled hardwood floors above him. In this place, Henry could almost feel the presence of his grandfather.

You see this, Henry? It's called a bayonet. A buddy of mine took it off a Jap soldier during the war. I fixed it up with this handle to make it into a knife. I want you to have it. Every boy needs a good knife. You see these notches?

Those are sharper than you can imagine. Be careful and don't ever play around with it. Maybe someday you'll give it to your son.

The power of memories began to overwhelm him, and Henry gripped the wooden railing to steady himself. A voice from the top of the stairs broke his meditation, and he turned to find his seven-year-old son David staring down. David was still wearing the black suit they had bought him for Grandpa's funeral.

"Dad? Mom says it's time to eat. You coming up?"

"Oh, yeah. I'll be there in a minute, buddy. Thanks." Henry looked at his watch and realized he had been entranced at the bottom of the stairs for half an hour. He took one last glance around, enjoying the heavy air for another moment before bounding up the stairs two at a time, as always.

***

Later that evening, with the crowds of family and friends long gone, Henry reveled in the silence of his grandfather's house. He lay in the guest bedroom next to Carrie, knowing that he wouldn't find sleep. It was in this room as a boy that he would lie with his Grandma Virginia and listen to her reading stories from an old Mother Goose storybook. Every room in the old house dripped with memory, deep and bittersweet.

A faint noise from beyond the bedroom door made him sit up on the creaky mattress. He knew instantly what it was: the giant furnace in the basement kicking on. Just another in a thousand familiar sights and sounds that accompanied his every second since setting foot back inside the house.

Fresh hot tears rolled down Henry's cheeks. The sense of loss was complete. The feeling that perhaps his happiest days were now behind him was unbearably strong. Henry sat upright for a long time, allowing the heartbreak to have its way with him.

He felt the soft left hand of his wife caress his right forearm. Henry squeezed her hand in response. In that moment, he envied her very much. Carrie's emotional strength was so much greater than his; he wished he could summon it within himself. Her ability to see the positives of any situation, and to fixate on only those things, had allowed her to weather a number of tough trials. She sat up and began playing with the hair on the back of his head – a habit that he once found annoying, but tonight it was immensely appreciated.

"Not sleeping, baby? I can't say I'm surprised. This house makes so many noises. Honestly, it's a little creepy. Maybe we should have stayed at a hotel after all," she whispered.

"It's not the noises. I'm used to all that. I just can't stop thinking about him. Grandpa was an exceptional person. I've never met...I'll never meet anyone else like him. I'll never be like him. I mean, I know he's in a better place, but Jesus, I miss him!"

"I know. I know how much he meant to you. And it won't be easy for a while, but it will get easier as time goes by. Herman wasn't just a grandfather to you, he was everything. Not many people have their father, grandfather, hero, role model, and best friend rolled into one man, but you had that. I just want you to know that I'm here for you, whatever you need."

"Thanks, honey. I know and I appreciate it. I wonder if David is getting any sleep. I should go check on him." Henry began to exit the bed. Carrie squeezed his arm and he halted with his feet now planted on the tough, worn carpet.

"Maybe that's not a good idea. The floors are so noisy you'll probably wake him. Besides, he knows where we are if he needs us."

Henry agreed and swung his legs back onto the bed. Carrie turned to him and drew a small breath. "Okay,

Carrie. What is it? I can tell something is up. Just lay it out there." In twelve years of marriage they had learned to recognize breathing patterns in each other. She smiled, acknowledging his discernment..

"Well, I'm not sure how to say this. Didn't you...did you ever feel like Herman was unhappy? I don't mean on an odd day or even after your grandma passed away. I mean in general, did he seem like he was trying to act happy but deep down wasn't really feeling it?"

Henry let her words float away in the darkness. The question surprised him, but he knew how perceptive Carrie could be and so considered the idea seriously.

"I'm not sure. Maybe. He did expend a lot of effort trying to make us all laugh, and I know sometimes that can be a sign. Why, did he say something to you?"

"No . . . I just feel like maybe there was more to his life than we realize. I believe he was carrying something, guilt perhaps or maybe shame, for something in his past."

"Huh. I can't say I picked up on that. I do remember him talking a lot about Jesus, about how he had so many sins to wash away and only Jesus could do that. He mentioned it more and more as he got older, in fact. But I just figured that was his faith talking. He always had a strong faith. But lots of people talk about having their sins forgiven."

"True. I heard him say that as well. I just hope that you realize that Herman was a man, just like you. I know you idolized him, but you're every bit the man he was. More, even, in some ways. You shouldn't feel like your life can't ever be as good just because he's gone."

Jeez, she really can read my mind!

"Thanks, honey. I think I know what you're saying. For me, when I think of the definition of a good man, I think of Grandpa. And yeah, I know he wasn't perfect. But he was pretty damn close from my perspective. He's set a pretty high bar for me to live up to." Henry wiped away another stray tear.

Carrie bent to kiss him on the lips, and they curled up together in what would be a futile attempt at sleep. Later, David would find his way into their bed, and his presence eased the atmosphere enough to allow them to nod off for a couple of hours.

***

Henry awoke early and found enough supplies to cobble together a breakfast of bacon, scrambled eggs, and toasted waffles. This was a Monday morning, and normally at this hour he would already be teaching in his first period U.S. History class at Powell High School in Evansville. As he whipped the eggs he thought about today's topic, the D-Day Invasion, and grimaced. Herman Bowersox had taken part in that attack on June 6th, 1944, which was one of the reasons why Henry regarded him as a hero. Herman never said much about his time in the war, other than to remark that "I lost a lot of friends" or "Just be glad you weren't there."

Henry also pondered the brief conversation with Carrie the night before. What was she getting at? Was there something his grandpa had been keeping from him? Or was Carrie just trying to assuage his grief? He felt it best not to bring up the topic again. The day ahead would be long, commencing with the cleaning out of seven decades worth of collected stuff. The goal was to complete the task in just two days, partly because that was all the time Henry had off from school for bereavement leave.

He was looking forward to the task simply for the enjoyment of sparking so many memories. But the job would be monumental for only a few people to handle. Though the Bowersoxes weren't hoarders, they came from the generation of Americans who never threw anything away. Their experiences during the Great Depression taught them the value of saving and recycling. He knew they would find relics such as old glass bottles full of ancient cleansers, and dusty board games not played since his mom was young. Two days might not be enough.

The morning passed in quiet, with garbage bags filling and souvenirs set aside for later claiming. In the basement he procured a treasure that he planned to share with David as soon as possible: an original electric football game from the early 1960s. What a stupid game. Set up the players, turn on the juice, and watch them wander aimlessly across the metallic field. But perfect for a seven-year-old boy.

David seemed to be enjoying his role of holding open bags and occasionally carrying them if they weren't too heavy out to the side breezeway. He had inherited some of his mother's intuition, and was doing his best to be a good boy because he knew Daddy was sad.

Joining Henry in the stale basement were his mother, Maggie, and her boyfriend Rick. Rick had been with her for so long that calling him a boyfriend seemed ridiculous. A good enough guy, Rick was always willing to pitch in, though he was mostly a quiet soul. Maggie, for reasons known only to her, seemed morally opposed to marriage and had never walked the aisle. She stayed with the father of her two children for nearly fifteen years without a license, and when their union ended, she played the "See, told you we shouldn't have been married" card liberally.

Henry's relationship with his mother had been rocky but based on a mutual respect. Though he kept ties with his dad throughout the years, he never found a bond with him the way he had with Herman. After their split, Maggie moved them within walking distance of her parents' house (in part for the free daycare they could provide), which led to Henry spending most of his spare time at his grandparents' house. It became a joke during his high school years for anyone answering the phone at

Henry's house to tell the caller, "I think he's down at his grandpa's," because most likely he was.

As they plowed through a spare bedroom located under the stairs, Henry unearthed another treasure.

"Holy shit! Stratego! You guys remember this game? Grandpa and I used to play this together sometimes..." Henry trailed off, remembering the hours spent on the porch with a game spread out on the card table and a baseball game playing far off on the old portable radio. He picked up the box, which he noted was still in near-mint condition, and carried it out of the room. This would be another in a growing pile of prizes he planned to bring back home.

As they continued to rummage, Henry heard the footsteps and talk of those working on the main floor: Carrie, David, his sister Lacey, and a male friend of hers who no one was quite sure of why he was there. Carrie believed it was a new boyfriend that Lacey wasn't ready to officially announce, while Henry was betting on him as a gay friend. Henry snickered as he heard his wife's voice, knowing she was doing her best to pry the information out of Lacey and her mysterious companion.

The day ran out quickly as they busied themselves with the routine of examining items, putting them in the trash or save piles, and then bagging. While their progress was efficient, Henry recognized it would take a massive effort for them to finish this job in another day. The group worked diligently until pizzas arrived around 7:30. Though he hadn't been sure of how this experience would unfurl, by that evening he was pleased by their success. The conversation was jovial and everyone, even Henry, enjoyed the rare atmosphere of camaraderie. No tears since last night either. That in itself was a minor miracle.

That night, Henry found sleep much more easily after a long day of physical stress. His body would be sore in the morning from all the squatting and lifting, but there would be no time to heal. Tomorrow he planned to tackle his grandfather's favorite—and private--portion of his property: the back garage. It had served as Herman's sanctuary and workshop for decades, and Henry wanted it all to himself.

***

The cool early spring air whipped at Henry's face as he strode toward the cinder block garage that was covered in fading and chipping maroon paint. The garage, or "the shed" as his grandfather called it, was a rectangular building that sat about fifty feet behind the main house. In this structure Herman had spent countless hours tinkering with "projects" that ranged from building birdhouses to attempting the maintenance of the tractor or his pickup truck.

While the rest of the crew stayed inside to continue their decluttering efforts, Henry took on the back garage as a personal mission. It would take an entire day at least to sort through the endless bins of tools and loose parts, but for Henry it was like a time machine. The memories of his grandpa were especially strong out here, where he'd "helped" with so many of Herman's projects. If catharsis was the goal, surely it lay somewhere within the dank walls of his grandpa's most treasured room.

As he unlocked the side door and stepped inside, the voice of Herman filled Henry's mind.

Can you hand me that screwdriver? No, the one with the funny tip on it. That's the one, pal! They call this a Phillips head for some reason or another. Having the right tool is pretty important if you're going to learn to fix things. I'm gonna make sure you're a handy boy, all right. You stick with me and I'll teach you how to work on almost anything!

Henry flipped on the fluorescent lights and opened the overhead door that took up most of the front of the building. Almost nothing had changed out here in decades.

To the left stood a large worktable with shelves above it filled with tools, rags, and a few odd aluminum soda cans Herman collected to turn them in for money at the recycling center. A drill press and a welding machine flanked the table.

All along the back wall, stretching nearly thirty feet, were endless shelves and cubbies reaching from floor to ceiling. The far right portion of the garage was a wasteland of old push lawnmowers, weed trimmers, and random items such as golf bags loaded with ancient real wood clubs, as well as a combination seat and desk that looked like it had been pilfered from a one-room schoolhouse.

Henry could have walked in blindfolded and found nearly any single item from memory. And though the garage had seemed much larger to him as a child, this job would be exhausting and perhaps overwhelming. A lifetime's worth of scraps and parts, collected on the off-chance that Herman might need them for something, sat waiting for his inspection. He panned around the garage, taking mental stock of a few things he needed to start pulling out right away. After another moment, he took a breath and dove into the business of cleaning out this historical warehouse of memories.

Two hours later, around ten in the morning, Henry paused to mark his progress. With the mowers and other large items removed, including several old bed mattresses he found under a tarp, the garage looked as empty as he could remember. The real job, going through each drawer and shelf, was only beginning. He considered taking a break to check on Carrie and the rest, but decided he was enjoying the quiet too much. The grime-covered AM radio from Henry's youth still stood on a tiny shelf above the worktable. He knew it would still be tuned to 860 WSON, known for carrying Cardinals baseball, but he didn't feel like testing it just yet.

Henry decided to start along the top of the back wall, figuring that most of these items would be the least likely to be "keepers." He ascended an old wooden stepladder that was a bit too rickety for comfort, and found a series of green metal lockboxes that he recognized as ones his grandpa has brought back from his Army days. Nearly all the materials Herman used to build their home and shed had come from a torn-down prisoner of war camp. Some of the original nails still sat rusting in a bucket next to the door.

The first few lockboxes were latched but not locked, and inside lay an array of randomness. One box held only a full jar of mercury. Shaking his head in disbelief and chuckling lightly, Henry carefully set the jar aside.

Why was this ever necessary? How the hell am I even going to dispose of this? Thanks, Grandpa!

Other lockboxes produced prizes such as drill bits of various sizes, ball bearings, electrical materials, and even a collection of bumper stickers and buttons that raved, "Nixon: Now More Than Ever!" Henry smiled again, thinking of the possibilities for using these in his history classes. Real 1970s artifacts!

Each new discovery confirmed what he already knew about his grandpa: he was a man of many talents and interests. Just as Henry had hoped, the job of cleaning out the back garage was lifting his spirits and helping him appreciate the man he loved so much.

On the far right of the top shelf lay one final lockbox. Henry moved the ladder over and retrieved it, immediately noticing that this box had a small padlock attached to it. His curiosity piqued, Henry searched in vain for a key. Not wanting to lose time, he decided to put aside the mystery box in favor of making more progress on the rest of the garage.

He managed to clear only one more shelf of items, which included a huge pile of rotting 1950s *Popular Mechanics* issues, before his attention returned to the small green box sitting on the workbench. With no key, Henry would have to be creative. Fortunately, he stood in a place where seemingly any tool one could imagine might be found. A few minutes later, Henry found a small, rusted pair of bolt cutters.

With a twist and a snip, the padlock fell to the ground. Henry took a moment to enjoy this small victory, then tossed the tool aside and unlatched the lockbox with growing anticipation.

I always wondered if Grandpa kept money out here...I'll bet this is cash. Or at least some bonds. Maybe like a thousand shares of Microsoft or something?

The lid flew backward and Henry gazed upon the contents. He was not initially disappointed. The box contained a small withered yellow envelope with a rubber band around it, and a smaller black box that he thought resembled one that would contain a ring or other jewelry. Before proceeding, Henry peeked his head out the front door and looked at the house. He saw no movement, no one to disturb him as he reviewed things that Herman obviously wanted to keep out of sight.

He went for the black box first. Inside he found a gold ring in excellent condition with a large rectangular stone in the center. Henry assumed this was his grandpa's class ring, and pulled it out of the box with only slight interest. He had never known Herman to wear jewelry, especially not a gaudy piece such as this. He bent to read the inscriptions, confident he would find a "Class of 19-something" etched somewhere, along with a basketball or another such school-related image. Instead, he found the ring's markings bizarre and unnerving.

A phrase wrapped around the center stone, one that Henry immediately recognized as Latin: *Corvus Oculum*

Corvi Non Eruit. He had no idea of the meaning, regretting that he had chosen to study German in high school. With his cell phone left inside the house, he had no way of solving the puzzle on the spot. Instead, he wrote the phrase down and continued examining the strange piece.

On the ring's sides, where he had imagined finding diplomas or basketballs, were two distinct images. One appeared to be the head of a crow, looking as dreary and menacing as any he had ever seen. On the other side, a robust flame was pictured. Looking it over carefully, Henry found no other markings or inscriptions. He sat staring at the object for a few minutes, twirling it back and forth, trying to wrap his mind around it. Did this belong to Herman? What could this possibly represent?

One thing was certain: the presence of the ring was making Henry uncomfortable. There was a stark quality to it that he couldn't fully grasp. If his grandpa had ever worn this ring, Henry couldn't possibly imagine why. This wasn't the sort of jewelry that a person would show off. It seemed more like a membership ring, perhaps for Freemasons or some other secretive group. After another moment, he placed the ring back into its original den.

Looks like Grandpa left me some homework. Later...

His mood no longer upbeat, but still curious, Henry grabbed the yellow envelope and carefully slid the rubber band off. He peeled open the envelope and reached in. In his hand was a stack of letters and photos, with the letters still inside their original envelopes. He counted four of these, noting the addressee was someone named James Bryant, Jr. and a return address in a place called Vicarstown, Tennessee. They appeared to be quite old, and he wondered why his grandfather would have kept letters that seemed to belong to someone else.

Setting aside the letters, he turned his attention to the small stack of black-and-white photos. Focusing his gaze on the top photo, Henry let out a wounded cry that must have carried out to the nearby road. Henry flipped to the next photo, and then the next, each one turning his guts and grinding the hideous images deep into his mind. His eyes welling up with fear, anger, and disgust, Henry reflexively threw the entire stack of photos back in the lockbox and slammed it shut.

Breathing heavily and hearing his own heart pounding in his head, Henry tried to walk around the garage to gather himself. But his legs weakened and he was forced to steady himself along the workbench.

Jesus Christ! What is this? That's Grandpa in those pictures. He's young, probably a teenager, but that's definitely him. What the fuck was he thinking? What...what...

After steadying himself for a few minutes, and checking again to see that he would not be disturbed, Henry removed the photos again, determined to study each one more carefully. There was no denying the evil in these images, and, more regretfully, there was no denying that Herman Bowersox was an active participant.

Chapter Two

August 1936; Vicarstown, Tennessee

"Tonight is the night, Junior. Are you ready?" Big Jim Bryant asked his son as they strolled through the wheat fields toward their home at dusk. Like most summer days on the Bryant farm, the work had been long, hot, and difficult. Junior – James Herman Bryant – thought of the evening ahead and broke a tiny smile.

"Yeah, Pops. I've been thinking about it all day! Right now I'm more concerned with supper. I'm starving!"

"No doubt. I'm sure your momma has something good for us. I believe she said there might even be pudding tonight," Big Jim spoke absent-mindedly. His true focus was on the night's events and how it would affect both of his families. Junior was sixteen now, and ready for the initiation. The boy was tall and thin like a teenager, but he knew Junior was much older mentally. He had been grooming his son for this night since nearly the day he was born. Jim was surprised by his own nervousness.

Inside, Ruth Bryant delivered what was expected of a good farm wife at the end of a long day: a hot and fresh meal. She was assisted by their only other child, a blond-haired ten-year-old girl named Hannah. Like her brother, she seemed older than her years, perhaps because Ruth had taken great pains to teach her kids to read, write, and most importantly, think.

The four gathered around their oval-shaped dining room table and silently scooped out portions of meatloaf, cabbage, mashed potatoes, and carrots from serving dishes. A basket of dark bread passed around the table, and then the family began eating.

The unusual mealtime silence was made bearable only by the radio in the living room, which Ruth kept on most of the day as she attended to her various jobs. The faint music of Cole Porter and Irving Berlin wafted over the tense family in soft waves.

***

Junior ate quickly but didn't notice the music. His eyes kept returning to his father's right hand, and the red-stoned golden band that clung to the ring finger. Junior knew it was only a short time now before he would have a ring of his own. That thought sent a jolt of both pride and fear down his spine.

The pudding rumor proved true, and the rare chocolate treat tasted as good as anything Junior had ever put into his mouth. He felt a bit as if he were celebrating before the victory, but no matter. As his father had promised him for so long, this would be a night to celebrate. This would be the first time Junior would attend a meeting of the small, secretive group of men that Jim liked to call "The Ravens." Though he had no idea what they did or talked about at these meetings, Junior had been waiting his whole life to find out.

As soon as he finished his dessert, Jim looked up at Junior with anticipation in his eyes. "Get yourself changed, son. Be ready in ten minutes."

Junior immediately scampered to his room to find clean pants and his Sunday button-up shirt. No one told him to dress up, but he felt it would meet with his father's approval. That benchmark—his father's approval—was the only standard of success in Junior's life. Working hard, studying according to his mother's lessons, obeying his parents, and not pestering his sister too much were the only goals he'd had to meet to this point in his life. Somehow, Junior felt tonight would serve to change that dynamic.

***

Big Jim, as the folks of Vicarstown called him, was a well-known and respected man in their town of nearly five thousand souls. Aside from farming, Jim was a town councilman who regularly went around door-to-door checking on constituents and taking stock of what needed to be on the council's agenda. To call him a proud American would have been an understatement. Junior had heard his father preach about American greatness often.

Son, there's something you need to remember about this country. America started from nothing. Just a bunch of immigrants with nothing but what they could carry. And by God, they worked their asses off and made this place into the strongest nation on Earth. Take our ancestors. Your great-great-grandfather brought his family here from Ireland and helped to settle this town. People back in Ireland could barely feed themselves, much less build anything. Here, we flourished. Built cities and towns, cultivated the lands, dammed the rivers...America is a testament to hard work and determination.

Vicarstown, named for the small Irish village where people like the Bryants originated, was a collection of farmers, shop owners, and furniture makers located roughly fifty miles south of Nashville. Junior had known nothing else in his life. Jim and Ruth seemed content to spend their lives there, and saw no need to travel. Junior had hinted at maybe going to college instead of staying on the farm. That was a conversation he would hold off for at least another year.

It was a bumpy, humid thirty-minute ride in Jim's old pickup to the house of Howard Devine, Vicarstown's sheriff. His home lay on the other side of town from the Bryants, surrounded mainly by woods. Devine was good at his job, handsome, smart, and well-built even though he didn't have the physically demanding job of a farmer. He had also remained conspicuously single, which was strange for a straight man nearing forty.

Devine also held the title of co-founder of The Ravens, though that title was known only to a very small group of men. Jim and Howard, along with two other men, formed the entire group. It was an idea they had hatched over ten years ago after a conversation about the future of America. And though their group remained small (on purpose), they believed their contributions to the local and greater society had been admirable thus far. Tonight, they would make yet another contribution to the cause.

Jim broke the silence as he navigated the gravel roads of rural Tennessee. "Son, I don't want you to be nervous. I don't expect you to know what to do or say. Just simply listen and be attentive, and you'll be fine. Okay?"

"Yeah, Pops. I got it. I won't say a word unless you tell me to."

"Good. Now I know I've said this before, but you need to hear it. What you experience tonight might . . . will disturb you. You may not understand what is happening or why. You may even feel the urge to stop what is happening. But you must understand, we only do what is right for our townspeople. We are the guardians, but in a way that people like the police can never be. You have to promise me again that whatever you see or hear tonight, you'll tell no one. Ever. This isn't like being initiated into the Rotary Club or something, this is for life. I'm bringing you into this because you're becoming a man and because I know you see the world the way I do. After you become accustomed to our ways, I believe you'll embrace them and you will be a great addition to us. I'm so proud of you. You're the first 'second-generation' member to be added to our ranks. It is a great honor for me, and it should be for you too." Jim turned the wheel and guided the truck down Howard Devine's long gravel driveway.

***

The gnawing whine of cicadas grew much louder out here in the wilderness. They covered the trees now that they had emerged from their underground lairs to mate, but fortunately they were not destructive to crops like locusts. Their synchronized mating cries would crescendo to an almost deafening level, then ease for a few moments of relief. The noise gave Divine's dark, secluded cottage an other-worldly feel that made Junior shiver as he exited the pickup.

Two other vehicles were already present, representing the other half of the group's membership. Junior had met them only once, and came away very impressed by both. Bob Barrett was the town's lone for-hire lawyer. He was a master of argument and debate, and it showed in his impressive legal record. He had begun his career in Nashville, but retreated to the rural setting of Vicarstown after a rumored nervous breakdown. Bob had a wife much younger than he and a six-year-old daughter.

The other vehicle belonged to Greg Harrigan, whose life in many ways mirrored that of Big Jim. Greg had a farm, was on the town council, was married, and had two kids, including a fourteen-year-old son. Greg and Jim spent their younger years as rivals, but in the end Jim decided to invite him into the group and make an ally out of an enemy.

Tonight, Junior was proud that he had been chosen over Greg's son to be the first of the next generation of Ravens.

Inside Devine's house, Junior found the small living room had been cleared of all its furniture and the dining room table dragged into the middle of the floor. Four chairs sat at the four sides of the table, with a fifth chair placed just off to the side. Howard, Bob, and Greg all enthusiastically approached Junior, shaking his hand, ruffling his hair, and congratulating him on his big night. Junior was immediately put at ease by this show of friendliness. He had never been treated as an equal by adult men, and he was finally beginning to feel like one. He couldn't wait to wear the golden ring that each of these four men bore on their right hands.

After another few moments of idle talk, Howard looked at his silver pocket watch. He moved toward the table and cleared his throat.

"Gentlemen, please. Let's go ahead and have a seat. We have some things to discuss . . . and some new business to attend to!" Howard grinned at Junior as he said this.

"Thanks, Howard. That's why you're the sheriff. Keep us on task," Bob joked.

Jim gestured for his son to take the seat set off from the rest. As soon as they were all seated, the jovial mood in the room changed. No one moved or spoke for nearly thirty seconds. Junior shifted in his chair, suddenly uncomfortable. The cicadas outside weren't helping with their eerie droning. Finally it was Big Jim who broke the silence, speaking like a judge preparing to deliver a sentence.

"The Order of the Ravens will once again commence. I see that all are present. Are you gentlemen prepared to carry out the work that God has set before us tonight?"

"Yes, I am ready." The statement was repeated by all three men. Junior stayed silent.

"As you know, tonight is a special one for me. Tonight my son, James Herman Bryant, will take his first step toward adulthood and toward becoming a full member of this order. Are you gentlemen prepared to allow my son to participate in the activities of this order tonight?"

"Yes, I accept him." Again, each man repeated the same phrase. Junior was strangely relieved by this statement of acceptance. Jim then turned to his son.

"James, are you prepared to join this order? To participate in its mission and carry out God's will for our town and nation? And to do these things in the absolute secrecy that is required among these, your brothers?"

Junior waited until he knew his father was finished, and then rose to his feet. Though he had envisioned this moment for many years, he now felt a pang of regret as he found it difficult to speak. "Yes, I am ready and I accept the responsibility."

***

The group moved slowly, purposefully out the back door and toward a weathered barn that was bigger than the house. Junior struggled to keep his cool, unsure of how he should be reacting. Inside the barn, several lanterns provided a welcome haven from the darkness and the crazed calls of the cicada hordes. Big Jim was the last to enter, and he slid the door shut behind them. The initiation was about to begin.

An old John Deere tractor and an even older Indian flathead motorcycle were the most prominent items in the space. Howard walked toward the center of the structure and bent to move a couple of bales of hay on the floor. He then found a handle and lifted, exposing the secret space underneath the barn: a cellar. Howard disappeared down the steps as a distant light emanated from the underground room. They heard the jangling of shackles, the rustling of feet, and finally the muffled sounds of a male voice.

Junior's eyes widened as a different man—a black man—ascended the steps toward him and the group. He looked desperate and scared, to say nothing of being filthy and ragged. The man looked young, perhaps in his mid-twenties, and his smell hit Junior so hard that he took an inadvertent half-step backward.

His mouth was stuffed with a rag, and a rope was tied to keep it in place. His hands were handcuffed behind him, and his face bore the marks of a recent beating. Dried blood caked his forehead, and his short hair was laced with bits of straw and dirt. This man had been down in that cellar, that dungeon, for some time. Perhaps a week or more. Junior observed these features without comprehension.

The prisoner stood looking at the group with a look of disbelief, but also some relief. Perhaps a part of him had been convinced he would die in that hole. Junior glanced at his father and saw him looking at him, likely trying to gauge his reaction. Junior tried to stay stone-faced.

"Shall we commence, gentlemen?" Jim asked casually. The group exited the barn, led by Howard and his weakened captive. The prisoner was trying to speak, but nothing could be discerned with the rag in his mouth. His denim pants were soiled, and he struggled to keep pace as they marched toward the woods. Junior walked in a haze of confusion, still processing the image of this poor creature being led out of an underground cell.

A single lantern held by Greg lit the path as they proceeded deeper into the forest behind Sheriff Devine's home. A sense of dread crept into Junior. There could only be one outcome from this excursion. The silent march continued for another ten minutes until they reached a small clearing with a steel post jutting out of the ground directly in the center.

Howard and Bob immediately went to work chaining the prisoner to the steel post. Greg kept the lantern hoisted as they completed the task. Junior stood motionless, hoping no one would ask him anything because he wouldn't be able to respond.

"He okay?" Howard asked Jim, nodding toward the swaying figure of Junior. Jim looked his son over, then approached him.

"Relax, son. All of this will be explained, and soon. Just take it all in. You need to experience this in all its fullness. You will be changed after tonight, but it will be for the better. I promise," Jim said, using his most reassuring tone. Junior simply nodded, never taking his eyes off the prisoner who was now tethered to the post.

The five men stood a few feet in front of the prisoner as if in judgment. Tears streamed down his face as he struggled against the chains. He was still attempting to speak. Finally, Howard lifted his right hand and the prisoner halted all movement and speech.

"Harlon Campbell...you have violated a law that runs far beyond the jurisdiction of our town, county, or even this great state. You have defied nature, God's own law, and that is something that must not be allowed to continue. You have impregnated a white woman, and in doing so you have contributed to the mongrelization of our society and the general decay that such acts lead to. Miscegenation is illegal . . . and unforgivable.

"I'm afraid there is nothing you can say or do, you must now accept your fate and know that we do this not for ourselves, but for all Americans. It is our mission to preserve the purity of nature, and the greatness of the society in which we live. By your actions, you have shown yourself to be in opposition to this mission. You must now pay the cost. Please bear in mind, we take no pleasure in this action. We are men in service of something greater than ourselves. We are simply following our consciences, something for which no man can be judged." Howard delivered these words calmly, self-assuredly.

Harlon stayed still for this monologue, then began struggling in futility against the heavy chains. Greg and Bob walked a few feet away to a pile of chopped wood that Junior hadn't noticed until that moment. As they began stacking the wood around Harlon's feet, Junior's brain erupted with comprehending horror.

This is an execution. A lynching. They're going to burn this poor man alive! Jesus. So this is what The Ravens do? This is what my father does? Is this really necessary? Are they really trying to help society? Is this . . .

Confusion coursed through Junior's body, which was becoming numb. At one point, Harlon's eyes locked with his and they stared into each other's soul. Junior tried desperately to justify the act to himself, to his God. *There must be a reason. This man must be a known criminal. A killer maybe, or rapist? There must be a reason . . .*

The muffled words became screams as the wood piled around him. There would be no last words. No time given for talking them out of this terrible deed. There were no insults or catcalls from the captors. Not even a smile. These men would have looked the same if they were preparing the grill for a barbeque. This was business.

Big Jim stepped forward, having produced a rag and a book of matches. "You die so that our society may live and thrive. You die because darkness cannot consort with the light. You die so that our purity, and the purity of future generations, can be maintained. This group stands united. Corvus Oculum Corvi Non Eruit."

The other three Ravens repeated the phrase in unison. Greg approached Harlon and began showering the wood with lighter fluid. He stepped back, and Jim took one last look into the eyes of the condemned. Then, in one quick movement, Jim struck a match, lit the rag, and flung it on the pyre.

The flames jumped to life in an instant, sending the prisoner into convulsions of shrieks and moans. His body lit up the forest around them, creating a burst of yellow heat that nearly singed Junior's face. His father's hand resting in the middle of his back both steadied him and coerced him to keep facing the horror of human torment. Junior struggled to breathe, and he put all his energy into not collapsing or breaking down in tears. Big Jim would be most disappointed at that reaction. He had to stay strong, even if he was terrified and confused.

Fortunately for Junior, the event did not take long. Harlon's maniacal dance in the flames was at an end. His body, still chained, lay limp as the clothes and flesh melted off of him.

Ashes to ashes. I guess I know what that means now, Junior thought. He continued to stare at the corpse long after Harlon's soul had escaped to what he hoped was heaven. Perhaps it was the methodical nature of the act, or the explanations given by men he trusted; but a part of him began to see the good in what they had just done. The man's face was burned into his mind, but the sympathy he had initially felt for Harlon was already dissipating.

As the flames died down, Junior took stock of Harlon's charred skeleton with both disgust and a small sense of something else. Accomplishment? Satisfaction? He wasn't sure.

Before he could explore the thought further, Greg broke the solemnity with a jovial request. "Gents, you know the drill. Take your places, please! Junior, you get in there too. This will be something you'll want to remember!" As if seeing a man eviscerated in flames would somehow slip from Junior's memory.

The men slowly gathered around the smoking remains, looking rather disdainful of this particular part of the ritual. Greg picked up his camera, complete with a large flashbulb, and snapped one blinding shot of the men as they posed with their newest victim.

"Got it. Now we can move on to disposal. Bob, I believe you have honors tonight." Greg's casual manner was shocking to Junior, but the others seemed used to it. They commenced with the removal of all evidence of their deed without another word. Jim approached his son.

"Son, I'm sure you have questions. I want you to know how proud of you I am. This is not easy, I'm aware of that. You held up like a champion! We can talk all you want later. I have to help with the cleanup. Why don't you have a seat, then we'll get going home."

Junior nodded and felt relieved to sit down in the tall grass of the clearing. The last twenty minutes had rocked his life to its foundation. There would be no sleep that night, and not much in the nights to follow. His initiation had been a success, though he wasn't sure he agreed with that assessment. One question kept pestering him, one that would persist for the rest of his life: *Was this murder? Or, was this a necessary death in the service of society?*

He wasn't sure if he wanted to know the answer.

Chapter Three

Sunday, March 13, 2016; 2:38 AM

Halfway through another sleepless night, Henry huffed as he threw his legs out of bed and walked out of their bedroom. Rubbing his face with no purpose, he trudged to the refrigerator and grabbed a bottle of water. He had hoped that being in his own home and into the familiar routine of teaching would help him find his way back. Back to any moment before he opened up Herman's lockbox and saw the horrifying evidence of crimes committed long ago. Back to when he saw his grandfather as a hero instead of a murderer. It wasn't going to happen tonight.

The images were emblazoned in his mind; permanently catalogued and protected against the ravages of time and experience. Henry would see those pictures again and again, every day, until his death.

There had been five such photos, oddly placed among other more pedestrian pictures of people whom Henry assumed were family. The five photos he was trying and failing to comprehend were all very similar. A group of men, some holding shotguns or rifles, others simply with hands on hips or at their sides, posing on either side of a smoldering corpse. Though the photos were old and yellowing, enough detail emerged to make Henry a little nauseous each time he pictured them.

In all five photos, the corpses were burned beyond recognition. They were held upright by a steel post to which hands and feet were bound behind them. Burned wood and ash on the ground surrounded each victim.

In each photo, the posing men were the same, but their clothing and positioning were slightly different. Although they held guns, Henry had become certain after some thought that the victims weren't shot but had been burned alive. There was something about the way their bodies hung, the way their melted faces contorted. These men had struggled against the flames and died in a fit of despair and fire that Henry could not imagine.

And in every photo, staring at the camera with no emotion, was the unmistakable face of a young Herman Bowersox. Henry thought he must have been a teenager when this took place, while the rest of the men looked to be at least around forty years old.

A second look had revealed a single set of initials and a date on the back of each snapshot. The sets of initials were all different, and none matched those of his grandfather. Each of the dates was also unique, ranging from 1936 to 1941. In the latest dated photo, Henry thought he could see a faint smile on the face of young Herman.

Henry stood in front of the open refrigerator, letting its light fill an otherwise dark kitchen, asking himself the same questions he'd been grappling with for nearly a week.

How could Grandpa be involved in something like that? Who were those other men in the pictures? Why were these people murdered? Why didn't he ever tell me?

He walked into the living room and sat silently in his recliner, lost in thought and desperate to put the pieces together. He had been close to telling Carrie after he first opened the lockbox, but found himself unable to speak of it. Though he was disgusted by what he had found, Henry still felt the urge to protect his grandfather's legacy. At least, that is, until he could figure out what exactly happened before those photos were taken and what part Herman played.

There were a couple of clues, enough to make Henry believe he could indeed put the puzzle together. He hadn't given it much thought while Herman was alive, but Henry was beginning to realize he knew almost nothing about his grandfather's life prior to his service in World War II. If the subject ever came up, Herman would simply say, "That was a long time ago" or, "They all lived a long way from here and they're all gone now."

No pictures of his parents, siblings, or grandparents were found in their extensive clean-out of Herman's house. No journals or diaries, no home movies, and no old letters had been found either. Except in Herman's secret lockbox in the back garage.

Included with the five gruesome photos was a picture of a young girl, perhaps ten years old, who looked like she could have been Herman's sister. Another photo depicted an older matronly looking woman (his mother perhaps?) standing on the front porch of a farmhouse. And there were those old letters banded together, with the return address listed as a place called Vicarstown, Tennessee. They had all been written by a Ruth Bryant and sent to James Bryant, Jr. while he was in Europe fighting the Nazis.

Henry flipped on a lamp next to the recliner and reached deep into the recesses of the chair. His hand emerged with one of those letters, kept hidden until he could wrap his mind around all he had discovered in that garage. The letter and envelope were in remarkable condition, probably having not seen the light of day in decades. He carefully unfolded it and read it slowly for perhaps the fifteenth time in a week.

August 9th, 1944
Dear Junior,
I was so relieved to get your last letter! When we heard about the invasion into France in June we were so worried because I know a lot of our boys didn't make it. Two weeks ago Mrs. O'Neill got a letter about her Charlie from the Army. I pray every day that I don't get one of those letters about you.
You have made us and the whole town so proud! Your dad can't stop talking about what it will be like when

you get back home. He misses you dearly as we all do. The farm is doing well and Hannah is getting ready to start her senior year of high school. Can you believe that? She sends her love.

Mary came by and had dinner with us again last night. I know you've been keeping in touch. She is such a sweet girl and I couldn't be happier that you two are planning to marry as soon as you get home from this terrible war. Everyone around here is hopeful that Hitler will soon surrender. I pray that he will and that you'll come back safe to us.

Please keep sending letters when you can. You're a brave and good man, and I'm proud to say I'm your mother.

With love and kisses,
Momma

From the envelope, Henry deduced that "momma" was Ruth Bryant. Rocking in his recliner and still holding the letter, Henry tossed all of this new information around in his mind. He wondered about this Junior. Who was he, and how did Herman know him? Or, could it be that Herman somehow was James Bryant, Jr.? He was missing a piece of the puzzle, but he had an idea of how that piece could be found.

The more he pondered these mysteries, the deeper the need to find answers grew. He owed it to Herman, secrets and all, to discover who he was and why he was in those photos.

Staring at the letter, Henry didn't notice his wife entering the living room.

"What's that?" Carrie asked as she settled on their micro-fiber, dark green love seat.

Henry looked up but was not startled. He made no effort to hide the letter.

"It's an old war letter written to someone named Bryant. I found several of these out in the garage. It's just so strange. His mom's name was Ruth Bryant. I've never heard about her, or anyone in that family from back then.

"Something doesn't make sense here. Maybe grandpa took these off an army buddy who died. Or, I don't know, maybe grandpa was a Bryant. I mean, I just don't get it. Did he change his name? She calls him 'Junior' in the letter, but I don't know what his dad's name was. In fact, I don't know anything about him as a young man. It's like he had this whole other life he didn't want anyone to know about. And..." He stopped before mentioning anything about the photos. He wanted no one, even his own family, to know of their existence.

"Yes," Carrie said, "the idea of him changing his name is puzzling, but that could be because something bad or unhappy happened to him back then. And that's why he never liked to talk about his early life. I know you've been struggling this week. You haven't been eating or sleeping much. You've been pretty quiet. What are you thinking?"

"Vicarstown, Tennessee. That's what I'm thinking. I want to go to this place and see what I can find. There must be records, at a library or a town hall or something. I really feel like I need to do this. If these did belong to one of his friends, I'm sure his family would appreciate having them back. And if my hunch is right, and grandpa really was a Bryant, then I have even more questions that need to be answered. Next week is spring break...I'm going down there then. In fact, I'm leaving Friday as soon as school ends. Do you want to come with me?"

Carrie hesitated, then responded. "Maybe it's best if you go alone. I don't want to be in the way, plus we'd have David with us. You go and do what you need to do to find some closure."

"Are you sure you're okay with that? I might be gone for a few days, I don't know. I feel like there's a lot here that I'm not getting. The Internet might help, but I doubt I'll find much. I need some answers, Carrie. I might lose my mind if I don't figure all this out."

"Yes, it's fine. Believe me. I want you to get back to being you, and if you need to make this trip to do that, then it's totally worth it. You know I love you, and I know how much he meant to you. I'd be making the same trip if he were my grandpa."

***

The office of Dr. Jeffrey Beck, professor of American History at the University of Southern Indiana, looked like the aftermath of a Civil War re-enactment. The walls were covered with battle flags, paintings, and memorabilia from the War Between the States. Curiously, Beck's main area of study was not the Civil War, but the racial consequences of the conflict. His published works concerned subjects such as southern lynchings and vigilante activity. It was for this reason that Henry sought out his former teacher and mentor.

When Henry arrived at the office door, Dr. Beck rose from his desk. Approaching sixty years old, Beck exhibited just enough gray in his hair to appear distinguished. His burgundy corduroy jacket, complete with elbow patches, and narrow spectacles resting on his head, gave him the stereotypical professorial appearance.

"Henry! Get in here! What's it been? Ten years? So glad you called. Can I get you some tea . . . or something stronger?" Beck winked at him.

Henry knew there would be a bottle of Johnnie Walker Blue in his bottom right desk drawer, just as there had been when he was a student years ago.

"Oh, no thanks, Doc. Great to see you, too. Thanks for working me in on short notice."

"Hey, no problem. You know you were one of my favorites. I'm always glad to see former students. I honestly don't have contact with many of them."

"Well, I had good intentions of keeping in touch with you. You know how things go. Get married, kids, career . . . time gets away from you."

Beck smiled. "Yes, I know what you mean. Aside from the wife and kids thing that is! I'm still holding out for Jennifer Aniston."

"Good luck with that!"

Henry took a seat and opened a small black briefcase. He sat staring into it, searching for the right words. Dr. Beck's smile faded into a look of puzzlement.

"What is it, Henry?"

"Doc, I've found something. Something that has rocked me to my core. I'm still coming to grips with it, and I felt like I needed an expert opinion."

"Yes, you sounded pretty concerned about it on the phone. You said this involves your grandfather?"

"Right. Herman Bowersox."

"Isn't he the one you wrote about for your term paper in my World Wars class? If I recall, he was a paratrooper who participated in D-Day as well as The Bulge. Correct? Sounds like he was a true American hero."

"Yeah, that's what I always thought of him as well. Until I saw these." Henry laid the envelope on the desk in front of Beck. The professor took a moment to study Henry's face, then proceeded to open the envelope.

"Jesus!" Beck recoiled after seeing the first photo. He carefully viewed each one, unable to hide his disgust. "Where did these come from?"

"My Grandpa Herman's garage. We were cleaning out his house after he passed away, and these were hidden in a lockbox. You see the youngest one in the picture? That's him. That's my grandpa."

"What do you know about this?"

"That's where I was hoping you could help me. You'll notice the varying dates and initials on the back of each one. I have a hunch each set of initials could be the victim's. Just a feeling, really. Aside from that, I've got nothing. He never mentioned anything about this to me or anyone else that I know of. I mean, I was completely stunned when I found these, as you can imagine."

"Of course, as I would be as well. So, what do you want to know? Are you thinking these could be racially motivated killings?"

"I guess, but I'm not sure. I've been thinking that these look a lot like some lynching photos I've seen in history books. I know that sort of thing was common in that time, and I've learned this probably took place in Tennessee. A place called Vicarstown."

Beck continued to study the photos as he replied. "Yes, I would say it's very likely we're looking at the aftermath of a lynching in each photo. They appear to be separate events, which means these men killed five people at least. And all in the same fashion."

"What can you tell me about lynching? I teach American History to freshmen, but we're always so rushed with the curriculum we don't really talk much about it. Honestly, I'm pretty ignorant on the subject. I know that's bad for a teacher to admit."

"Well, Henry, these types of photos aren't as uncommon as you might think. I've seen hundreds of them in my research, many of them quite similar to what you've brought me. In fact, there was a time, around the end of the 1800s, when these pictures were actually put on postcards and printed in newspapers. It got so prevalent that the U.S. Post Office had to ban them from circulation.

"Lynching a black man in the south in the decades after Reconstruction ended was as common in some areas as a town hall meeting. Many of these killings were public events, with parents bringing a picnic lunch and their children to watch it happen. These public lynchings were mostly hangings, but there were plenty of instances of what you've shown me here. People being burned at the stake, or even beaten to death and dragged through the streets. Pretty macabre stuff."

"Hard to believe that went on in America."

"It should also be noted that these kinds of activities weren't confined strictly to the southern states. Lynchings happened all over the country. One example is the Duluth Lynching of 1920," Beck stated, still going through Henry's photos.

"Duluth, Minnesota? Really?"

"Oh, yes. It was a group of African-American circus workers. They were accused of holding a couple at gunpoint and beating and raping the young lady. Her doctor found no evidence of the alleged abuses when he examined her, but that didn't stop a crowd of over a thousand people from massing at the jail where the men were held. They stormed in, with little resistance from the police I might add, and put the men through a quick sham trial. Naturally, they were found guilty and marched down the street where they were hanged gleefully by the mob. I tell you, people get worked up today about seeing some protestors at an Occupy Wall Street or Black Lives Matter rally. But this country's history is rife with mob rule. Our history is a lot uglier than most people realize."

Henry sat looking at the photos on Beck's desk but not really seeing them. He had heard much of this before while a student in Beck's classes. The racial history of the United States, much like other tragedies, sickened and fascinated him simultaneously.

Beck continued, "It's important to know that in most cases, it wasn't just the KKK or some small group involved, it was the whole community. Those groups did kill people, but they were allowed to flourish because of the culture, not in spite of it."

Henry shook his head. "I just can't believe that my grandpa would be a part of this. I mean, look at those guys. They're posing like they just caught a bass or something.

That's sick. Every time I think about it I just want to vomit. How could he do it?"

"I can only imagine what you're feeling. We all want to idolize someone we love, think of them as better than we are. Someone to look up to. But they're just humans, and we all have demons. And even those of us who haven't indulged in actions like this have committed them in our minds countless times. How often have you wanted to shoot someone who cut you off in traffic? Or beat someone else's kid for misbehaving? We all have those urges. It's just that most people are better at reining them in."

Both men sat silent for a moment before Beck produced the Johnnie Walker bottle along with two glasses. Without a word, he poured out a double into both and pushed one toward Henry.

"Please . . . I think we could both use one," Beck said. Henry obliged, and they sipped the high-end Scotch in silence. Henry tried to put the events in perspective.

What if he were pressured into it? What if he didn't have a choice? He was young . . . maybe his dad made him take part. Maybe I shouldn't place final judgment on Grandpa until I know more.

Henry broke the silence. "So, do you think these were public killings? It's hard to tell where they are, but it's only those few men in each picture."

"Most of the public lynching photos I've seen show the crowd quite clearly. The photographer would include the crowd in the picture to show how big of an event it was. These pictures look private. These men . . . they're not wearing sheets and hoods, so they're not too concerned about being identified. Then again, these photos could be some sort of trophy. This group, whoever they were, obviously did this often. I wouldn't doubt they were involved in more killings that we don't know about. Just a guess, but I'd say these guys did it the same way every time. Like a ritual. And I'd bet, even though they're not wearing hoods, they had some sort of identifying symbol to show their membership in the group."

Henry looked up abruptly and reached into his front pocket to produce the gold ring. Beck's eyes widened as he took the ring and began studying it.

"You were right, Doc. I found this ring with the photos. If what you say is true, then all of those guys in the picture would have a ring like this."

"What is this Latin phrase? I assume you've looked it up already."

Henry pulled a folded paper from his other front pocket and began reading. "Corvus Oculum Corvi Non Eruit. It loosely translates to 'A raven will not pull out the eye of another raven.' From what I can gather, it's a phrase used to describe a group of people who are extremely loyal to each other and who would never forsake or betray another within the group."

"Huh. Makes sense. So these men, if we're to continue with our theory, consider themselves to be some kind of a brotherhood or fraternity. Most likely sworn to secrecy for life. And . . ." Beck cut himself off and began looking around his office. He rifled through the desk's drawers, finally finding a small magnifying glass in the back of the middle drawer.

Beck examined one of the photos again, looking for one small detail. "There . . . right there. Look at the guy on the far left, his right hand. The hand holding up the rifle . . . he's got that same ring on!" Henry took the magnifying glass and saw for himself. In every photo, they discovered the ring on the right hand of each of the perpetrators.

"You're right. My God, why didn't I think to look for that before? Okay, so what does this all mean?"

Dr. Beck leaned back in his chair and rubbed his chin. "It means your grandfather was involved with a group of very dangerous men. They obviously had a common goal, racially motivated, and were extremely loyal to both the cause and each other. Other than that, there's not much left to say."

"I need more. I need to know why Grandpa was a part of this, and who these other guys were. He may have been forced into it for all we know. Look how much younger he was than the others!"

"I'm afraid I've done as much as I can, Henry. What's your next move?"

"I'm going down there. There must be records, newspapers, something. I'm going to find out who all of those men were. And I'm going to find out who my grandfather really was." Henry stood and gathered the photos and the ring.

Dr. Beck extended his hand. "Henry, it was wonderful seeing you again, even under the circumstances. If you have any other questions you think I can help with, you know the number."

Henry shook his hand and departed, filled with new energy and more determined than ever to find the truth about Herman Bowersox.

Chapter Four

March, 1938; Vicarstown, Tennessee

Big Jim Bryant reached into his gun cabinet and found his favorite weapon: the 1895 Model .405 Winchester rifle. He had purchased the gun because of its fierce reputation, and because he'd heard that Teddy Roosevelt had used it during his African safaris. Tonight he and Junior would be engaging in a kind of safari of their own.

Jim's decision to bring his son into their secret brotherhood--The Ravens--had been an apparent success. Junior had accompanied the group on their last two "outings," and tonight he would be more than just an observer. Jim knew the only way his son would ever truly become one of them was by spilling impure blood. Junior's final trial was about to begin.

Jim went out the front door of their small farmhouse and found Junior already waiting at the truck. He smiled when he saw how anxious his son was to begin the night's activities. Jim approached Junior and held out the rifle to him.

"Son, this is my .405. I want you to keep it with you tonight. Careful you don't nick it up!"

"Sure, thanks! You aren't bringing a gun for yourself?"

"Nah. I'm sure we'll be fine. That's a fine gun, and I know you know how to use it."

***

Junior Bryant had spent the better part of two years grappling with his new role as a member of The Ravens. They met monthly, but most of the time it was just to play poker and smoke cigars. His father was adamant about his presence for each meeting, even when it seemed they were simply passing the time. He felt it was important for Junior to feel that he belonged.

It was their "special" meetings, their once-a-year ritual of racial purity in which a man had to die by fire, which kept Junior from feeling good about his acceptance. He agreed in general with his father's arguments about keeping the races separate. He felt strongly that blacks and whites were clearly different and unequal, and therefore should never intermarry and especially never bond sexually. But killing them . . .

What about Thou Shalt Not Kill? What about Jesus' command to love our neighbor? This can't be what God wants us to do. Can it?

The two murders that Junior had witnessed were permanently at the forefront of his mind. He saw those men's faces and heard their cries in the fields, in the house, and in his dreams. Then again, those men were guilty of raping white women. One of the women had become pregnant as a result of the crime. A mixed child would almost certainly grow up to become a criminal or a burden on society in general. The Ravens, he constantly told himself, were doing a service for society that few were willing to do. It was dirty work, but in the end it was justice.

If that's the case, why don't I sleep? Why can't I look myself in the mirror? Why do I hate being in the same room with, much less talking to, my own father? This isn't right, and it isn't going to end well. You know that, don't you?

Junior let the confusion in his mind run wild until they reached their destination. It was the same location they used for all their meetings because it was the furthest from civilization: Sheriff Howard Divine's house. The trip here had been a silent one, with both men knowing what was to take place. As he exited the pickup, Junior forced himself to clear his mind and focus on the task ahead.

Tonight you are a soldier. Act like a soldier and do your duty. Don't worry about the consequences...be a man. Be a Raven.

The night commenced just as they had in each of the past two years. Pleasantries were exchanged between Howard, Big Jim, Junior, Greg Harrigan, and Bob Barrett. After a few minutes of talk, the five men carried their guns and lanterns outside and toward the back barn. Once again, Howard moved a few bales of hay and revealed the secret door in the floor.

He descended the steps as the others watched. Junior began to feel something that both scared and excited him: anticipation. He was impatient to see the victim. Hungry to see his face. The heart of a true murderer was beginning to grow inside him.

It occurred to Junior that he had a full erection, but he didn't want sex. This was a different kind of lust. One that could only be satisfied by pain and blood. His grip on the Winchester tightened as the victim came up the steps and into view. Junior nearly gasped as he realized that he knew this one, and he was a teenager. Probably even younger than Junior. With his head down in resignation, the kid didn't notice Junior's presence.

Wearing only a filthy pair of denim overalls, the teenage prisoner bore all of the signs of being a farmhand. His muscular physique made him seem much older, until one looked at his face. It was the face of a child, of an innocent. His hands were bound behind him with rope as Howard prodded the prisoner forward with his shotgun.

The prisoner moved in silence as they slowly moved toward the path that would lead to his ultimate demise. Junior couldn't take his eyes off the prisoner. He knew why they had captured him.

His name was Darryl, at least that's what the other farmhands called him. Junior had worked with him a time or two in the fields around their home. Darryl seemed, from their limited interactions, to be a hard-working and respectful kid. But recently there had been rumors.

Darryl had allegedly been caught with the daughter of another local farmer, Samuel Wagner. Though the details in these types of stories always changed and grew more salacious, Junior assumed that something serious must have occurred. He didn't know how Howard came to possess these men, and he didn't want to. But he knew that Howard and the rest of their group would never proceed with their ritual if they weren't sure it was necessary. Whether it was rape or just plain old sex, Darryl knew the unwritten code of the south and he willingly broke it. More than that, he had contributed to the further mixing of the races, which Big Jim always said was the root cause of most of our country's problems.

A shotgun blast from a few feet ahead ripped Junior from his thoughts. Walking at the back of their procession, Junior didn't see what happened. Suddenly the men were shouting and running ahead. His feet feeling as if they were encased in concrete, Junior slowly broke into a sprint. Light bounced crazily back and forth from the lanterns as the five ran forward into the blackness of the forest.

"What the hell happened, Howard?" Jim yelled.

"The fuckin' nigger cut through the rope and kicked me. I got a shot off as he was running, but I'm pretty sure I missed. We gotta find the bastard! Spread out! This son of a bitch has to be weak. He can't run too far. Just spread out and shoot his ass if you get the chance."

The sounds of crunching leaves and branches filled the forest. With no lantern of his own, Junior stepped carefully while keeping the Winchester close. His heart pounded with the excitement of the chase. As the minutes passed, he hoped more and more that he would be the one to catch Darryl. The doubts, at least for the moment, had been flushed from his mind. His soldier mentality had transformed him into the hunter. Searching these woods, looking for their prey, Junior had never felt stronger or more convinced of the rightness of their cause.

Over an hour passed. The darkness was nearly absolute. The moon was covered by clouds, and the other Ravens had passed out of view. Junior was beginning to believe that Darryl had found a way out of the woods. The fear of what could come next descended on him.

Did he recognize me? Will we go to prison if he tells his story? This could be the end of all of us.

Junior froze. He heard hard breaths nearby, the kind that came from near total exhaustion.

"Darryl? Is that you," Junior called out, wondering if he should give away his position.

No response, but the breathing abruptly halted. Junior stayed as still as possible, arching his neck to hear any sign of the escapee.

"Darryl, I know you're out here. I know you're scared and tired. Why don't you let me help you?" Junior's words were greeted by more silence. He decided to walk forward a few steps, then froze when he heard something else: the faint sound of muffled crying. He moved a few steps in that direction, and the sound became clearer.

Five minutes later, Junior spotted his prey. Darryl was on the ground, leaning against an oak tree. In the darkness, he couldn't see Darryl's face, but his crying was still evident. Junior came closer and found that Darryl had tripped and split his head open on the oak that now supported him. Blood trickled down his forehead, mixing with the tears and sweat as it flowed.

The two stared wordlessly at one another. The confusion that Junior had successfully tamped down was now returning. He was unsure of how to proceed.

"I know you. You're the Bryant kid, right? Ya gotta help me. Please! I don't know why this happened. I didn't do anything wrong! Can you please help me?" His pleas hit Junior hard. He took a deep breath, never taking his gaze from Darryl's face. His eyes had adjusted to the darkness enough to see the damage to Darryl's face, and to see the absolute fear in his eyes.

You could let him go right now. He won't tell anyone. Look at him. He's so scared. He just wants to be left alone. You know this isn't right. You know…

Before he could finish the debate in his mind, Junior found himself yelling as loud as he could. "I got him! He's here! Can you hear me? It's Junior! I got him right here!"

"Oh Jesus, oh please. Why are you all doing this? I tell you I'm innocent. I never touched that girl. I swear to God I never did!"

"Darryl, just stop." Junior could hear the men calling out to him and each other, making their way toward him. "I'm here guys! I got him!"

"Junior, please! I know you're a good guy. You're not a killer! Please, man. Please just let me run off. I swear I won't – "

"Darryl, enough! You need to shut up. This will all be over soon, I promise."

With that, Darryl's pleas became sobs. His words became unintelligible, replaced by the moans and cries of one who knows they are going to die. Junior looked at Darryl and felt the sensation of rage trickle into his brain.

What a pathetic show this is! Dad is right. These people have no dignity, no class. They have no business consorting with our kind. They can only drag us down. I can see now why Howard chose him.

He could hear the others approaching from all sides, now locked on to the sounds of Darryl's hysteria. The chorus in Junior's mind grew louder and more confident with each passing second. With no conscious effort, he raised the Winchester and aimed toward Darryl, still lying at the base of the tree.

This is why you were born. You have to fight. You have to destroy people like this, people who cannot and will not contribute anything good to our society. You were born for this. You were born for this!

A single, deafening blast rang out through the dark woods. Jim and his fellow mates stopped in an instant. He was close enough to see his son, and the rifle pointing downward in front of him. No one moved as the seconds crept by like hours. Finally, Jim responded.

"Junior? That you? You okay?"

His vision still fixed upon the now deceased Darryl, Junior stood silent for another moment. "Yeah, I'm okay. I...I got him, Dad. He's dead."

Jim approached his son and looked upon the body. Shock quickly turned to relief, and relief turned to pride. He placed his hand on Junior's left shoulder.

"You did good, son. You did what had to be done. If he had escaped, God knows what might have happened. You . . . you truly are now one of us." Jim's voice choked up as the realization set in. Junior said nothing, only continued looking at the aftermath of his hate and rage. His mind was blank. No feelings of pride or regret. Just a knowledge of what had just occurred.

They congratulated Jim on his son's courage. They greeted Junior with "Great job, kid" and "Welcome to the family."

Though the prisoner was dead, the ritual of burning still commenced. The men glanced between the light of the pyre to the young man who had just saved them all from what could have been a disastrous outcome.

Junior looked at his father and noted the pride in his gaze. He knew this was a moment Big Jim had looked forward to for many years. Junior was now a man, and a full-fledged member of The Ravens.

Chapter Five

Sunday, March 20, 2016; Vicarstown, Tennessee

Henry sat in a lonely side room inside the Vicarstown Public Library. An elderly assistant had set him up and showed him how to use the microfiche machine. He hadn't seen one of these since college, and had never needed to operate one until today.

He was perusing old editions of the Vicarstown Democrat, the town's only newspaper which had once been a daily but had been reduced to a weekly paper in recent years.

As he grew accustomed to the old machine, Henry's speed increased as did his frustration. He wasn't seeing anything about the Bryant family. He skimmed through several months of dailies from the 1930s without success. This was going to take more time and patience than he'd first thought.

As the day wore on, Henry considered giving up and seeking alternative methods. He took a break and went out for lunch, but returned and dove back into his work, his confidence waning with each passing minute.

Finally, in the late afternoon, he caught a break. A small announcement from "Big Jim" Bryant asking for a few temporary farm workers to help with the coming harvest. The address listed matched those on the letters that had been sent to James Junior.

His pulse quickened at this revelation. Still, he needed more confirmation. He continued sifting through the editions for another hour before he was stopped cold by a headline on page five of the edition from January 4, 1942: BRYANT IS FIRST TO HEAD TO BASIC TRAINING.

The short article that followed indicated James Bryant, Jr. was soon to be officially the first young man from Vicarstown to report for service during World War II. A grainy photo showed what must have been a school picture of a boy whom Henry had known only as Herman Bowersox.

He sat frozen for minutes, staring at the photo and remembering the same young man's face from the horrific photos he'd found in the garage.

So it's true. Grandpa was never a Bowersox. Which means I was never one either. We're Bryants. My God, I'm a Bryant!

***

By the time Henry's well-traveled silver Honda Accord pulled into the Greenbriar Apartments parking lot on Tuesday of spring break, the second-guessing had already commenced.

This is a mistake. You don't have to contact this guy. Just turn the car around and head back to Vicarstown. Hell, go back to Indiana. You've learned all you needed about Grandpa and his past. Just leave it alone now.

But the car didn't stop, and Henry found himself gliding up a flight of steps and toward apartment 2C. Here he would find the home of Ty Lockwood, a man whom Henry believed he owed an apology for the sins of the past. This was going to be incredibly awkward, and Henry braced himself for the possibility of confrontation. He hated awkward interactions, even avoiding answering the phone when an unrecognized number came up. But this went beyond his personal needs or wants. This was about family, and legacy.

The past four days had been draining but enlightening. Henry visited numerous libraries in the Nashville area, and spent more money than he cared to admit on ancestry.com. Henry found the process of research and discovery thrilling. Though a procrastinator,

Henry excelled in college when writing papers because of his passion for fact finding and analysis. Dr. Beck wasn't just being nice when he called Henry one of his best students.

But he wasn't just researching his own family history, he was also searching for answers about Herman's five victims and their descendants.

The initials and dates on the back of the victim photos had been the crucial clues. He was able to match missing person reports and local newspaper articles from around the time of each murder to their corresponding initials and dates. It wasn't a hundred percent confirmation, but the matches lined up too well to be a coincidence.

Only two of the victims had been mentioned in any newspaper of the time, and none had received more than a few printed lines of coverage. Apparently the disappearance of a southern black man in the 1930s did not warrant front page headlines.

In his search over the past few days, Henry also visited approximately two dozen jewelry stores in towns all around Nashville. He was especially looking for older, family-owned shops that might have some record of creating the rings worn by Herman and his fellow Ravens. Admittedly, it was a long shot. But if he could find where the rings were made, he might be able to procure the names of the other men in those grisly photographs.

Henry approached the door to 2C with hesitation. It was just after noon, and most people would be at work. An hour ago, he'd felt confident that he was doing the right thing. Now he felt the urge to run.

I should have called first. It's crazy to just show up like this, especially with the news I'm about to deliver. What if he wants revenge? Oh, God . . .

He conjured the image of a charred body with the simple label of "H.C. 8/18/36" on the back. Someone had to answer for those acts, even if it was nearly eighty years later.

Henry stopped at the door and let out one long breath. He knocked three times and did his best not to flee before anyone could answer.

"Be right there!"

Shit! Here we go.

The door swung open, and Henry was eye to eye with a young-looking thirty-year-old African-American man wearing a dull green U.S. Army T-shirt and khaki shorts. He tried to smile at the man, who looked genuinely curious.

"Can I help you?" Ty asked, sounding only mildly irritated.

Henry cleared his throat. "Ah, yes, Hi. My name is Henry Bowersox. Um, I should tell you I'm not selling anything and I'm not recruiting for a church or anything." He smiled and was greeted with a look of confused relief.

Henry continued, "You see, well, I'm from Indiana. My grandfather used to live near here many years ago and . . ." *And he burned your grandfather alive just for being black. I'm really sorry about that! I had no idea my grandpa was such a racist bastard...*

This was going to be much more difficult to explain that he first thought.

Ty interrupted, "Okay, that's nice. But what's this got to do with me?"

"Your name is Ty Lockwood. Is that correct?"

"Yes. My full name is Ty'Wan, but I like Ty. Employers seem to prefer Ty as well."

"Good. Um, I hate to ask, but could I come in and speak to you for just a couple of minutes? What I have to tell you is of a highly personal nature. It involves our families' histories. You see, my grandfather knew your grandfather," Henry explained, straining to keep looking Ty in the eyes.

Ty hesitated, then stepped back and waved Henry into the clean and well-kept apartment. The wall above Ty's television was dominated by Tennessee Titans posters and pennants. A huge Fathead Titans helmet formed the focal point of the room. This was clearly the apartment of a single man.

"Titans fan, huh?" Henry asked as he sat on Ty's dark leather couch.

"Oh yeah. All my life. You?"

"No, I'm afraid my team is the Dolphins. I guess we're both accustomed to disappointment then."

Ty smiled and nodded in recognition of a fellow long-suffering fan. "No doubt! It's been what, thirty years since Miami won a Super Bowl?"

Henry smiled back. "Forty-two, but I'm not counting." This friendly exchange came as welcome relief. Perhaps a personal connection would soften the blow of his impending bombshell.

Ty shuffled to the kitchen and quickly returned with two glasses of iced tea.

Southern hospitality . . . it is real after all, Henry thought, gladly accepting the beverage.

Henry looked around and sipped the exceptionally sweet tea. "I'm surprised to find you at home. I figured you'd be at work and I'd be leaving a note."

"Oh, I work from home. I'm a web consultant for a few companies in the Nashville area. Pretty sweet gig. No commute, and I set my own hours."

"Nice," Henry replied, more and more impressed with Ty by the minute. "I'm a high school teacher up in southern Indiana. Mainly American history. I love working with the kids, but teaching from home would be amazing!"

"I like it. I sort of fell into it after I got discharged from the Army. I was a communications specialist, so I spent some time working on networks. Frankly, what I'm doing now is pretty easy in comparison."

"So, did you serve overseas anywhere?"

"Yeah, two tours in Afghanistan. Not the most fun I've ever had. But probably not as bad as you're envisioning, either. Like *Lone Survivor* or *American Sniper*? I never faced anything like that. I was lucky though." Ty looked at the floor. Henry could see there was much more to Ty's time in Afghanistan than he was letting on. Still, he decided not to pry.

Henry sipped his tea, more comfortable than when he'd knocked on the door, but still dreading what he'd come there to say. He took another gulp and then straightened up.

"Okay, Ty, here's the reason why I'm here. This is . . . this is going to be painful to hear and I won't blame you for wanting to throw me out of your place. What I'm going to tell you happened many years ago, and it's something I just recently found out myself."

Ty sat back in his plush recliner. "Fair enough. Please continue."

"Your grandfather on your father's side . . . do you know anything about him? His name was Harlon Campbell, I believe," Henry asked.

Ty sat staring for a moment.

"Uh, not much. I know he died way back. Dad told me once that he disappeared when he was a baby. No one seemed to know anything about it. Dad said that's what happened to black men sometimes back then, though. You know, Jim Crow and all that. My grandmother was white, so maybe someone got pissed and murdered him over it. Wait . . . is that what this is about?"

"I'm afraid so, Ty. It seems that my grandfather, a man named Herman Bowersox, was part of a group of men who . . . who killed black men on a regular basis. I wouldn't have believed it if I hadn't seen the photos for myself. I found them after he died, locked away for decades. I've been doing some research over the past few days, trying to piece together the clues. It appears that Harlon Campbell was one of their victims. I . . . I don't know what else to say except that I'm sorry." Henry started to say more, but stopped himself. He slowly brought his eyes up to meet Ty's, and the mixture of emotions was plainly evident.

Ty slowly shook his head. "Wow. I mean, wow. So, you didn't know this about your grandfather until you saw the pictures?"

"No. In fact, he was my role model. No, more than that. He was my hero my whole life until I found those. It's hard to explain. Everything I ever thought I knew about him, just destroyed. There were five photos, with five different victims. Your grandpa was one of those five."

"Do you have the pictures?" Ty asked, surprising Henry.

"Well, yes but . . ."

"I want to see them. Please let me see them."

"Ty, they're awful. They're the most disturbing pictures I've ever seen. Are you sure?"

"Look, I know it's going to hurt. But I've always wanted to know what happened to him, and now I can know. Please, I can't explain why. I just really need to see the pictures. Do you have them with you?"

Henry slowly reached into the back pocket of his jeans and produced a small white envelope. He thought the chances of Ty wanting to see the photos remote, but something had told him to bring them anyway. He reluctantly handed the envelope to Ty.

Stone-faced, Ty scanned the monstrous images. He flipped from one to the next, never flinching or giving any verbal reaction. After viewing all five, Ty laid the photos in his lap and brought his hand to his face as his eyes began to well up with tears.

"Henry, I'm sorry. Could you please leave now?" His voice was barely above a whisper.

Henry immediately stood up, understanding the need to be alone. He desperately wanted to say more, to apologize again for the blood that was spilled. But nothing he thought of seemed appropriate and Henry allowed himself to be shown out of the apartment without another word from either man.

The door to 2C closed behind him, and Henry made the slow trek back to his vehicle. The conflict began again within his mind. *This was a mistake. The guy knew his grandfather was probably murdered. That was enough. He didn't need the details. You just ripped open old wounds. But what if it were reversed? I would want to know the truth, wouldn't I? Yes, of course! He deserved to know what really happened, and he deserved an apology. You did the right thing.*

Through his research, Henry had found out more about Ty than he'd admitted. His father, Lionel Lockwood, died of cancer five years ago. Ty, along with his younger sister Deja, were the last living descendants of Harlon Campbell. Now, at least, the two could live without the veil of mystery surrounding their family's history.

As Henry pulled away from the Greenbriar Apartments, he wasn't sure how to feel. One thing was clear in his mind: he hoped fervently that this wouldn't be his last encounter with Ty Lockwood.

***

That evening, back at his motel room in Vicarstown, Henry ate a pizza from Domino's and replayed the meeting with Ty. Though still not convinced it had been the right move, he felt more at ease about what had transpired. The bigger question was what now?

Though he had uncovered a few details, Henry felt that his investigation was stalling. He had discovered the possible identities of three of the five victims, mainly by matching newspaper and police records with the initials on the backs of the photos.

Ty and his sister were the only direct living relatives of the victims that Henry could find. With the apology complete, there seemed to be nothing left to accomplish on that side of the equation. However, there was much more work ahead. Who were the other men in the picture with Herman? Were any of them still alive?

Plus, there was a pilgrimage awaiting Henry that he'd intentionally been putting off. The address on his grandpa's letters, 614 Old Orchard Road, the Bryant family home, still existed. The navigation app on his phone said the house was twenty-three minutes from his current location. Henry knew he had to visit the home, if only to satisfy a curiosity about how Herman grew up.

While contemplating another slice of pizza, Henry was halted by the *Twilight Zone* theme blaring from his phone. It was an unrecognized number, but he answered knowing that he had left his contact information with numerous people over the past few days.

"Hello?"

"Henry, hey . . . it's Ty."

"Oh, hello Ty! Did I leave you my number?"

"I'm a communications specialist. It wasn't hard to find your number. Do you have a minute to talk?"

"Of course. I'm sorry about today, I really am. I was conflicted about whether or not to tell you about it at all. I just figured you had the right to know, and certainly the right to an apology from me. I realize that's a pretty weak and meaningless gesture."

"No, no. Henry, I called because I wanted to thank you. I was upset for a while, but I realized I was glad to know the truth. That was a pretty ballsy thing, coming to face me directly like that! I know that took guts, and I appreciate your apology. It was a long time ago, and I don't hold my grandfather's death against you. Truly, I don't."

Relief swept over Henry as he lay back on the motel bed. "I'm so glad to hear you say that. I just didn't know how you would react, but now I'm glad I went through with it."

The conversation began to dry up quickly, and the two searched for a way to end the call gracefully. Henry decided to blurt out what he was thinking. "Hey, I know this may be weird or even inappropriate to ask, but would you maybe want to, I don't know, hang out sometime? You seem like a good guy, and I'd like to get to know you better."

Jesus, just blow him a kiss over the phone, why don't you?

The line went silent, and Henry bit his lip in anticipation of a polite rejection.

"You know what, I'd like that. To be honest, I don't have many people that I consider friends. Who knows? Yeah, what the hell, let's do it. I'll call you and we can set up a lunch or something. You going to be in town for long?"

"Maybe just another couple of days. Just let me know. If not, no problem. I'm glad to know you, Ty."

"You too, Henry. And thanks again for today. It means a lot to be able to have some closure, even for something that happened so long ago."

His business with Ty concluded, Henry laid the phone down on the bed and wondered how Herman would have reacted to the knowledge of the day's events. He had never known his grandfather to be the slightest bit racist. For someone of his generation, Herman seemed downright progressive in his views toward women and other races. The image of a young Herman taking part in a ritual killing seemed totally out of character.

How can the Herman that I knew have committed these acts? It's almost as if he led two completely unrelated lives. I need more time to sort this out.

Henry looked at his phone and saw that it was nearly 10:30. Carrie and David would be in bed already. He hadn't spoken with his wife much since he left for Tennessee. He told himself he would make time tomorrow and update her on his progress.

He grabbed the remote and flipped through the channels on the thirty-two inch flat screen sitting on the dresser. He found the tail end of the Nashville local news and repositioned himself on the bed. A few minutes of television would help him get to sleep. The seven-day weather forecast flashed on the screen for a moment, and then the camera switched to an attractive blonde anchorwoman in a dark blue blouse.

The box next to her head exclaimed 'Breaking News' as she sternly launched into her monologue. "Now a story that has just broken during our broadcast. An Amber Alert has been issued for ten-year-old Vicarstown resident Aleah Mattingly. She was last seen earlier today at the Sellers Park playground, which is about four blocks from her home. Authorities have no leads at the moment and are requesting the public's help. If you have any information regarding the whereabouts of Aleah Mattingly, please contact the Vicarstown Police Department immediately."

A picture of the missing girl appeared on the screen. She was sporting a big, bright smile, thick braids, and a light pink T-shirt. Henry thought from her skin tone that she might be mixed, but it was difficult to tell. He listened intently, but there was nothing more about the story. The news quickly gave way to Jimmy Fallon, and Henry allowed sleep to overtake him before he could shut off the TV. He was growing accustomed to his new rituals as a lonesome stranger in Tennessee.

Henry awoke at 7:30, groggy from a night of rancorous dreams. As he showered and shaved, Henry deliberately distracted himself with thoughts about the upcoming Cardinals' season and school issues. He wasn't quite ready to ponder his mission for the day: finding and entering his grandfather's childhood home.

After taking advantage of the motel's less than impressive complimentary breakfast of cold rolls and donuts, Henry returned to his room to retrieve his wallet and keys and begin his trek. He glanced at his phone: one missed call. It wasn't Ty's number, but the area code told him it was from the Nashville area.

He dialed the number with no expectations. After three rings, a gentle male voice answered. "McLaren's Jewelry. How may I help you?"

"Yes, hello. My name is Henry Bowersox. I have a missed call from this number."

"Oh, yes Mr. Bowersox. I meant to leave a message but was interrupted. I wanted to tell you that we found a match on that ring you brought in the other day."

Henry froze, nearly dropping the phone. He managed a weak reply, "Uh huh."

"Yes, I was intrigued by the ring and its unique markings, and so I spent a good deal of time yesterday looking through some old files. They needed to be sorted anyway. So, I have a name for you if you're still interested."

Henry had told each store manager he was working on a project for his grandfather. According to his fictional account, Henry was searching for members of a high school club that Herman and a few close friends had been a part of. He had indicated to the store owner how important it was for his grandfather to reconnect with these friends before he died.

"Wow, frankly I'm stunned that you found anything. Especially something made so long ago. This order was from the 1930s, is that correct?"

"No. This order was for four rings identical to the one you showed me. The date of the order is April 16th, 2001."

Henry stood silent and uncomprehending. *2001? That can't be right. He must be mistaking this for some other ring. If he's right, that means . . .*

"Sir? Hello? Are you still there?"

"Oh, yes. Sorry. It's just...are you certain this order in 2001 was for the exact same kind of ring that I showed you? With the red stone and Latin phrasing?"

"Yes, I double checked based on the picture you left for us. There's no mistaking them. Same ring, each one of them."

"My God. Um, okay. Could you please give me the information on it?"

"Sure. The name is Phillip Kaiser. 2193 Kingsmont Drive, Vicarstown, Tennessee, 37251. I normally wouldn't give out this information, but your story was so compelling. I really hope you find some answers. Anything else I can do for you, Mr. Bowersox?"

"No, thanks. I appreciate it." Henry forced the words from his mouth and quickly hung up. He sat down on the bed and stared at the name and address.

New rings, made just fifteen years ago. There was no chance of coincidence. The only remaining possibility began to dawn on Henry: the murderous group of his grandfather's era was still active.

Then he thought of the newscast and the missing little girl, and a shiver went through him. *Is it possible? This group is* still *killing for racist reasons? Could this girl be their latest victim? No way. There's no way this girl is connected.*

But those thoughts lingered, and the dread began to build. Even if little Aleah Mattingly wasn't their victim, one terrible fact was still true: the tradition of ritual killing had been passed to a new generation, and he might be the only person on the outside who knew it.

Chapter Six

January, 1942; Vicarstown, Tennessee

Suddenly, a way out. Junior Bryant, the son of a farmer and a killer five times over (including the first one in which he was only an observer), could finally see an escape route. The war that raged in Europe and Asia had finally come to America in the form of a surprise bombing at Pearl Harbor, Hawaii. The nation called for its young men to respond, and Junior was among the first to act. He reported to the recruiting office in Nashville only days after the attack and enlisted in the Army.

The night before his departure, Junior and his girlfriend – and secret fiancée – Mary Gilpin lay in the loft of the Bryant barn naked and panting. Their heavy breaths formed vapors in the frigid air of the barn as they rested on a layer of straw. They were both shivering, somewhat from the cold of the evening but more from the intensity of their first sexual experience together.

Having once promised to hold out until marriage, their plans adapted to the reality of war and Junior's impending service. Mary didn't want Junior to lose his virginity to some French prostitute or, worse, a gorgeous American nurse whom he would fall in love with and forget all about little Mary from nowhere.

Junior, still feeling the aftershocks of an orgasm he would never forget, brushed Mary's strawberry-blonde hair from her freckled face. She smiled and kissed him forcefully. They stayed silent for another minute, trying and failing to brush away thoughts of the next morning.

Mary spoke first. "Now you've got something to tell your Army buddies about. You think this will hold you over 'til you can get back here, soldier?"

He grunted. "Oh, no doubt. That was . . . that was . .
."

"Yeah, I know." She giggled and they kissed again.
Her caressed her thighs and she moaned.

"Jesus. Now I don't want to leave. Every night
when we're packed into our little bunks I'll be thinking
about how I could be here doing this with you," Junior said
and smirked.

"Well, I guess you'll just have to do it yourself and
pretend I'm there with you."

"Yeah. Hey, look at me for a second. I want to tell
you something." Mary's face was only an inch away from
his, and their eyes locked. "It's about the future. Look, I
may not make it back. I mean, this is a big war, and
anything can happen. I don't want you to just wait around
for me while I'm gone. I want you to live your life. Go
somewhere. Live in Nashville or Memphis, live out on your
own. Meet people. Hell, even go out on dates. I hate
thinking of you with someone else, but if I don't come back
. . ."

Mary's brow furrowed and she rolled herself on top
of him. "That's not going to happen. You'll be back, I
know it. We're going to have a great life together. You'll
be telling our grandkiddies your war stories while I'm
baking cookies or something in the kitchen! Don't talk like
that, okay? Let's just enjoy this time now while we have
it."

"Yeah, okay. Here . . . I have something for you."
He reluctantly removed his right hand from her butt cheek
and held it up to her face. She glimpsed the familiar gold
and red of his ring, an object she had never asked him
about although she was curious. He slowly pulled it from
his ring finger and offered it to her.

"Something to remember you by?"

"You could say that. You don't have to wear it, but
I want you to keep it always. Even if . . ." Junior trailed off.

She accepted it and placed it on her middle left finger. "Are you kidding? I'm never taking this off."

Junior could feel himself getting hard against the soft warmth of Mary's body. He ran his hands down her back and tried to do exactly as she said. Enjoy the moment. Let the future worry about itself. But he knew something no one did. Even if an Axis shell didn't take his life, Junior wasn't coming back to Vicarstown. Not ever.

"I'm sorry, Mary. I know it sounds like I'm being pessimistic. It's not that. I just want you to take some time and plan for your own future . . . even if it's without me in it. Promise me you'll do that."

"Sure. I promise I'll think about it – later. But as for right now . . ." Mary straddled Junior and began passionately kissing him again. He was back inside of her in seconds, his hands feeling the curves of her body. He lied and told himself that somehow, in spite of his plan to exile himself from his old life, this wouldn't be the last time they made love to each other.

**

The next morning was a Monday, and Junior stood on the front porch of the family home preparing to say goodbye to it all. His father, Big Jim, busied himself with starting the truck and pulling it around to the front of the house. He would drive Junior the forty miles from Vicarstown to Tullahoma, the home of Camp Forrest, named for the famed Confederate General Nathan Bedford Forrest. At the camp, Junior would learn to be a soldier, and then ship off to help avenge the bloodletting at Pearl Harbor.

Ruth Bryant, the hard working matron who had seen Junior and his younger sister Hannah through so many seasons, shook as she fought the chilled air and the warmth of her tears. She ran her fingers through Junior's hair, ignorant of the mortal sins committed by her son and husband.

"I'm not going to break down. I know you'll just be a few miles away. It's just . . . you're a man now. And you're going to be fighting. Just . . . please be careful. Please come back to us. I'm so proud of you for doing this. But please come back to us, Junior."

"I will mom, I will. I promise. I just want to do my part."

"I know, baby. You're going to be a great soldier! You're so brave and strong." Ruth's voice caught and she bit her lip as she embraced him. After a moment, she released him and retreated to the warmth of their parlor. Hannah immediately took her place in Junior's arms.

"Goodbye, bro. Don't forget to write. And when you do, send me some pictures of the cute guys that are in your unit!" Hannah was just entering the time of life when boys appealed to her, and she gave Junior a smile to confirm she was joking.

"No problem. I'll write as much as I can. Just take care of Mom. And stay out of trouble." Junior gave her a gentle peck on her cheek. Hannah joined her mother inside, and Junior turned to find his father waiting inside the rattling pickup. He grabbed his second-hand suitcase, trudged down the porch steps, and flung it into the bed of the truck.

The ride to Camp Forrest would be long and silent. As the truck bounced down the country roads toward his future, Junior looked out at the fallow fields and tried to summon a few words for his father. None emerged.

Finally, Jim spoke. "Son, I hope you know your mom and I are proud of you for this. You're going to be a great soldier. The only thing as important as fighting for your race is fighting for America. You're a soldier in both wars now, I guess."

Junior nodded but did not reply. He kept drifting back to the night before, when Mary gave him two very special gifts. The first was her virginity. The second was a promise that she wouldn't wait around for him, but would pursue her own life as if he weren't coming home. He wasn't sure she could keep that promise, but hoped with time she would see the wisdom in it.

Mary had provided the only comfort and pleasure in Junior's life over the past year. She, like the other females in his life, was unaware of the horrific acts he had committed. She was a pure soul who loved Junior sincerely and saw him as the perfect man to spend her life with. Though she did her best to conceal her sadness, Junior knew she was devastated. With day breaking, she had sprinted from their hidden nest in the Bryant barn loft with tears streaming down her face.

Though he would miss Mary every day, Junior also felt a great sense of relief at their parting. No longer would he have to look his loved ones in the eyes and pretend he wasn't a monster. Perhaps he would now be given the chance to kill for a valid reason: the protection of American citizens and those abroad. Maybe spilling the blood of America's enemies would somehow make up for the blood of the five lives he had helped to destroy.

Why did I ever think that killing those men was the right thing? The Ravens aren't about racial purity and saving our culture. That's all bullshit. The ritual is all about satisfying our fucking sick need to see a man die. Well, I've seen five men die and I enjoyed every one of them. Got off on it, in fact. It felt so good, so just, to put those men down. Like we were Templar Knights protecting the Holy Grail. We were the heroes, they were the criminals. But I had it all backwards. We are the murderers. We are the ones who should be put to death. If I had any balls at all, I'd put the shotgun barrel in my mouth and end it. If I didn't think it would crush Mom, Hannah, and Mary, I'd probably do it. Hopefully there's some Jap or Nazi bullet with my name on it. I can't come back here, can I? How could I possibly pick up this life again? I can't. I won't.

"You nervous at all, son?" Big Jim's question broke Junior's meditation. He took a deep breath and thought before answering.

"Nah. Not really. I don't honestly know what to expect, so it's hard to be nervous. I'm just ready to get started."

They continued to drive without further comment. There would be no hugs or exchange of emotional goodbyes between father and son. Their relationship was a tangle of secrets, and oaths, and, of course, rituals. The regard that Junior had once held for his father was now reduced to disdain and resentment. If not for this man, this killer, Junior would never have developed his lust for murder or his self-loathing. There was nothing to be said or done. They were no longer really father and son, but rather like two ravenous wolves in a pack that forever roamed the wilderness.

It's the look in their eyes that is so hypnotic. That look of pure terror, and of pure understanding. Understanding their life is about to end. That's what I really crave. When their cries and convulsions end, and they're forced to confront the inevitable truth that their lives are about to be taken from them – that's the moment that I look forward to most. There is a righteousness, a sacredness about our ritual that makes it feel right. The brotherhood. The feeling of working together to right a wrong.

No. We never righted any wrongs. We weren't saving anyone. We destroyed. Lives, families, future, ourselves . . . we destroyed it all. God will have no forgiveness for us. The pastor likes to talk about 'God's grace' and 'blessed assurance.' But that won't apply to men like us. We are the enemy. I will burn for what I've done, just as I burned those men. But the fire that consumes us will never cease, will never be quenched. I deserve it. In fact, in a strange way, I'm looking forward to it. How could a just God forgive anyone for the things we've done? It wouldn't be right. It wouldn't be just. Grace applies to people like Mary, whose only sin was giving herself to me before we could officially marry. I think God will forgive her for that.

The pickup pulled out onto Highway 16, heading east toward Tullahoma. Perhaps twenty more minutes until Junior would arrive at Camp Forrest. This was the furthest Junior had ever traveled from the place of his birth. He eyed the distant green Smokey Mountains and let the sadness overtake him.

No matter what, no matter if I live through this war or not, I'm never going to have a normal life. I should have run away the day after the first ritual. Why didn't I? Because I liked it. I didn't want to admit it at first, but now there's no doubt. I'm addicted to the kill. And now nothing can feel good. Nothing will take the place of that high. I'm ruined.

Junior turned and looked at his father, who was singularly focused on keeping the truck on the right side of a faded yellow line that divided the winding highway.

You son of a bitch. You disgusting monster. You've taken everything from me. I'm running to a war just so I don't have to see your twisted face. I'd rather die in some ditch on the other side of the world than go on living with you. If there's any way possible, I will make sure that this will be the last time I have to see you. God, let me be killed in action before letting me walk back into this man's life.

The drive on Highway 16 seemed to take hours for Junior. The road noise kept their lack of conversation from seeming too awkward. Junior stayed lost in his thoughts until a large wooden sign on the right side of the highway came into view: Camp Forrest, U.S. Army Training Center, Next Right. Junior shifted and felt a bolt of energy pass through him. The reality of his future as a soldier suddenly came into focus. A calm settled into his mind, and he made a new commitment to himself.

From this moment forward, I am not James Herman Bryant, Junior. I am a soldier. A nameless soldier with no past and no future. I will put every ounce of energy I possess into being a good soldier. I will not dwell on the past, because there is no past. I am a warrior, and nothing else.

This new vow, unlike the one he had taken years before in the presence of four murderers, felt good and right. In this new world of the soldier, there was no such thing as The Ravens. There was only the next order, the next battle, the next objective. This tunnel vision would save Junior's sanity and make him an excellent weapon against the Axis Powers.

"Not long now," Jim uttered. Junior did not respond, but continued looking out of the passenger window and seeing his future as a simple soldier. He would take orders, train hard, and think of nothing but what lay ahead.

The truck veered right onto a freshly paved road and sped toward a large metal gate. After clearing the checkpoint, Jim guided the truck another mile until arriving at a featureless registration building to the left. The truck stopped and Junior hesitated. After a second of thought, he opened the passenger door and proceeded to gather his suitcase from the bed.

He slowly walked around toward the driver's side. Jim stayed seated at the wheel, but rolled down his window. Junior struggled for words. The urge to spit in the man's face and curse him battled with the strange need for a proper goodbye. With the words held hostage, Junior simply extended his right hand toward his father.

Jim, looking genuinely perplexed, grasped the hand and gave it three firm shakes. For a moment, Junior thought he could actually see tears in his father's eyes.

"Son, I'm just so damn proud of you. Go out there and kick those goddamn Nazi asses! We'll all be waiting for you when you get back. And when you do, you'll be a hero around here."

Despite his best effort, Junior felt a surge of pride at hearing his father's words. Even after all that had transpired, the need to make his father proud wasn't yet dormant. He looked at the ground and responded.

"Thanks, Pop. I'll do my best. Tell Mom and Hannah I'll miss them. And I'll write when I get the chance. Well, I guess I should get going."

"Yeah, go ahead. I better be getting back to the farm anyway."

Junior turned and carried his suitcase toward the small building that appeared to be made out of aluminum. He fought the urge to turn back and watch his father drive away. Not because he would miss him, but because he understood it was the final scene of his old life.

As Junior entered the building and headed for a nearby check-in desk, one thought overwhelmed all others: *By God, I'm never going to see that man again. Live or die in this war, I can never come back here.*

Chapter Seven

Wednesday, March 23, 2016; Vicarstown, Tennessee

Henry thought of his students and colleagues from Powell High School back in Evansville and sighed as he drove. The beach vacations, the camping trips, the all-day video game marathons some of the freshman boys were no doubt participating in . . . any of those would have been a fine alternative to his spring break. Delving into long-hidden dark family secrets, and discovering new and even more frightening horrors, was quickly turning Henry's "vacation" into an arduous journey.

The drive to the outskirts of Vicarstown and the former home of the Bryant family added to the unpleasantness. The roads were gravel and pocked with holes and shallow trenches. The scenery was simple: miles and miles of emerald farmland. Henry thought it probably resembled the original homeland of the Irish who had settled this area over two centuries before.

Henry barely saw the roads or the fields. His mind was focused on two names: Phillip Kaiser and Aleah Mattingly. Were they connected? Was Kaiser really a part of some new version of the murderous crew that his grandfather was apparently involved with? Was little Aleah's disappearance simply a coincidence? Henry's grip on the steering wheel tightened. There had to be a way to find more answers. But before he could focus on the present, he first had to face his family's past.

Finally, the ancient farmhouse came into view. It was similar to what Henry had imagined. The two-story home was covered by chipping, faded white wooden siding. Its grimy windows were flanked by freshly painted black shutters. The small porch on the front slumped toward an unkempt yard that featured more weeds than grass. A large red barn sat to the right of the house, and to the left Henry spotted a sagging but still useful clothesline. He thought there must be homes like this scattered throughout nearly every county of every state in America. Henry could almost see young Herman striding through the fields as the car creaked to a stop in the driveway.

Before he could make it to the first of three uneven concrete steps leading to the porch, the storm door opened and a youthful looking pregnant lady in a turquoise sundress appeared. Henry thought she couldn't be older than twenty-five, and not more than two months from a due date. Her shoulder-length blonde hair fluttered in the breeze, while her cornflower eyes darted between Henry and his dust-covered vehicle.

Henry put on his most friendly smile as he began to sweat. He hoped that his casual apparel – an old Jim Edmonds Cardinals T-shirt and even older relaxed-fit jeans – would deflect any worry that he might be a salesman.

"Hello, ma'am. My name is Henry Bowersox, but my relatives were the Bryants. They used to own this farm. I'm doing some family research and I figured I needed to come and see this place for myself. I'm sorry to have disturbed you. Perhaps I should have called first."

"Oh, no, that's fine. So you're one of the Bryants, huh? I didn't think any of them were around since the widow Bryant died a few years back. How were you related exactly?" She squinted while studying his face.

"My grandfather was Herman . . . well, he was always Herman Bowersox to me. You see, well, it's a bit complicated. I've only recently found out that his real name was James Herman Bryant, Jr. From what I've seen, he mostly was known as just Junior. We were very close, and since he passed away back in January I've been finding out a lot of things I never knew about him."

"Wow, I'm sorry to hear about your loss. I lost a grandmother just last year. There was nothing better than her chicken and dumplings! I loved her a lot, so I know how you must be feeling. I'm sorry, I'm being rude. My name is Katie, Katie Offerman. And you're Henry, right?"

"Right. Nice to meet you, Katie. I'm honestly not sure what I was hoping to accomplish by coming here, but it just felt like the right thing to do. I don't mean to be forward, but would you mind if I came in and looked around for a minute? I know you don't know me, but it would mean a lot." Henry attempted to read Katie's face.

She hesitated, but quickly softened. "Of course. I just hope you're not a clean freak!"

Henry followed Katie through the open storm door and into a sunlit sitting room. He looked right to find a narrow dining room which led directly into the kitchen. Ahead of him stood a closed door which he assumed led to a bedroom or perhaps a short hallway.

"Would you like some sweet tea? I always try to have some on hand for guests, but mostly for myself." Katie smiled, and Henry noticed how attractive and vibrant she was. Aside from her prominent bump, Katie had a slim but athletic frame with shapely legs and ample breasts.

"Sure. Sounds great. So, is there a Mister Offerman around? I don't want to seem like I'm intruding on a married woman."

"My husband Jake should be home anytime now. He's an electrician. Well, still technically an apprentice. But he'll be official in a few months. I work a little in town at the bakery, but once our little Anna gets here I'll be a full-time housewife." Katie looked lovingly at her belly. She poured some tea into two tall, yellow plastic cups and handed one to Henry. The sugar and cold blasted his mouth and created an instant rush.

"Mmm. Thank you. This hits the spot." Henry scanned the hopelessly dated but still cozy kitchen.

"Don't get many visitors out here. I'm guessing you're not local?"

"Right. My accent, or lack thereof, gave me away, huh? I'm from southern Indiana. It's pretty similar to here in many ways. Lots of farmland. I'm surprised your husband isn't a farmer."

"Yeah, we bought the house three years ago at auction. The farmland around us got sold in separate auctions, but we didn't have the money for that. I loved this place from the moment I saw it. I've always had a thing for old farmhouses. So much character and history. So yes, we live on a farm but we don't actually grow anything!" Katie flashed that beautiful smile again and Henry felt it pass through him like a pleasant breeze. They sat for another few moments, enjoying the tea and the pleasant environment.

"So, did anyone aside from the Bryants live here before you?"

"No, I don't think so. We were told after we won the auction that it sat empty for three or four years because Mrs. Bryant was still alive but living in a nursing home. When she passed, there were no known living relatives, so all the property and belongings were sold off."

Henry's mind began to churn. Perhaps something, he had no idea what, but some sort of clue to his grandfather's past might yet be found here.

"If you don't mind me prying, what was included in the sale? Did the house come furnished, or is this all stuff that you guys brought in?"

"Um, yes some things were included. The big items, like tractors and cars, were sold separately. But quite a bit of the furniture stayed with the house. I can show you, if you'd like."

"Please. I don't even know what I'm looking for, but maybe we'll find some things to help me fill in a few gaps."

Katie seemed pleased to have a new objective for the morning. She walked him through both levels of the house, the boards creaking beneath them at every turn. Henry observed beds, nightstands, a couch, a rocking chair, some barstools, and a few other items that had all been used by his family in the distant past. Still, nothing stood out. Drawers would have long since been emptied, mattresses looked under. Henry smiled as he thought of the movie *National Treasure*, and how he wished the clues came as easily as they did for Nicholas Cage.

The two adjourned back to the front sitting room where Katie offered him a seat on a modern-looking beige couch. Henry wasn't sure which he was more upset by, the lack of clues to his grandfather's past or the fact that he would soon be leaving the presence of a genuinely beautiful person. Her looks were easily matched by her good humor, and Henry sensed that she was an old soul from the way she responded to him and carried herself.

That's two pretty great people I've met on this trip. At least that's something.

Henry took in the wood-paneled room, stopping at an antique clock sitting atop a cherry wood bookcase. He could tell from the face it was an antique, and he was impressed to find it was still keeping the correct time. The bookshelves were filled with old volumes, some appearing to be encyclopedias.

"I noticed your ring, Mr. Bowersox. How long have you been married, if you don't mind me asking?"

Henry looked down at the thin white gold band on his left ring finger. He immediately pictured the much thicker gold ring from Herman's lockbox and bit the inside of his bottom lip.

"Going on twelve years. We have a son, David. He's seven. Super sweet kid. You're going to love being a parent. I can tell you'll be a great mother."

"Well, thank you! I'm a little scared, but I figure that's normal. My mother promised to come down and stay with me for a while after she's born." Katie once again flashed her very white teeth in a charming smile.

"That's nice. Carrie, my wife, would love to be a stay-at-home mom. But I'm a teacher so . . ." Henry trailed off, assuming Katie would understand the universal truth that teachers are underpaid.

As the conversation drifted on, Henry's eyes repeatedly came back to the bookcase with the obsolete tomes of knowledge jammed into every available space. This was all original, no doubt. The books would have been here when Herman was around.

Katie said something that Henry missed in his distraction.

"I'm sorry, Katie. I . . . how long have you owned that bookcase? Was that part of the auction?"

She turned to investigate and began to nod. "Yes, it came with the house. We liked it so much where it sat that we didn't even move it!"

"So, no one has touched the case or those books since you've been here?"

"Not as far as I know. Not much use for eighty-year-old encyclopedias what with the Internet being available. I kept them because I think it lends a certain classic quality to the room. Like an old study. Before the words had left her mouth, Henry was on his feet and moving toward the bookcase. It was a beautiful piece and still in excellent shape. Most likely it had sat in this very spot for decades. The Offermans had kept the original hardwood floors and had found no need to move it.

Maybe. Just maybe. It's at least worth a look.

"Mind if I have a look through some of these? Probably nothing, but I came all the way out here," Henry asked, already crouched in front of the shelves.

"Fine by me. They belonged to your family anyway. You can feel free to take them if they might mean something to you."

"I don't think that will be necessary. I just have a hunch."

Henry pulled out the book on the far left on the top shelf. It was the "A" volume from the 1935 Funk and Wagnalls encyclopedia collection. He blew a thin layer of dust from its top, and then began flipping through its well-preserved pages. He marveled at the topics and images, realizing that these books were literally the only source of knowledge for most people in that era.

"You know, people in the 1930s would go door to door selling these sets. Not cheap either. It was good money for men who couldn't find regular factory jobs during the Depression. My grandpa Herman had a set of these from the 1960s. I used to look at them a lot when I was a kid, not realizing that we'd be using computers to look everything up in the future. Crazy to think that this was Google for people for generations," Henry remarked, still flipping through the "A" volume.

"I can't believe I haven't looked at these since we've lived here! Can I have one?"

Henry handed her the book he'd been examining, and then pulled off the next volume from the shelf. This was going to take more time than he had imagined. He enlisted Katie's help, and together they started flipping through each book systematically. Neither of them knew what they were looking for.

Inside the "H" volume, tucked into the page mainly devoted to hummingbirds, Henry found a folded piece of lined paper with numbers written all over it. He determined they were most likely scores from card games, perhaps Clabber or Bridge. He quickly set it aside and continued the search.

The score card brought vivid memories into Henry's mind of card games on the breezeway of his grandparents' house. Low Rummy and Rook were their two favorites, and they showed no mercy to him even though he was a kid. He thought those games were among his most treasured memories.

Minutes passed, taking with them Henry's brief glint of optimism. They were running out of volumes with nothing but an old score card to show for their efforts. He handed the "Q" volume to Katie and grabbed the "R" for himself. He opened the front cover and froze. There, on the title page, written in a hasty man's penmanship in black ink, was the familiar phrase: *Corvus Oculum Corvi Non Eruit.*

"Oh my God," the words tumbled from Henry's mouth. He sat staring at the phrase, remembering the gruesome deeds of his family's past. Katie looked up immediately.

"What is it?"

Henry continued to stare at the inscription. Finally, he looked over at her.

"A clue. Look at this. This phrase is the same as on a ring I found that belonged to my grandfather."

"What does it mean?"

"It's a reference to ravens. A raven will not pluck out the eye of another raven."

Katie frowned. "Okay. What does that mean?"

"Hold that thought." He flipped through each page, hoping this was the break he needed. Then, it occurred to him.

R for Raven . . . find the page about ravens!

He began furiously flipping the pages . . . raccoon, radio, Raleigh, ram. He turned to the page that he thought would contain the entry about ravens, and was stunned again: a recess carved into the pages contained a small book. It was a tan journal with a brown strap holding it together. The cover was blank, but appeared to be in excellent condition.

Nearly gasping for breath, Henry carefully pulled the smaller book from the encyclopedia and turned it over in his hands.

Katie's eyes widened. "Oh my God! I can't believe we found something! To think that's been sitting there this whole time. I would have never known. This is unbelievable! What is it, Henry?"

He didn't speak for a full minute. He was almost afraid to open it, knowing that it most likely contained many disturbing details. Finally, he unstrapped the journal and opened to the first page. In the same black ink and handwriting, Henry read the page out loud.

"The deeds herein are those of James Herman Bryant and the God-fearing Brotherhood of The Ravens. 1931 to 1968." Henry stared at the words as "Oh, Jesus" fell from his lips in a whisper. He looked at Katie and saw her lack of comprehension.

"Brotherhood of the Ravens? Sounds like a cult or something. Do you know what that's about, Henry?"

"Unfortunately, I do. I'm afraid I don't have the time or the will to tell you the story right now. I'll just say that my grandfather and great-grandfather were into some very . . . unethical things. I need to go. I'll be taking the journal. I promise I'll explain things further when I know more. Okay?"

"Yeah, I get it. You need some time to digest it all. I would definitely like to hear the story sometime. Perhaps you could stop by again?" Katie's inviting eyes gave Henry a momentary case of amnesia.

"Uh, yes. Yes, of course. I'll give you a call." Henry quickly placed the scattered volumes back onto the shelf and then stood up. His mind was ablaze with excitement and disbelief. What were the odds of finding something like this after all these years? He was torn between desperately needing to read the journal and never wanting to open it.

"Well, it was very nice meeting you, Henry. I'm glad you found what you were looking for." She extended her hand.

He gave it a strong shake. "The pleasure was all mine, Katie. Thanks so much. I honestly can't believe we found this. I have a feeling there will be more questions after I read it! I want to tell you more, but I really do need to leave. Please give Jake my regards."

With that, Henry broke for the door and exited without looking back. He genuinely hoped to see young Katie again, but he doubted he would be back. Sitting in the car, he had the urge to begin reading the journal right there. He forced himself to lay it on the passenger seat and start the engine. He raced back to the motel with a newfound sense of both purpose and dread.

***

July 4, 1931

On this, the anniversary of the beginning of this great nation, we have struck a small victory in the cause of preserving it. Our group, which we are calling The Ravens (at least for now), is a band of men brought together by the need for moral justice. Our race, the Caucasian race which first took hold and settled this land, is under assault from the inferior black race. Our jobs are being taken, our neighborhoods invaded, and, most critically, our women violated. The mixing of the races, which we have seen more and more of in the decades since the fall of the Great Confederacy, is slowly yet steadily destroying this nation. Our white women are seduced and raped by the black scourge, producing a weak mixed race that can only serve to drain our resources and quicken our fall from God's grace.

My fellow brothers (Ravens) and I have just concluded the first of what I hope will be many cleansing exercises. We disposed of a vagrant nigger who was going door to door asking for food and work. Our Vicarstown is already infested with enough white refugees who are desperate for work.

Some would say that we committed murder tonight. I would argue that we have simply rid our country of one more pathetic being who would have only caused our townspeople grief. We have destroyed a life, yes. But we have also defended our community against the hordes of mongrels that roam this country and feed on our young girls like wolves.

I intend to record our actions in this journal in order to show future generations how we fought the good fight and, hopefully, kept the inferior elements from ruining America. I feel no remorse for what we've done. In fact, I feel more alive than ever. The races must be kept separate if we are to preserve liberty and democracy. The Ravens will, from this day forward, be the defenders of those values. And we will also serve as the Wrath of God, striking those who would upset the delicate natural balance that He has created. May He ever bless us in our efforts!

James Bryant

Henry read the opening passage of the journal with utter disgust. These were the lunatic ravings of a racist killer. A killer who likely was his great-grandfather. Anger and sadness flooded his mind as he paged through the entries, taking note of dates and counting the number of entries. The journal contained twenty-four separate entries, each one dated at the top and signed by James Bryant at the end. Though it would take him hours to read the entire work, it was obvious from his brief overview that each entry represented a murder.

As he read, he was astonished at the care that Bryant had taken in describing details, places, and names. The entire original roster of The Ravens were listed by name, something Henry thought the other men in the group were probably never aware of. Bryant had also taken the time to describe their victims. Their names, when they knew them, occupations, and, most importantly, their "crimes." In many cases, it seemed their only offense was coming in too close contact with Vicarstown. In others, the men were accused of rape or sexual activity with white women.

Though Henry was sickened by the diary's entries, he was also excited to find new clues with which to continue his investigation. What if some of the original Ravens, or perhaps their sons, were still alive? Would they be willing to talk to him?

He began writing two lists on a legal pad: one for the killers and one for their victims. The name Harlon Campbell jumped off the page. Ty's grandfather's supposed crime and terrible punishment were spelled out in thorough yet detached detail. Though little doubt about these crimes had existed in his mind based on his own research, the sudden confirmation made Henry's stomach churn. It also emboldened him to continue his work.

He fully intended to find as many of their victims' descendants as he could and face them, just as he had with Ty.

By the time he had finished the final entry, dated April 19th, 1968, Henry's head felt as if it would split open and his brain would simply ooze out onto the cheap motel carpeting. The grim details of his ancestors' deeds careened through his mind, forcing him to close his eyes from dizziness.

I shouldn't have read it straight through. This is too much. So much death. So much pain caused by my family. This is . . . overwhelming.

Henry felt the sudden and desperate need for sleep, though the clock on the nightstand said it was only three in the afternoon. He fell onto the bed, letting his face burrow into the overly soft pillows. Disturbing images of fiery death and unbridled hatred followed him into his dreams.

After two fitful hours, Henry arose feeling blasted physically and emotionally. He stumbled to the shower and stayed in it twice as long as usual. Standing under the spray, with the water as hot as he could stand it, Henry tried desperately to think of something good to take his thoughts away from his family's evil legacy.

Finally, he remembered those waiting for him back in Indiana: Carrie, the gorgeous English-Lit major who had taken pity and married him even though she could have had any man she saw; David, his bright and sweet son whose future held unlimited promise. Thoughts of his loved ones pulled Henry from the pit and back to a level state of mind.

After the shower, he lay back down on the bed and called Carrie. He needed to hear a familiar and loving voice, but her greeting didn't cooperate.

"Tell me you're calling from the interstate and that you're heading back home," she demanded without first saying hello.

"Well, I can't lie. I'm not on the road, and I'm not coming home yet." A deafening pause followed.

"Why? Why, Henry? You've been gone for almost a week. We've barely spoken since you left. You've had all this time to figure things out. What's left to do? I miss you. Your son misses you terribly! Your Magnum, P.I. role is over now. You're needed back in the real world, Henry," she finished, softer now.

He gave a deep sigh before responding. "Carrie, you don't understand. I've learned so much. I've had a big breakthrough today. But I need more time to sort it all out. I know you know what this trip means to me. I'm trying to restore my family's legacy if that's possible. Please try to understand that."

"Yes, I get that. And I support what you're doing. I really do. But this is getting ridiculous. Your spring break will be over soon and you'll have missed a whole week with us. Wouldn't you rather be spending your time with people you love, and people who are still alive? Don't you want to be home, Henry?"

"Don't do that, Carrie. Don't lay the guilt trip on me. Of course I miss you and David! I think about you all the time. But I need to be sure of why Grandpa changed his name. I can't share everything with you yet, but it looks like my family was involved in some criminal activity. And I won't be able to live with myself, or look you or my son in eye, unless I at least try to make amends. Please, Carrie...I just need two or three more days. I promise I'll be home soon and we'll at least have the weekend to share before I go back to school. Okay, baby?"

"Yes, okay. Fine. I'm not trying to make you feel guilty. I just don't want to you lose sight of what's really important. You sound really tired. Are you sleeping?"

"Honestly, not much. I doubt I will until I get back in bed with you. I tell you, the more I dig, the worse it gets. I don't want to discuss it right now, but it's bad. Unbelievable, really. I wish I had never found those pictures."

"What pictures? Of your grandpa?"

Henry gritted his teeth in frustration. He hadn't meant to divulge any details yet. He wasn't ready.

"Yes, they involve him. I can't say more right now because I still don't have many answers. Please just trust me and know that I'm trying to do this as quickly as possible."

"I know. Just remember that I'm here, and David is here, and we love you more than anything."

Henry smiled, marveling at his wife's ability to make him feel like a great man.

"I love you too, baby. So much. Say hi to David for me. I'll call tonight and help tuck him in!"

The call ended, leaving Henry alone again with the ghosts. He decided a walk would help him piece together all the new data and decide on his next moves. He had been intentionally vague with Carrie. She had no idea what he'd found, and he hadn't decided yet if he would ever tell her.

On his way out the door, Henry took one more look at the two lists he had created. He knew what needed to be done next, and it scared him. He felt as if he were hovering on an event horizon, unable and unwilling to escape the black hole in front of him. Dark days were ahead, and he wasn't at all certain that light existed on the other side.

Chapter Eight

April 11, 1945; Ludwigslust, In Northern Germany

Sergeant James Herman Bryant surveyed the lush forests of the Mecklenburg region from the balcony of a two-story hotel that had been converted into a makeshift barracks. He found the sight peaceful and out of place in a nation torn apart by war. The swaying of the branches and the rustling of the leaves sent a strong surge of homesickness through Junior's body.

He was thinking of home even more than usual lately. It had become obvious that the Second World War was rapidly coming to a close, at least in Europe. Hitler's armies had been beaten back on both the eastern and western fronts, and reports said the Soviets were already at the doorstep of Berlin.

Every one of Junior's mates in the 507–the Parachute Infantry Division attached to the 82nd Airborne Division – would have gladly given a year's pay to be the one to put the bullet in Uncle Adolf's brain. Though Junior was no fan of the Nazi leader, he would not have asked for that hypothetical assignment. He had lost, regained, and then lost again any desire to kill.

As a paratrooper who served in multiple units, Junior had been involved in some of the most intense action of the European war. In Italy, as a member of the 504, he parachuted onto the beach at Salerno, helping to save the beachhead position for the Allies. Later, he lost more than a few friends during the bloody Anzio campaign.

Having survived Italy with only minor wounds, Junior transferred to the 507 in time to take part in the greatest of all land-sea-air invasions: D-Day. Dropping into

Nazi-occupied France, Junior narrowly escaped capture and death several times. With his unit scattered across the French countryside after a chaotic night jump, Junior eventually teamed with remnants of other units and helped to pave the way toward liberation.

His greatest challenge, and closest brush with death, came near the end of 1944 in the snow-covered Ardennes forest. Somehow, Herman survived the bone-chilling Belgian winter, a relentless and reckless Nazi assault, and a severe lack of basic supplies. The Battle of the Bulge, as it would become known, made Junior agree with the old cliché that war is hell.

But today, with a cool early spring breeze on his face and a serene setting fit for a painting, Junior believed for the first time that he would live to see the war's end. When he joined in the weeks following the attack on Pearl Harbor, Junior had been committed to the notion of willingly sacrificing his life for his country. After all the pain he inflicted on those innocent men back home in Tennessee, it would be his penance. God, however, seemed to have different plans for him.

Is it possible to have a life after all this? All I've thought about for three years is the mission. Take that beachhead. Destroy that railroad track. Defend this bridge. What is there to do if I don't have an objective? After all of this destruction, all of this killing, how can I go back?

The thought was too much, and Junior retreated from the balcony into his tiny shared room. Alone for a moment, he had an opportunity for reflection. The idea of returning home to Vicarstown, where everyone in the world that he loved resided, was at once incredibly enticing and utterly repulsive. A beautiful young girl eagerly awaited him, with plans for a big wedding. A lonely sister and a worried mother prayed for his safe return. The homecoming would be sweet, if not for the man who taught him to enjoy murder.

Junior closed his eyes and tried to see the faces of the Italian and German soldiers who died by his hand. There were too many to count or remember, but a few stayed with him. Their faces, contorted and surprised at the realization they were hit and probably going to die, still lingered as if they had just walked out of the room. Those faces were entrenched within his mind, and somehow he understood he would be seeing them again and again for the rest of his life. But he had no remorse over their deaths. War is an ugly thing, and good men die in battle every day.

It was the five black faces, tortured by fire and screaming for mercy, which poisoned Junior's dreams. Those men weren't soldiers, and they had done nothing to deserve the fate that befell them. Killing in battle was for God and country. Killing in the woods of Tennessee had been only for himself. He had committed the ultimate act of selfishness: taking a life only to satisfy his own twisted desires.

I'm never going to have a normal life. I'll never find real happiness. Not after all of this. But I won't go back to being a killer. I'll shoot myself before I become a Raven again. James Herman Bryant, Jr. is dead. And good riddance. He was a monster.

His thoughts then turned to the plan which was only hours away from commencing. He'd had the idea months ago, but couldn't proceed until he knew his unit was done with combat. He would not abandon his brothers when they needed him most. But now there was nothing left to do. Having paid its dues in combat, the 507 now guarded the thousands of German soldiers who had recently surrendered. There would be no more beaches to storm or drops to make.

The plan was more than a little risky. Under cover of night, Junior would sneak away from the camp and hike five miles through the forest to a small military airstrip. At midnight, assuming their schedule didn't change, a Douglas

C-47 Skytrain would take off and fly to its destination in Scotland. The aircraft, having delivered its payload earlier that day, would be empty save for its two pilots. Junior planned to be aboard that C-47, but he would not land with it. He would parachute into the darkness over Scotland and, from wherever he landed, find a way back to the states without anyone finding out his identity.

The more he turned the plan over in his mind, the more nervous he became. Getting away from the camp undetected would be difficult but certainly not impossible. The C-47's pilot, Captain Terry McDaniel, knew of the plan and had actually been the one to suggest using his plane. Terry and Junior had known each other since their training days at Camp Forrest. Terry was the only person whom Junior had confided in about his dark secrets. He knew Junior's pain and his guilt, and he knew there was absolutely no way that Junior could return to that life.

Terry promised to have a parachute pack waiting on board, so at least he didn't have to bring that with him. He figured he could survive for five days on the meager rations that were stuffed into his uniform. It wouldn't be the first time he'd gone hungry. During his time in the Ardennes forest, their unit had gone four days without food or water before being resupplied – ironically by airdrops from C-47s.

There's still time to call this off. You don't have to do this tonight. There will be other chances, other ways. They'll lock you up, maybe even shoot you for abandoning your post.

Each time Junior's doubts emerged, the faces of those helpless men whom he helped to destroy crushed them. Risking arrest for going AWOL was nothing compared to the risk involved in returning to Vicarstown. There could be no more debate. He would make his escape tonight or never.

***

Junior planned ahead, trading his patrol duty with the newbie Shannon by bribing him with a pack of cigarettes. He wanted Shannon's patrol because it took him near the Elde River.

Though their position lay far behind the lines of battle, there had been reports of sniper fire coming from the dense forest across the river. No one had been hit to his knowledge, but their unit had been advised to stay alert.

Junior stepped onto his room's balcony for the last time, looking out at the forest, now completely shrouded in darkness. Luckily, it was an overcast evening, though that would make his trek through the woods even more perilous. He gathered his courage and reported for his final duty.

Junior walked the perimeter of the town for a few minutes before veering off toward the Elde. He kept expecting to hear a voice asking where he was going, but none came. There was only darkness and silence as he approached the river's edge.

For a moment, he hoped that a Nazi sniper had him in his sights and would take the shot. That would simplify things.

Junior took another look around, then produced a small knife from his belt. He gathered himself for a moment, then dug the blade into the top of his left hand. He needed a decent amount of blood to make this believable, so he continued cutting despite the pain.

Blood poured from the wound, and Junior took the opportunity to drip it along a wide area on the river's bank. Fighting the urge to cover the wound and stop the bleeding, he instead twisted and squeezed the hand.

He grunted, but kept his composure until satisfied with the amount of blood on the ground. He quickly bandaged the hand while checking again for any signs of life around him. If he didn't appear back on his patrol soon, someone would come looking. He had reached the decision point.

He removed his helmet and laid it strategically on the bloody river bank. He hoped this scene would be enough to create the illusion he had suffered a sniper shot and fallen into the river.

This was his only hope of escaping his unit, and his old life, without word getting back home that he had gone AWOL.

Junior then jogged along the river for about a mile, staying low and watchful as he approached a clearing to the west of town.

From here, he crawled over five hundred yards until he felt he was far enough into the darkness. He stood and sprinted toward the woods, unable to see more than five feet in front of him.

He reached the edge of the forest by nine-thirty. From his pocket he produced a compass and a pen light. The airport lay approximately five miles due north. Though Junior did not think there were any patrols through these woods, he couldn't be sure. If he were spotted, he would surely be fired upon. Without looking back at the town he walked into the woods and toward a new life.

The darkness and thick undergrowth impeded his progress, and he started to worry he had taken too long. If the plane left without him, he would be caught for sure. One doesn't simply just walk out of an occupied country without being spotted, especially when that person is supposed to be a part of the occupying force.

At eleven-thirty, Junior began to make out the sounds of aircraft nearby. His pace quickened, and the airstrip came within view by eleven-forty. One last hurdle remained: find the right plane and get on it without anyone seeing him. He trudged closer, making sure to stay at the edge of the forest that surrounded the strip. He saw two planes on the ground, and only one was a C-47.

Back on his belly, Junior crawled from the trees over flat ground toward the aircraft. He saw no one standing on the runway, but couldn't tell if Terry and his co-pilot were yet inside the cockpit. When grass turned to asphalt, Junior looked up to see the plane was only about fifty feet ahead of him. He took a knee and surveyed his situation. The C-47's nose was closest to him and facing to his left. From here he spotted Terry in his captain's hat seated inside the cockpit. The tiny control center lay behind the plane, so anyone looking out would not see him on the runway. He also noticed the door near the back of the plane hanging open.

Junior looked down at his watch and was barely able to see the face: eleven fifty-five. Taking one last look around, he stood up and began running toward the open rear door. Junior dove through the opening, then quickly doubled back to secure the door. He heard a friendly voice echoing from the front of the plane.

"Nice of you to join us, Bryant! I was starting to worry! You okay?"

He took a moment to calm his breath before answering. "Yeah. Holy shit, yeah! I made it! Hey, let's get this bird in the air, pal!"

"You bet! Settle in, brother. It's gonna be a long, dark flight!"

Terry eased the plane down the lighted runway and Junior could feel it picking up speed. He crawled up toward the cockpit and looked at both pilots as the bird took flight.

"Terry, I don't know how to thank you for this. You know what this means to me. I just hope I don't get you guys in any trouble."

"Nah, no sweat. Hard part's over now, at least for us. You've still got a hell of a journey ahead though. I wish I could find a way to get you on a transport direct to the states," Terry said.

"You've done enough. I'll always be in debt to you, no matter what happens next."

"Don't sweat it. And don't worry about Bowersox here either. He's cool. He won't mention a thing to anyone, will ya Ace?" Terry's co-pilot shook his head and gave Junior a reassuring glance.

Bowersox? Interesting name.

"Thanks. My parachute? I want to check it and make sure I'm ready to make the jump."

"It's in a storage compartment in the back on the right. I had to be careful not to let anyone see it. Should be ready to go, but you're the expert."

Junior crawled along the dark metallic floor of the plane until he discovered a panel just where Terry had said. He found his pack waiting inside. Even in the darkness, Junior was more than adept at examining the pack and making certain it would open once he jumped from the plane.

I guess it doesn't really matter if the chute opens. Either way, this is my last jump.

The C-47 sped through the night, crossing the North Sea toward RAF Alness, a British Royal Air Force base in northern Scotland. Junior hoped to make his jump sometime before dawn and certainly before they got close to Alness. In the meantime, he would have several hours to sit and ponder his suddenly limitless future.

He sat crouched against the wall of the plane, letting the phantoms of the past rush through his mind. Most of all, he saw the faces of his mother and his fiancée, Mary. They would be crushed by his disappearance. There would be no wedding day, no honeymoon, no kids, no grandkids. No Sundays visiting the farm with his family, sitting in rocking chairs on the front porch drinking lemonade. Every good thing in his life would vanish the instant he jumped out of that C-47.

But the scales of Junior's life were unbalanced. The bad, the evil, outweighed the good by such a margin that it wasn't even an argument. Whatever happiness he thought might be waiting for him back home had to be sacrificed in order to right the scales.

I don't deserve those things. Mary deserves a better man than me. Mom deserves a better son. In the long run, my absence will be a blessing to them.

Still, the tears came. At first slowly, trickling one at a time down his smooth cheeks. Soon, the flow of tears increased, and Junior began wiping his face on the sleeves of his jacket. Then, all at once, he was weeping openly and uncontrollably. He rolled onto his side and instinctively assumed the fetal position as the crying overtook him completely.

He wept for those he was leaving behind, for those he was running from, and for those who would never be born because of his decision. The sudden realization he was totally alone in the world made him cry as he hadn't since childhood. It felt good. In fact, it was the first pleasurable thing he'd experienced in a long time. Junior let the waves of sorrow overtake him without a fight.

After about ten minutes, the urge to cry finally passed and Junior sat back up against the wall. He appreciated the silence from up front. Terry was a good friend, and yet another person whom he would never see again after this night.

The rest of the flight passed slowly. Aside from some chit chat between Terry and "Ace," the roar of the engines was all Junior heard. Finally, Terry called his name.

"Junior! Hey, Bryant! We're now over the Scottish countryside. Only a few minutes until daybreak. If you're gonna do this thing, you better get ready!"

"Got it," Junior replied, and promptly strapped on his pack. His heart began to race, though not because of the jump. He'd made plenty of combat night jumps, a few under fire. This one would be cake. What had him shaken was the knowledge that once he left the airplane, there was no going back. He would jump out as Junior Bryant, but land as someone completely unknown to the world. The thought both terrified and electrified him.

With his pack and his mind secured, Junior walked toward the cockpit to say his goodbyes.

"Okay, I guess this is it. Terry, I don't have the words. Thanks again for doing this. You've always been a good friend. Have a . . . good life."

Terry firmly shook Junior's hand. "Man, I don't know what to say either. If you're ever in Buffalo, look me up, will ya? I hope you . . . well, I hope you have a good life too. It's out there, ya know. There's a good life out there for you . . . you just have to find it."

Junior kept Terry's last sentence in his heart for many years after that night. He nodded and turned toward the rear door. Trudging ever closer, he did his best to clear his mind and think only about the jump. He unlatched the door and stood for a few moments, letting the cool air above Scotland hit his face. After three deep breaths, he lunged forward and fell into the black void.

Chapter Nine

Thursday, March 24, 2016; Clarksville, Tennessee

Henry arrived at Grace Methodist Home outside of Clarksville at a little past eleven in the morning. His Internet search confirmed one second-generation member of the Ravens could still be alive, and a few phone calls had led him to a shabby-looking nursing home with a large screened-in porch on the front. Perhaps there was a time when the porch gave the home a certain charm, but now its dingy appearance added to the sense of dread Henry felt as he approached the door.

This was the final residence of Jacob Harrigan, the ninety-year-old son of Greg Harrigan, an original member of the Ravens. Henry had no idea what condition Jacob was in mentally or physically, but he hoped the man would be "with it" enough to shed some light on the Bryants' sordid history.

Henry checked in at the front desk and then slowly maneuvered through a maze of wheelchairs, beds, shuffling residents, and pale-faced relatives. The stench of urine made his eyes water, and he fought the urge to cover his face.

Please God, whatever happens, don't let me end up in a place like this!

He found room 37 and noticed that the wide wood-paneled door was already open. Jacob sat on the edge of his bed, staring at Drew Carey performing the hosting duties on *The Price Is Right*. Henry rapped on the door and waited in the entryway until Jacob noticed him.

Jacob Harrigan looked every bit his ninety years. His veiny bald head was laced with random sprouts of white hair. He wore thick bifocals, a navy blue terrycloth bathrobe, and brown leather house shoes that were beyond worn. He had the old man look down cold, but when his eyes met Henry's they were young and sharp. Rather than look Henry over from head to toe, or simply ask who he was, Harrigan held his gaze and challenged Henry to look away. Finally, Henry blinked and the old man seemed to relax.

"Um, hello sir. My name is Henry Bowersox. I believe you may have known my grandfather and great-grandfather. Would you mind if I came in and talked with you for a little bit?"

Jacob didn't answer immediately, but turned off the TV with the remote, signaling his interest in this unannounced visit.

"Sure. Come on in. As you can see, I'm not especially busy at the moment." Jacob's voice was gravelly and hoarse, just as Henry had imagined. Those eyes, though. They followed Henry as he sat down in a ragged beige recliner that must have been brought from Jacob's house. They were the eyes of a predator, or at least had been at some point in the past.

"I appreciate it. I promise I won't take too much of your time."

"Bowersox, eh? I don't recall ever knowing anyone by that name. I think I would have remembered such a name. But, of course, my memory isn't what it used to be!"

"Well, maybe you'll remember my true family name. Bryant? James Bryant and his son James Junior, or Junior Bryant? Do those names sound familiar?"

The blood ran out of Harrigan's face in an instant. He let out a half grunt, half sigh and stared down at the ceramic-tiled floor. He seemed to whisper something to himself, and then grabbed a dark-stained wooden cane that leaned against his bed. Pulling himself up painfully, Harrigan stood hunched over facing away from Henry and toward a small window giving a view of a sad little courtyard. He turned and trudged toward the door.

I knew it. He won't talk about it. It's either too painful or too shameful for him to discuss. I shouldn't have come here.

Henry prepared to rise and leave the man in peace, when he saw Harrigan use the cane to swing the door closed, leaving them together in silence. He was breathing heavily. Without turning to face Henry, Harrigan spoke.

"Yes, I knew those men. I suppose you know exactly *how* I knew those men as well. But . . . I thought Junior was lost in the war. Thought he didn't have any kids. Just where do you come from, Mr. Bowersox?"

Henry spent the next five minutes filling him in on his findings. Harrigan strained to hear each word but never asked Henry to speak louder. His face was a combination of fascination and horror. He obviously never thought he would be answering for his past sins, certainly not in this life. Once Henry finished, he found it difficult to look Harrigan in the eyes. He had just laid bare the man's most hidden and terrible secrets, and, to his surprise, felt a twinge of guilt for having done it.

"Jesus," Harrigan muttered. He sat staring at Henry, stunned by the revelations of both the past and present. "The Ravens are still at it? Are you certain?"

"No, not entirely. I haven't yet had a chance to look into this Phillip Kaiser and why he might have had those rings remade. But why else would someone want that particular ring? And four of them at that. Were there any members named Kaiser that you were aware of?"

"No, never. I thought I knew everyone who had ever worn that ring. I was among the last, in fact. My son . . ." Harrigan stopped himself, biting his lower lip hard. A heavy silence permeated the stale room.

"What about your son, Mr. Harrigan? No sense in holding back now. Please . . . I need to know everything. There could be lives hanging in the balance."

The last sentence seemed to jar Harrigan back to the present, and he rubbed his forehead while searching for his next words. "My son, Kevin, joined our group right after his nineteenth birthday."

"If I may, what year was that? Do you remember?"

"Well, he was born in '55, so this would have been the fall of '74. Anyway, he was hesitant to join even though he believed in our cause. By that time there were only two of us left, and our . . . activities had long since ceased. We were more like a club at that point, just getting together here and there talking about how things needed to change and about how good we used to have it. In fact, Kevin was the first new recruit we'd had in over twenty years. I thought maybe he could get us going again, you know, start a whole new generation."

Harrigan paused and reached for a bottle of Dasani that sat on his nightstand. It had clearly been a while since he'd talked with someone at length. Henry sat quietly, allowing the old man to gather himself.

"Well, things never work out the way you plan. We put together the initiation for him. The blood initiation. But he couldn't go through with it. I ended up having to finish the job, and Kevin was . . . he was upset. He wasn't ready and I should have known it." Harrigan's eyes began to well up, but he defiantly refused to wipe the tears away. "He was weak, but he had a good heart. I should have seen it. Should have seen it." His voice trailed off as he lowered his face.

"What happened to him? Do you ever see him," Henry asked.

"He just wasn't the same after that night. He . . . he couldn't look at me the same. We were always close, but that night tore us apart. He started drinking a lot. Usually with his college friends, but even by himself. He got depressed. Of course, back then, I just wrote it off. I figured he would snap out of it. But things just got worse. One night he left the house and didn't come back. The next day a sheriff showed up, said he had rolled his car on the highway. He was drunk. Killed instantly. I can still see that sheriff's face, like he's standing in the room with us right now." Harrigan looked up at Henry, who was involuntarily shaking his head slowly.

"And that was the end of the Ravens, I take it?"

"Yes. How could I possibly carry on with that wretched ritual after it killed my own son? I buried my ring in the backyard and never spoke of it again. My partner, Michael Suhrheinrich, wasn't sad to see it end either. He was older than me and had no sons to pass it on to anyway. He died a few years later. I never saw him after Kevin's funeral. I think he felt as responsible as I did for his death. A good man."

"I take it Kevin had no kids?"

"Nah. He was just a kid himself. He was never much for girls. I actually wondered if he might be gay at one point, but who knows? He was a sweet kid. I miss him every day. God, what I wouldn't give to take that night back. To just let the Ravens die quietly the way it should have."

"So, would you say you still hold the same feelings? I mean, regarding the race issue."

"Now? No, sir. I think old age softens a man. I was a true believer in the cause for most of my life. I did some terrible things in service of that cause, but I always put it in context of being a soldier. The Ravens were on the front lines of the race war, and we did our part with vigor. But, as we started to lose the war in the sixties, the drive went out of us. We realized we had lost. There wasn't much point in continuing the fight after that."

Vigor. The word stuck in Henry's throat. The look in Harrigan's eyes as he spoke of their war was evidence enough. He was a man still consumed by hate. Suddenly, Henry felt a strong urge to get the hell out of there. Old or not, a killer sat only a few feet away.

"So, to your knowledge, no one picked up the Ravens' mantle after you and your partner quit?"

"No. I have no idea when this Kaiser fellow would have even gotten a ring. He must have been a relative of one of us, but I can't imagine who it might have been. Like I said, there were no Kaisers in our ranks. You say it was an identical match to Junior's ring?"

"Yes. Sounds as if I have more research to do. I'm afraid I've taken too much of your time, Mr. Harrigan. I'll be leaving you now." Henry stood.

"No need to rush off. I don't get visitors anymore. My family and friends are long dead. It's a lonely life here, but I suppose I shouldn't complain. I've only got hell to look forward to after this."

This made Henry freeze. He wanted to turn and get out of that room, but as he looked at Harrigan he saw his grandfather's face. Herman had spoken often of his sins and how he was so thankful for Jesus' saving grace. But unlike Herman, Jacob Harrigan didn't seem to feel apologetic or guilty.

"How well did you know my grandfather, Mr. Harrigan?"

"We were pretty close, up until the war started anyway. Of course, I wasn't old enough to be in the group yet. He always made it a point to play ball with me whenever there were get-togethers. I liked him a lot. I'd say he was a better man than his father, from what I could gather."

"And what about your father, Greg Harrigan? He was a founding member along with my great-grandfather, correct?"

"My father was a son of a bitch. He never liked me, and he made those feelings quite clear on a regular basis. When I joined the Ravens, I thought it would make him proud of me. Thought I could earn his approval, you know? It didn't matter. I hated him when he was alive and I don't feel any different today."

"I'm sorry to hear that. Well, I should probably . . ."

"One more thing, before you go. Do you know why we called ourselves The Ravens?"

"Not really. I figured one of you just made it up because it sounded cool."

"No, it was my father, Greg, who coined the name. He told me a story when I was young, a story he said had been passed down from his grandfather, who was a sheep herder before he came over from Ireland. One year, for whatever reason, they had a huge surge in the number of raven flocks. They began singling out and attacking the younger lambs, pecking them to death and leaving nothing but a few bones behind. They got really brazen after a while, even attacking one of the farm hands! He survived, but lost an eye. His grandfather claimed to have witnessed several ravens attacking a lone baby lamb. According to him, they simply picked it up off the ground while it screamed helplessly, and carried it away.

"My father said that people who have been around ravens much knew they are really very smart creatures. They can coordinate their movements, attack quickly and without warning, and are scared of nothing. And they never forget when someone has wronged them. He believed the raven was the perfect symbol for what we wanted to become. Hence, The Ravens were born."

"What about the Latin phrase? Corvus Oculum Corvi Non Eruit. Where did that come from?"

"I'm not sure which of the original guys came up with it. I just know it stands for solidarity and brotherhood. We were united as one against our enemy. We recited it each time we . . . completed a ritual," Harrigan said, half smiling at Henry.

Instant goose bumps rose on Henry's skin, and he realized he stood in the same position as when he had first attempted to leave. This time, he was determined.

Clearing his throat, Henry moved toward the door.

"Mr. Harrigan, thank you for your time." Unsure of what else to say, Henry turned, pulled open the door, and nearly scampered into the hallway. He had no wish to take a last look at Jacob Harrigan, last surviving member of The Ravens. But what if he weren't the last?

With his spring break almost over, and his wife seeming less and less supportive of his mission by the day, Henry knew his next move had to be quick and decisive. He must find Phillip Kaiser, and determine if he was merely an enthusiast for racist memorabilia, or a modern-day Raven commanding a new flock of murderers.

Chapter Ten

June 23, 2006; Outside Detroit, Michigan

Herman and his loyal grandson exited off of I-94 toward the eastern suburb of Grosse Pointe. It was an eight-hour excursion from Evansville, but Henry couldn't say no when his grandfather asked if he would drive him. Herman's reasons were vague, something about a girl he knew before the war. Henry tried to pry more details from Herman about her and about his life before World War II throughout the road trip, but with minimal results. He revealed almost nothing, except that her name was Mary.

They had a lively conversation during the trip, straying from Cardinals baseball to politics – both were conservatives, but no fans of President Bush – to war stories. Herman rarely spoke of his time in combat, but for some reason was being receptive to Henry's inquiries today.

As far as Henry's grandmother Virginia knew, the two men were on their way to Tiger Stadium to see a ballgame. Evansville had once been home to the Triplets, the Tigers' Triple-A affiliate, and Herman spent several seasons working at Bosse Field as an usher before the team relocated in 1984. The Cardinals were making a rare appearance in Detroit, and Herman made sure this series coincided with their trip. It wasn't a lie. They purchased tickets for that evening's game months ago.

But Virginia didn't know about their first stop, an old, well-established subdivision in Grosse Pointe. There, they would find the residence of Mary Laurence, once known as Mary Gilpin, a widow whose children lived nearby and kept tabs on their eighty-two-year-old mother.

As they entered the city limits, Herman's demeanor began to sober. He took several deep breaths and watched as the homes and trees passed by in colorful blurs. If Mary were home, this would be their first interaction since one passionate night together in a barn in Tennessee. He hadn't called ahead, hadn't written. He wanted the option of bailing out if the feelings became overwhelming. He had no idea what to expect.

The idea to find and visit his former fiancée formed months ago, when Herman finally began to understand what the Internet was. He made frequent trips to the west-side branch of the Evansville Public Library, and noticed more people glued to computer screens than looking for books. One day, he asked the attendant on hand to assist him, and he began to learn why America had fallen in love with Google.

His online search for Mary hadn't been easy. He had no way of knowing her married name, where she lived, or even if she were still alive. Finally, he caught a break when an article emerged from The Grosse Pointe News about Mary and her husband's fiftieth wedding anniversary in 2000. It listed her maiden name, along with the names of their four children and ten grandchildren.

Herman shed tears as he read the article, thankful that she had kept her promise and built a life with another man. At the same time, it tore at his heart to know that she was his first. They had both found love with other people, but what if he had come back for her? Would that be Mr. and Mrs. Bryant listed in the paper, celebrating their beautiful life together? He knew the answer.

The car turned into a sprawling, hilly neighborhood that featured acre lots and large stone houses built during Detroit's glory days of the 1950s. Mary and her husband Pete had done well for themselves. Pete worked for thirty-five years at the Ford plant, while Mary taught elementary school in Grosse Pointe. Their children, all grown, lived no more than twenty minutes from their ancestral home. It appeared to Herman that Mary recovered nicely from his disappearance.

Henry pulled Herman's Buick Regal into the driveway and threw it into park. They sat silent for a while as Herman assessed the house's features and gathered his courage. He hadn't felt nerves like this in decades, not since the war and his dramatic exit from it. The urge to vomit and scream hit him simultaneously.

"You okay, grandpa? You look white, and you're sweating. I can take us back to the hotel if you want."

"No, I'm all right. We've come this far . . . no turning back now. I have to do this." Herman turned to face his grandson. "Henry, I need to do this alone. Please understand, it's no disrespect to you. It's just . . . there's a lot that I need to say to her, and it's very personal. Do you understand, bud?"

Henry nodded. "Sure. Uh, no problem. Let's make sure she's home first, then I'll give you some time. Maybe I'll find a diner or something."

Herman patted Henry's shoulder with affection, then took one more long breath before exiting the car. His heart pounded in his ears as he marched slowly toward the front door. What would she look like? What would he look like to her? Would she slam the door in his face? Would she even remember him?

He lifted a heavy arm and rapped at the door three times. The waiting was agony. He knocked again. Finally, he heard movement from behind the door. A lock unlatched, and suddenly Herman's first love stood before him.

Still beautiful. That was his first thought. Her strawberry blonde hair had turned a light grey, but the face seemed almost too youthful to be real. Some small wrinkles around her mouth, hopefully from years of laughter and smiles, and she wore bifocals, but otherwise she was the same old Mary. Remembering to breathe, Herman shifted his feet to keep his knees from locking up. He was tearing up, but also smiling for how generous time had been to Mary's appearance. It was as if nature had rewarded her for moving on from her love of a murderer.

Mary stood motionless for a moment. Then her eyes went round and she let out an audible "Oh." He thought she might faint, but she used the door to steady herself. They continued to study each other for a few moments, both unsure of how and where to begin.

Mary spoke first. "Junior? Is that really you? Oh, my God. It *is* you, isn't it? Oh, Jesus. How? How?" Her eyes began to well up.

"Hello, Mary. Yes, it's me. I, uh, well, it's a long story. In fact, that's why I came here. To tell you the story. I know this is probably a shock. Maybe I should have called first. It's just . . . I wasn't sure I could go through with this. I . . . ." Herman stopped, gauging Mary's reactions. She didn't seem angry, but the shock still hadn't worn off.

"I can't believe it. This is . . . you know, a part of me always knew you were out there. For a lot of years I fantasized about you showing up, just like this, and sweeping me away. And now, here you are."

"Yeah, here I am. Been a long time, Mary. God, you still look great. There's no way you should look this good at our age! And believe me, I thought about you every day. *Every* day. I know it's crazy for me to show up after all this time, but I need to tell you some things. Things I should have told you back in the old days in Vicarstown. What do you think?"

"I . . . I think you should come in. I suppose an explanation is better late than never. Come in, I'll put on some tea."

Herman spent the next half hour laying his soul bare. Every detail about The Ravens, their rituals, his father's influence, his crushing guilt. It felt good to have it out in the open, to have a confessor. She took in the entire story without a word. She didn't touch the cup of Earl Grey on the coffee table in front of them. Neither did he.

As he told of his final jump from the C-47 over Scotland, and his transformation from Junior Bryant to Herman Bowersox, she began to weep softly. She took both of his hands in hers and let the tears roll down her cheeks and onto her lap.

Herman whispered, "I'm sorry. I'm so sorry, Mary. Can you ever forgive me?"

"My God. You must have been in so much pain. I can't imagine having to live with that. I don't . . . I can't blame you for what you did. If you had come home, you would have fallen right back into that life. Our marriage would have been in the shadow of all that death. You wouldn't have been happy, and that means I wouldn't have been happy. You did the right thing."

He began to cry, and she threw her arms around him. The joy and relief in that moment were absolute. Six decades of guilt and second-guessing slid from his shoulders. Though the feeling wouldn't last, he felt absolution.

"I forgive you, Herman. I forgive you. Oh, what a struggle that must have been. Starting a new life from scratch all alone. How did you do it?" She released him and wiped her tears away.

"Well, it was tough for a while. I bounced around from town to town for a couple of years after the war. I ended up in Evansville and found a job working for Whirlpool making refrigerators. I liked the town, liked the work, so I decided to put down some roots. Met a girl, got married, had kids . . . a lot like you. My grandson Henry drove me up here. He's a great kid. Well, he's no kid, he's twenty-five, and a history teacher. He's more like a son. But he doesn't know about any of this. And I don't intend to tell him. I don't think he would understand. I mean, he'll find out someday, but I'll be in the ground first."

"And your wife, does she know?"

"No! No, in fact, you're the first person I've talked to about this since the war. I've had to bury it deep inside, but lately it seems like it doesn't want to stay buried. I dream about them . . . their faces. I still see them. Can hear their screaming. I see my dad watching with pride as we burned those people. I think I could live ten lifetimes and not be able to forget. If I told Virginia, she wouldn't be able to look at me the same. I couldn't bear that. I think I would rather die than see a look of shame on her face."

They continued the conversation for another hour, trading stories about spouses, kids, grandkids, accomplishments, and regrets. Mary seemed satisfied with her life, and was adjusting well to being without Pete. It was impressive. Herman thought he might jump in the coffin with Virginia if she went first.

He heard Herman's Buick pull into the driveway. A vintage grandfather clock standing in the corner of the living room told him how quickly time had passed. Herman gave his former lover a warm smile.

"That would be Henry. The curiosity is probably killing him. It's going to be tough to fend him off on the way home." Herman stood and stretched.

Mary stood as well and grasped Herman's hands. He paused and looked again into her familiar eyes. "Junior . . . Herman, I'm so glad you came here today. You know, I never stopped loving you. And I'm honestly happy that you were able to make a great life for yourself after all. Hey, look at me. No regrets. You hear me? No regrets." She brought her hands up and caressed both sides of his face.

"Thank you, Mary. I think both of us came out all right. It killed me to not go back and see you. You can't imagine how many times I thought about it, planned it out. I wanted to come back for you, but . . ." He stroked her thinning hair and remembered how it used to glow in the sunlight.

He leaned in and kissed her on the left cheek. He held his lips there for a long time, both of them breathing heavily as in the old days.

A moment later, he broke free and took a half step backwards as if to steady himself.

"I guess you need to go. Oh, wait just a minute. Please wait." Mary turned and briskly walked down a hallway. He stood waiting, both anxious to get going and dreading their final goodbye. This would certainly be their last encounter in this life.

She returned more slowly, focusing on a small object that she held in her right hand. He couldn't tell at first, but then he noticed the glint of faded gold and understood. It was the ring. She slowly brought it up to his eye level. He gazed at it with fascination and terror. Another life's worth of bad memories were attached to this object.

"Herman, I know you probably don't want to see this again, but I want you to take it. I never knew what it meant, but I kept it all these years because it was yours. Now that I know, and now that I've seen you here, well, I feel like I need to let it go. Please take it."

He hesitated, then reached out and took it between his fingers. She was right, he didn't want to see it again. He used to wonder if she kept it. He liked to think, in spite of what it stood for, that she sometimes took it out and put it on her middle finger. That she would stare at its ruby center and strange markings and think of him. Now, he just wanted to destroy it.

"Oh God, Mary. Why don't you just throw it out? I don't want it. Why would you give this to me now, knowing what it means to me?"

She continued to look at the ring as she replied. "I don't honestly know. I just feel like something is telling me that you need to take it. Like maybe something good will come of this somehow. I'm not sure. Please, just take it."

He reluctantly followed her request. He shoved it deep into the left front pocket of his jeans, safe from the prying eyes of Henry or anyone else.

"I suppose it's the least I can do for you, after all I put you through. Mary, it was incredible seeing you one more time. You're still beautiful, and still an amazing woman. I . . . I love you." He embraced her in a long and warm hug.

"I love you too. You've still got that boyish face. So, I guess this is it?"

"I guess so. Take care of yourself, Mary. I wish we could have done this a little sooner!"

She gave a half-hearted laugh. "Me too. Herman, I hope you can find peace in whatever time you have left. You're a good man. You always were."

He turned to look at her face one last time, but didn't reply. He waited a moment longer, then proceeded out the front door and toward his waiting car.

He looked at Henry but didn't speak. As they rolled down the street and out of the neighborhood, Herman fought the urge to cry again. The mix of relief and sadness was nearly overwhelming, but he kept it to himself.

This was one of many stories he never wanted his grandson to hear.

Part II:

Shaking Hands With The Devil

"…those who torment us for our own good will torment us without end for they do so with the approval of their own conscience."

~C.S. Lewis

Chapter Eleven

Thursday, March 24, 2016; 11:50 PM; East of Vicarstown

The dark, cavernous interior of the former McGathy rubber extrusion plant was suddenly lit with the pull of a lever. The former owners had been kind enough to build their plant in a remote setting, surrounded on three sides by forest with a lifeless pond on the other. The current occupants knew nothing about rubber extrusion, nor were they interested in restarting the factory. They used it for its location and spacious design.

On the factory floor, long since cleared of any useless machinery, stood four men dressed in well-tailored suits. Each sported a large gold ring with a ruby centerpiece on his right hand.

All had just emerged from a black Audi A6 belonging to their leader. The ride from his house to the factory took less than half an hour. Still holding his keys in his hand, the owner looked over the large, empty space that had once bustled with industrial activity.

While he stepped to the panel that controlled the massive garage-style door they had just entered, the others turned and moved toward the Audi's rear. The trunk popped open, and two of the men scooped up their "cargo." After the owner closed the outer door, the four men then proceeded toward an office containing an ancient desk and little else. They placed their cargo inside, then locked the door.

The smell of rubber, acid, and mold still heavily permeated the entire building. Back on the factory floor, the men stood facing each other, awaiting further instructions. Each of them understood the seriousness of their job, and therefore kept the small talk to a minimum. This was not a time for jokes or meaningless chatter; this was a time for absolute concentration and commitment.

This night marked the ninth time the crew had performed the "ritual," and all four of them had become exceedingly efficient in their roles. The only difference tonight was the venue. The abandoned factory was a new twist, and the three followers looked to Phillip Kaiser for assurance. He acknowledged their curious stares.

"I know you have questions, gentlemen, and I appreciate your waiting until we arrived. I recently acquired this old building for a number of reasons. First, as you have already surmised, the location is ideal for our purposes. The ritual can be accomplished with minimal risk of interference, which is more than we could say in the past. Second, on that note, I believe we have been carrying undo risk by performing the ritual inside Michael's home. While it has been sufficient thus far, I'm sure you will all agree that it was less than ideal. It was only a matter of time before something went awry." Kaiser looked at the black-suited Michael Nix as he spoke.

Nix had been the first to join Kaiser in his mission ten years ago. Though he was a successful Nashville lawyer, he had never married, and so his home had become the unofficial headquarters of the group. Though they had considered using other locations through the years, Nix's basement functioned as both a den and a dungeon for all eight of their previous engagements.

Kaiser continued, "Most importantly, this building represents a new beginning for our group and our cause. The Ravens must evolve or die. Simply put, this building will function as our new permanent headquarters. We four have been carrying on the good fight for many years, but, as we have seen recently, the battle is being lost. The past seven years have seen us slip further into the abyss of mediocrity and impurity. I believe we have reached a point at which we must choose.

"The choice is stark and will require each of you to ponder deeply before responding. The first choice is the simplest . . . we surrender. We go our separate ways after tonight and never again visit or correspond with any other member for as long as we live. I have to admit, this choice is tempting on a certain level. We have labored, risked our lives and freedom, and spent huge sums of our hard-earned income, only to see our cause set back more severely year after year. None of you is as frustrated as I at this realization. I believe if we are to give up the fight, we should assume that posture immediately and never question the decision.

"However, there is a second choice. This choice is considerably more difficult. It will require all of us to redouble our efforts and place risks on ourselves as never before. Here is my vision: we expand our ranks, perhaps doubling or even tripling our current numbers, within a short span of time. Next, we invest heavily in the newest forms of media, both social and traditional, to make the world understand what is at stake. Finally, and this is most crucial, we must initiate an event, or series or events, that will force this nation to clearly see the damage that their capitulation to the black race has inflicted on us all. I have more specific plans regarding all of these steps which I will spell out in detail quite soon. For now, I would appreciate your initial thoughts."

Kaiser locked eyes which each of the three men whom he had personally groomed as his disciples. He saw the fear and confusion on their faces, but he also sensed a growing exhilaration as they processed his words. After nearly a minute of silence, Grant Kessler, the newly-elected sheriff of Vicarstown, spoke.

"Guys, I don't know what you're all thinking, but this is what I've been waiting to hear. I think we have to step up our game if we want to survive and keep making a difference. Phillip, count me in!'"

Kessler had joined Kaiser's group while still a young officer in the Nashville Police Department. Upon Kaiser's urging, Kessler took the job of deputy sheriff of Vicarstown five years ago. He was a true believer in Kaiser's racial views.

Kaiser sensed Kessler aspired to lead the Ravens, but knew he, as well as the others, would not be up to the task and challenge his authority. Kaiser had intentionally surrounded himself with followers, not leaders.

The next to speak was Logan Feury, the proprietor of Feury Motors, a large and successful used car dealership in Franklin. Feury was the newest member, having joined at his friend Grant Kessler's request in 2008. Of the four, Feury had the most to lose financially. His parents died young, leaving behind a six-figure inheritance which he shrewdly invested in real estate as well as the dealership. At forty-three years old, Logan Feury was a millionaire, as well as a husband and father to three teenage boys.

Feury's motives for joining and staying with The Ravens were purely murderous in nature. He had a bloodlust that suited the group perfectly. He enjoyed every part of their ritual, but didn't honestly care if the victim was black or white, male or female, grown or a child. He liked to spill blood, and Kaiser had opened a world to him in which he could satisfy that need while still maintaining a normal life. Without the outlet the activities of The Ravens provided, Feury knew he most likely would have already been imprisoned or perhaps even executed by the state for murder. He was in no hurry to leave that outlet behind.

"I'm with you, Phillip. You know that. If you think it's time to take this to the next level, I'm all in."

Kaiser gave a genuine smile of gratitude at Logan's reply. He then turned to Michael Nix, the only one who still had not responded to Kaiser's speech. He had told Nix some of the expansion plan and knew the lawyer was nervous about the added risk.

"Well, Michael, what say you? Are you willing to soldier on a bit longer?"

"I trust you, all of you. Most of all, Phillip, I know you have a grand vision that is exciting and ambitious. How could I possibly walk away now, when our culture is dying and our cause is so apparent? I am with you."

Kaiser nodded approvingly and then responded. "I had no doubt you would all make the right decision. My plans are already in motion, and we have much to discuss. If you'll follow me, I have set up one of the offices upstairs as our 'nerve center' so to speak."

"Phillip, what about the girl? Aren't we going to finish the ritual tonight as planned?" Feury asked, attempting not to sound desperate for the anticipated blood-letting.

"Not to worry. We will indeed finish the ritual this evening. First, I feel that I should enlighten you all as to what exactly this group's future will look like."

Kaiser turned and led the men up to their new main office. A table with four wooden chairs had been set up, and a Windows Surface tablet rested in the center of the table. It became clear that Kaiser intended to give them a full multi-media presentation that would spell out their future as self-appointed culture warriors.

***

Ten-year-old Aleah Mattingly sat shivering in the dark and cold of a side office of the former McGathy rubber extrusion plant. She was old enough to be aware of her situation. She knew that at least three white men had her locked in this office, and probably meant to rape or kill her. Her mom had warned her about playing in the park near their apartment building when there weren't any other children around. She had been swinging facing toward the street and away from the handful of other kids on the playground. She hadn't been careful enough.

Her next memory was of waking up inside a bag in the trunk of a car. Her screams had gone unanswered, and at some point during the ride she lost consciousness. Tears streamed down her face as she looked around and tried not to panic. Why her? Did they need a reason? She could only think of one possibility: she was mixed and the men whom she had caught glimpses of were all white. They must be racists. Or maybe they were just sick assholes who got their kicks abducting little girls. The kind of men her mother always told her about but that Aleah never believed actually existed.

For a while she heard them talking just outside the office door, but now all was silent. The frosted glass in the top of the door allowed in just enough light for her to begin to see. She was on the floor, the room empty except for an old wooden desk pushed up against the far wall. Her hands were bound with rope behind her, and a handkerchief served as a muzzle.

She slowly approached the door and tried to turn the knob. Locked, of course. She futilely pulled on the knob for a few seconds, then withdrew to reassess the situation. Her heart had finally ceased pounding, and her survival instincts were kicking in. Her mother taught her to be smart and strong, and she tried to recall those lessons as she surveyed the room.

Her first move was to search the desk. Nothing there. No closet, nothing on the walls. She began to believe the situation was hopeless, when she spotted an object sitting in the corner next to the door. She was delighted to find it was an iron-shaped doorstop. Though very small, it must have weighed ten pounds. She put her ear to the door and listened for a few seconds. She still heard nothing. Maybe they planned to keep her here for a while…maybe they had left for the night.

Next, she worked on the ropes that bound her hands. They were tight, but her arms were thin and it wouldn't take much slack for her to escape them. After a moment's thought, she returned to the old desk and began furiously rubbing the ropes against one corner. She adjusted her strategy several times before finding a method that worked. After a few minutes of struggle, she had freed herself from the rope and then from her muzzle.

She checked again for any sounds from outside the door, then returned to her quickly evolving plan. Giving the desk a test push, she determined she was capable of moving it the ten or so feet to the door, but it took longer than she expected to get the desk across the room. Her energy level was sagging from the trauma of the experience and the fact she hadn't eaten in half a day. Finally, the desk was in place. She grabbed the metal doorstop and then climbed up onto the desk.

The glass portion of the door was decorative, and the width of the opening was perhaps only a foot at most. She wasn't sure if even her little body would fit through it, but it was her only chance. Taking a deep breath, she drew back the doorstop and swung it by the handle at the frosted glass. It shattered easily, but made a terrible sound that she was sure would bring the men running. Quickly, she did her best to clear the jagged edges around the small opening at the top of the door. Looking through, she saw no one around and heard no footsteps approaching.

She dropped the doorstop onto the floor on the other side, and then proceeded with the most treacherous part of her plan: fitting through the window and then running for her life. She managed to squeeze through and drop down onto the factory floor with the grace of a child who had spent long hours climbing and swinging in the Sellers Park playground. Her left arm sustained a minor cut, but she was otherwise unharmed. She was now convinced that the men had left the factory. Surely, if they were anywhere near here, they would have heard the window shattering.

Aleah looked around the cavernous space, her eyes darting in search of the fastest way out of the facility. The lights were still on, and she spotted several possible exits. The black car they had thrown her in was also still parked in the middle of the floor.

After checking the cut on her arm, she hurried toward what looked like an exit on the far side of the factory. Those men had taken her phone, so she had no way of contacting her mother or even knowing where she was. Still, she knew the only way she would survive was to stay calm and run as far away from these maniacs as she could.

As she ran, she noticed there were a couple of offices upstairs with lights on. With any luck, she could slip out of here before they broke up their little meeting. She tried the first door. Locked. Not panicking yet, she proceeded immediately to the next door about a hundred feet down along the same wall. Also locked. Now a tiny droplet of panic began to creep in. She could attempt to hide inside the factory, but the place was almost completely empty and it wouldn't take them long to find her.

"Shit! I thought I heard something! Guys get out here, the girl's loose!" She heard this and broke into a sprint until she was underneath the staircase and out of their view for the moment.

Only seconds now before they get down here. Think!

The few windows she had spotted were covered with plywood fastened to the metal walls around them. No use trying those. Then her eyes flew back to the largest exit in the room, the one she had somehow managed to miss until now. The garage door. It was large, but maybe she could push it up just enough to roll under and then run like crazy.

Footfalls came rumbling down the metal stairs above her. She immediately understood this was her only chance of escape. They wouldn't take any chances on her getting away a second time.

"She broke through the fuckin' window! That little shit! Where the fuck is she?"

Without further hesitation, she broke into a full sprint while doing her best to keep her feet light as they touched the ground. Thank goodness she hadn't been wearing her favorite sneakers, the ones that blinked with red lights with each step she took. Halfway to the garage door, she allowed herself to look back. The one in the black suit was just turning around. None of them had spotted her yet. A few seconds more was all she needed.

As she approached the door, she was now in the open and easily spotted if they looked her way. Way past time to worry about that now. She half-slid, stopping at the base of the garage door as quietly as she could. Now, the moment of truth…would it open?

"Look! There's that little bitch! Go get her!"

Her heart skipped.

She tugged on the bottom of the garage door once. No movement. Again, nothing. She looked toward her pursuers. Time for one more try. She fixed both sets of fingers under the rubber stripping along the bottom of the door and lifted with her back this time. She felt the door move and her heart jumped even higher. It wasn't much of an opening, maybe a foot or so, but it would have to be enough. Instantly, she dropped and started rolling, just as she learned from the fireman who visited their school earlier that year.

She emerged on the other side and got to her feet. She knew she needed to run, but which direction to turn and what would she be running into? Finally, she spun herself left and prepared to run full-bore into whatever lay in front of her.

Her left foot hit the ground, but her right one couldn't match the stride. Her mind struggled for a moment to understand what had happened, then the bleak realization hit her. Her right ankle was caught in the hand of one of the kidnappers.

"Holy shit, that was close! Phillip…where did you learn a move like that?"

Kaiser lay on the floor of the garage, his torso partway through the opening, his right hand grasping the girl's ankle.

Her cries were audible only for a second, and in the wilderness there was no one to hear them.

Within seconds, she was pulled back inside and the garage door was closed. Her mind flooded with two repetitive thoughts: *I was one step away from getting out!* and *They're going to kill me now!*

The other men held Aleah, now panting and trying her best not to break down in front of them. Kaiser looked annoyed as he attempted to dust off his suit. It was ruined, but a necessary casualty. Better a wrecked suit than a loose hostage. All was quiet as Kaiser composed himself and the others pondered on the what-ifs of their situation.

Finally, Kaiser spoke. "I must applaud your efforts, young one. You gave us quite the scare. Most resourceful! No one has ever attempted, much less nearly succeeded, in escaping us. However, as in life, there is no reward for almost succeeding. Your efforts, I'm afraid, were futile. And now…" He trailed off and signaled for them to move her. They followed Kaiser toward the darkened back portion of the factory. He produced a key and opened a door that led into a large squared space that resembled a shower room, but with no nozzles protruding from the tiled walls. She noticed a circular drain in the middle of the floor.

The last thing she saw was Michael Nix producing a menacing looking serrated knife, while the others removed their jackets and began putting on latex gloves. The last thing she heard was what sounded like a chant, with all four men speaking in unison.

"As we prepare to spill the blood of the impure, we do this in remembrance of those who came before us. We honor our brothers who first waged this conflict, and we look ahead to a time when our race can live in peace. Corvus Oculum Corvi Non Eruit!"

The last thing she felt, as she struggled and wailed against her killers, was cold steel piercing her chest, and the hot flash of pain exploding throughout her body.

Chapter Twelve

Friday, March 25, 2016; 8:15 a.m.; Vicarstown

Henry stood in line at McVee's Coffee Hut, half-dazed from the rich aromas and the knowledge that he was standing less than ten feet from Phillip Kaiser. He should have been on his way back to Indiana, back to his family and the routines of an average teacher's life. Instead, he was waiting to order a large café mocha while staking out a man who could very well be a murderer.

Henry had parked outside Kaiser's surprisingly upscale townhouse at six in the morning, waiting for activity. Almost falling asleep, he was stirred when one of the twin garage doors opened to reveal a slick, black Audi rolling toward the street. Henry followed, trying to remember every cop show he'd ever watched for tips on how to tail a car without being caught.

Ten minutes later, the Audi parked on the street. The driver, a tall, blond man who from a distance reminded Henry of a middle-aged David Bowie, emerged from the car wearing a long, black overcoat which covered an equally black suit. The man quickly disappeared into the coffee shop, allowing Henry to gain an even closer look at his target.

The faint sound of Nena's "99 Luftballoons" came from an unseen speaker as he waited for his coffee. Finally, a stressed but friendly young lady handed over his drink. Henry gladly accepted the hot cup and looked around the small but tastefully decorated shop for a seat.

He spotted Kaiser, who had nestled into the Hut's prime location in the corner. He was sipping coffee while gazing at the front page of the *Wall Street Journal*. Henry found a spot along the opposite wall, near enough to Kaiser without taking the chance of raising suspicion. He pulled out his iPhone and mindlessly scrolled through his Facebook feed while doing his best to keep an eye on Kaiser.

He found that Kaiser did indeed resemble Bowie. He had the build of a runner or a swimmer. Lean, but not skinny. Henry gauged Kaiser's height at around six feet and his weight about one-eighty. From his suit, townhouse, and car, Henry assumed that Kaiser was pulling in paychecks that featured more zeroes than his own.

The more Henry looked him over, the more impressed he became. Was this guy really a racist psychopath? He looked a lot more like a Wall Street broker than a potential Charles Manson. Just as the doubts began swirling, Phillip Kaiser finally removed his black leather gloves.

A bolt shot through Henry's body as he instantly recognized the gold ring on Kaiser's right ring finger.

Oh, Jesus. This is real. That's Grandpa's ring, no doubt. Still, doesn't mean he's a killer. What the hell do I do now?

Henry spent another ten minutes trying not to stare at that ring. He tried to come up with any plausible explanation for why a man would be wearing a copy of a ring that symbolized hate and death.

Because he's a murderer, pal! You're staring at a murderer. And now you're officially in over your head. Get up and get the fuck out of town . . . now!

But Henry resisted the urge. Though he was scared, he hadn't felt this invigorated in years. Just as quickly as the flight reaction hit him, it was replaced by thoughts of family bonds and fate. Maybe he was meant to find Kaiser. Maybe this was all part of some cosmic plan to cleanse the blood from his family's legacy.

Or maybe you'll get yourself killed and leave a wife and son behind with nothing.

As Henry silently struggled, Kaiser rose and walked swiftly past him. He deposited his empty cup in the trash and left the Hut. Henry fought the urge to follow him, sensing that a man like Kaiser would probably be able to spot a tail if given enough opportunities. He waited a couple of minutes more, then stood up. He gripped his coffee and realized he hadn't even tasted it yet. He approached the young lady behind the counter and waited to get her attention.

"Excuse me. The man that just left a minute ago, I believe his name is Phillip. I think I recognize him from high school, but I didn't get a chance to talk to him before he left. Does he come in here often?"

She smiled. "Actually, yes. He's a regular. He comes in almost every morning around this time. Says we have the best blend he's ever tasted!"

"Great! Maybe I'll catch him sometime. Thanks for your help."

Henry made his way to the car, and then back to his hotel room. Time to check out and get home, before Carrie took David and moved to her mother's.

Kaiser's not going anywhere. Time to get home and face what's coming.

While packing his duffle bag and double-checking the bathroom for any stragglers, his phone rang. A curious smile crossed Henry's face as he answered.

"Ty! To what do I owe this pleasure?"

"Well, Hank. Can I call you Hank? I always liked that name and never knew anyone named Henry until now."

"You know, surprisingly you're the first person who's tried to call me that. Sure, why not?"

"Sweet. Hey, I was wondering what you're doing tonight. I wasn't sure if you're still down in Dixie, but if you are, you want to get together? I'd like you to meet my sister. She was pretty stunned when I told her about our first encounter."

"I can imagine. Well, I was planning to drive home today. In fact, you caught me just in time. I, uh . . . yeah! I think that would be nice. Just name the time and place."

"Cool! Just come to my place around seven. We can talk for a while and then grab some dinner. Dee likes Mexican. That good for you?"

"Absolutely! Count me in. See you tonight."

Henry put the phone back in his pocket feeling genuine excitement at his burgeoning friendship with Ty; and genuine dread for the conversation he'd be having later with Carrie.

***

Henry arrived at Ty's apartment feeling none of the anxiety that had accompanied his first visit. He sensed a definite connection with Ty, and perhaps an opportunity to gain an ally in whatever he was getting himself into.

The door opened to reveal a young woman seated on Ty's couch. She stood and gave a hesitant smile as Ty led Henry into the living room, and offered her hand. He shook it and immediately took note of her face. She was beautiful, and seemingly without a hint of makeup.

"Hank, meet Deja. I call her Dee, but she hates that so I'm the only one who can do that!"

"Great to meet you, Deja! Pardon me for saying, but I can tell who got the looks in the family."

She grinned as Ty said, "Damn, why does everyone say that? Don't they see this face?"

They sat and chatted for a few minutes, Henry learning about Ty's sister.

Deja Lockwood was twenty-three and in the second year of law school at Belmont University. She paid the bills by working nights as a mutuel clerk at a Nashville off-track betting facility. It was clear almost immediately that she and Ty shared a strong sibling bond.

At the restaurant, they waded through the Friday night crowd – half-price margaritas kept Los Bravos filled to capacity – and were fortunate to find an empty booth. A large, stuffed water buffalo's head decorated the adjacent wall. The waitstaff wore colorful sombreros. Across the room, a few of them were serenading a guest with their own special birthday song.

"So Hank, you got any other massive bombs to drop on our family tonight?" Ty attempted to keep a stern look, but it quickly dissolved into a full smile. That was one of the reasons Henry liked him right away; Ty was quick to smile.

"Well, yes and no. No more revelations about the past at least. But . . . I do have a bomb for you." No smile from Henry. Ty quickly leaned in and focused. Deja, seated next to Ty and facing Henry, did the same.

"What do you mean?" Ty asked.

"Look, if I tell you this, then I'm opening you up to possible danger. It wouldn't be fair to either of you. I just want you to know that before I go any further."

Ty's eyes widened. "Dude, what the hell are you talking about? Are you serious?"

"Yeah, I'm afraid so. Look, maybe I should just go back to Indiana and leave you alone. You both seem like really good people, and I don't want to get you mixed up in anything."

"Wait, just take a breath. Why don't you tell us, and we'll decide what to do with it, okay? You've piqued my interest now pal, there's no going back." Ty once again flashed a smile that Henry assumed had gotten him past first base with more than a few ladies.

"Please, tell us," Deja said without hesitation.

Henry launched into his explanation of all he had learned about The Ravens, the new rings, and Phillip Kaiser. Ty and Deja sat entranced as Henry explained how he just may have stumbled onto a hidden terror cell. When he finished, their food, which arrived mid-story, still sat untouched.

Ty spoke first. "You actually staked out his house? And then followed him? Dude, you're ballsier than I thought!"

"Thanks, I guess. Yeah, probably not my wisest move. I just had to see him for myself. And there he was, wearing the ring. I tell you, it was surreal. It's like they've resurrected the evil from my grandpa's generation. God, my grandfather was an evil man. Or at least did evil things. I still can't wrap my mind around that. But dammit, if these guys are trying to somehow repeat the past or bring it back or something, they have to be stopped." Henry surprised himself with the emotion. He still hadn't had enough time to fully grasp how his hero had turned so quickly into a villain.

Deja spoke next. "Have you thought about going to the cops? Maybe they could tie in the ring this Kaiser is wearing to the rings your grandpa and his group wore. Admittedly, it's not much, but it would at least put him on their radar."

"Yes, but I just don't think that's enough. I'm no detective, but I think they're probably going to need a little more proof than that. And we're not talking about some thug off the street. This guy, Kaiser, looks like a legit dude with a lot of money and more than likely a lot of influence."

"I'm sure you're right. You're going to need some hard evidence against a guy like that," Ty replied.

"So, that's all I've got so far. Like I said, I don't want to cause you two any more trouble. I won't be mad if you decide to walk away from this."

Ty and Deja looked at each other and nodded. Ty said, "Hank, we're in. Whatever you need. I think we owe it to our grandfather to help if there's even the slightest chance that this Kaiser dude is really a killer."

"Thank you so much! I guess our first move should be to find out as much as we can about Kaiser. Ty, that's probably your department. Deja, maybe you could do a little homework on missing person cases in and around Nashville over the past few years. I noticed one on TV...a little girl kidnapped in a park I think. This is pretty overwhelming. I mean, I'm a history teacher for God's sake. I'm not cut out for this kind of thing."

"Hey, you've got help now. We'll do everything we can. Now, what about you? What's your next move?" Ty asked, looking down at the shredded beef burritos cooling on the plate in front of him.

"Well, my first priority is damage control with my wife. She's probably throwing my clothes on the front lawn as we speak. I haven't called or texted her all day, and I was supposed to be home today. She's been incredibly understanding, but I screwed up. I should have called her. But, as they say, it's easier to ask for forgiveness than permission."

"You mean you blew off your wife just so you could go to dinner with us? Why didn't you tell us you needed to leave town?" Deja asked.

"To be honest, I didn't want to ruin the chance to get to know both of you. I don't have any black friends back in Indiana. Ty seemed like a really good guy, and I figured he might want to get involved with my little investigative project." Henry raised his eyebrows at them. "Is it okay to say black?"

Deja flashed another smile. "Yes, Henry. It's okay for you to say 'black.' And I think I speak for both of us when I say we're glad you were willing to take some heat from your wife to be here. That means something."

"Yeah, it means I might be getting a divorce." Henry shook his head and gave them a tight smile.

They dug into their meals with a vengeance, and the conversation bounced from Titans football, to President

Obama, and finally to settling the check. Henry insisted on picking up the tab.

Henry drove back to the hotel and retrieved his phone from the nightstand drawer behind the Gideons Bible. Three voicemails and seven texts, all from Carrie— the reason he hadn't taken the phone to Ty's place. He didn't bother checking them; he knew it wouldn't be pleasant.

Time to take your medicine, Hank!

He punched the Home button on his contacts list, and prayed that his wife was in a forgiving mood.

Chapter Thirteen

Saturday, March 26; Bowersox Residence; Evansville, Indiana

Henry's prayer was not answered quickly. After getting no response to his calls and texts – *touché, Carrie* – he drove home early on Saturday only to be greeted by an empty house. No note, no call or text. At least there weren't packed suitcases in the foyer! Later that afternoon, Carrie arrived home with David, explained coldly that they had been at the mall, then ignored Henry completely.

His reunion with David was sweet, but swift. Carrie ushered the boy off to his room, where he would most likely busy himself with Star Wars Legos until it was time for supper.

After Henry's attempt at a contrite apology, Carrie walked past him to the kitchen.

She pulled the dishwasher open and began to unload the clean dishes.

He stood in the doorway to the kitchen, totally mute and incapable of finding a way to break the ice in an effective way. After an interminable five minutes, he could take no more silence.

"So you're just not going to talk to me? I know I should have called yesterday. You know I'm sorry. I had more things to take care of before I left Tennessee. I met a couple of folks who are helping me with the search. Ty and Deja Lockwood. Really good people. The whole experience was . . . illuminating. I'm really glad I went down there. And I thank you again for letting me go. Can you please forgive me?"

She continued sorting cups on the counter as she listened to Henry's mea culpa. She stopped and wheeled around to face him. "Look, I understand why you went down there. I was totally behind the idea. What I don't understand is why you needed to be there the whole week, and why you felt it necessary to keep me in the dark all day yesterday when I was expecting you home. What if you had a wreck on the interstate? I was going crazy around here last night, and you can't even fucking text me? You're an asshole!"

"I know. I'm sorry. I just don't know what else to say. You know I hate it when we fight."

"Yeah, apology not accepted. You told me you were definitely going to be home on Friday, and then you no-show, no-call me? Your wife? What kind of man does that? How do I know you weren't screwing some Nashville skank in your hotel room all week? Why would you not call me? No, just stop. Don't try to make this all better. I don't want to see your face right now. I'm going to my mom's for a while. You can feed David and tuck him in. I'll be back . . . whenever I feel like it!" Carrie grabbed her purse and slammed the back door on her way out.

That went well. Now what? Flowers? A spa pedicure? No, this is just going to take time and a lot of patience. Welcome back to Indiana, Hank!

***

Henry spent a large portion of his Sunday watching the NCAA men's basketball tournament on TV. His beloved Hoosiers had failed to make it to the second weekend, but he was still interested to see how the other Big Ten teams fared. Carrie still wasn't speaking to him, and he knew his best option was to stay out of sight as much as possible.

A lazy Sunday also gave Henry the chance to reflect on what had been the most intense and memorable week of his life. He kept replaying his observations of Phillip Kaiser, wondering if he would ever see him again. Wondering if he had been in the presence of a murderer. He also found himself missing the presence of Ty and Deja. He was positive he would see them again, but unsure of when.

Henry also wondered how he was going to handle getting back to his old routine. He hadn't thought about teaching at all over the past week, which was unusual for a man who enjoyed planning lessons and finding new materials to help his students learn about history. Monday was going to hit hard.

While dozing in his worn, but still cushy Lay-Z-Boy, Henry was awakened by the *Twilight Zone* ringtone on his phone. Henry thought there was no more appropriate song for what he had just been through. His bleary eyes cleared in an instant when he saw who was calling.

"Ty! This better be good. You just interrupted a four-hour nap!"

"Ha! Glad to be of service. Resting up for your triumphant return to teaching?"

"More like girding my loins for battle. The kids will be boisterous after not seeing each other in a week. You been watching any of the tournament games today?"

"Why would you assume I like basketball? Because I'm black?"

Ty's stern response caught Henry off guard. He sat wordless, unable to form a quick response.

"Dude, I'm just messing with you. You've got to loosen up, my man! Yeah, I've been watching a little."

"You're right. I gotta lay off the white guilt. I'm not on my game today, anyway. Carrie didn't appreciate my little disappearing act on Friday. I could probably replace most of the polar melting with the ice that's formed in my house this weekend."

Ty laughed. "I'm sure you'll smooth things over. Just give her some time, and then bury her in flowers and candy and all that. Thankfully I don't have any female issues to speak of . . . at the moment."

"No, I'm guessing you do fine with the ladies. Never met the right one, huh?"

"There's been a couple of promising ones. I don't know, it just never quite worked out. Maybe my standards are too high. Mostly I just don't like to play games. I tend to be frank and direct, and that doesn't always make the ladies howl with delight, if you get me."

"I hear you. And thanks for checking on me. It was really great hanging out with you and Deja. Hopefully, once things are more settled here, you two can come up to visit."

"Copy that, good buddy! But I didn't just call to chitchat. Unlike you, I've actually been productive today. I've been researching your guy Kaiser. Care to hear what I've got?"

Henry sat up, suddenly wide awake. "Yeah, of course. What did you find?" He looked around to see if Carrie was close by. She still knew nothing of Kaiser and the new rings, and he wasn't sure how or when he was going to explain it all.

"Okay, first, don't worry about writing any of this down. I've got this all typed up and I'll email it to you when we're done. I have to say, if this guy's a killer, he's really good at covering his tracks. On paper, he's about as far from criminal as you can get."

"Doesn't surprise me. He looked pretty legit in that coffee shop, but that doesn't change the fact that he's wearing Grandpa's ring. That's not an accident."

"Right. Anyway, Kaiser works as an investment banker in Nashville. He has a LinkedIn account, but nothing else in the realm of social media. He's forty-five. Not married. No kids. He's in excellent physical condition. He ran the Nashville marathon two years ago. Let's see, what else? Bachelor's and Master's degrees from Vanderbilt, both in business. Owns a 2014 Audi A6."

"Any club affiliations?"

"What, like the KKK? No, not really. He's involved in a couple of online groups that deal with investment stuff, but that's it. No American Legion, no church, no Moose Lodge. The guy seems to be a lone wolf. Oh, and no criminal record to speak of. Not even a traffic ticket. At least on the surface, Phillip Kaiser is a successful professional and an up-standing, law-abiding citizen."

Henry sat silent for a few moments, digesting Ty's report. "So, what to make of the fact that he's got a Raven ring? There has to be a connection to one of the older members of the group. How else would he have known what the rings look like in the first place?"

"I don't know, man. I'll keep digging on my end. I will say this though. He seems to be highly intelligent and capable. If he's a racist of the kind you think he is, then he's incredibly dangerous. You need to think hard before you figure your next moves."

"I know. We've got nothing that the police would take seriously. You're right, I need some time to think. I wish I didn't have to go back to school, but the bills won't pay themselves."

"I hear that, big dog. I'll keep prying, but I can't make any promises. If he's hiding something, he's probably very smooth and very calculating. Just stay in touch, man. Let me know when you're planning to come back down to the Volunteer State."

"Will do, Ty. Thanks for everything. Catch you later."

Henry relaxed into his chair and exhaled audibly. An idea began to form. He'd been considering it for days, and now he began to believe it was his only choice. As he ran through the possible scenarios, his stomach churned.

If you do this, you're crazy. You'd be putting your whole life, and maybe even your family's, on the line. You've worked too hard. Carrie and David are worth too much. You can't, you just can't.

But Kaiser's face, and the golden ring on his slender, white finger, kept invading Henry's thoughts. Then, more images. Proud men posing with guns, standing over burned carcasses. The charred remains of human flesh, destroyed by men of Henry's own blood.

As he twisted and rolled through a sleepless Sunday night on the couch, Henry played these pictures over and over like a perpetual slideshow. With each rotation, his heart pounded faster and his mission became clearer.

At around three a.m. Henry still hadn't found sleep. He paced the floors of his darkened living room, wrestling with arguments from both sides of his mind.

It made no sense for him to risk his life, and perhaps the lives of his family and new friends, simply because he felt guilt over his family's past transgressions. But it wasn't only guilt.

There was also a profound sense of duty.

Since the moment he saw those photographs in Herman's garage, Henry had known these crimes were his burden to bear. The more he analyzed it, the more he thought of the old biblical adage about the sins of the father.

He remembered a sermon he'd once heard describing what the Bible said about those sins. Though he couldn't quote it verbatim, Henry recalled the overall message vividly. The iniquities of the father would be visited on the third and fourth generations.

If I do nothing now, nothing changes. This curse passes to my son. How can I allow that to happen?

Three hours later, sunlight broke through the windows to find Henry still pacing, still wrestling with a decision he knew would likely change his life.

He'd never done anything dangerous in his life. In fact, if he were being honest, he was a bit of a coward. But this was the most important and personal conflict he had ever faced. People's lives—people he didn't even know— could conceivably be saved by his actions.

Henry had finally come to an inescapable truth: the cost of doing nothing would be much greater, and much more painful. The new Ravens would, if his belief was correct, continue to spill innocent blood. And his family legacy would carry on besmirched and cursed for untold generations to come.

As he gazed at the framed portrait of Herman still sitting on the mantle, Henry's conviction strengthened.

I have to meet Kaiser face-to-face, but that's only the beginning. I have to get close. I need to be in his life. Get close enough for him to trust me. Close enough to share in his plans. Close enough to know the mind of a killer.

Chapter Fourteen

Saturday, May 21

In years past, this day was circled on the Bowersox family calendar as the best day of the entire year. The day after graduation, the first day of summer vacation. Normally, Henry would spend the afternoon on the back deck, sporting a Tommy Bahama T-shirt and cargo shorts, grilling hamburgers and smoking cigars. Relatives from both sides of the family would converge on the Bowersox home for an evening of eating, playing cornhole, and complaining about President Obama. Henry would down a few Angry Orchards and try his best not to get pissed when he lost to his father-in-law in the cornhole tournament. It was an annual tradition, and the pinnacle of relaxation for Henry after a long and stressful year of teaching.

But not this year.

The morning was appropriately gray and unseasonably cool. It perfectly matched the mood inside the house. As Henry packed their largest suitcase, Carrie sat glaring on their bed. The last half-hour had been most unpleasant. David, thankfully, had agreed to stay the night with her parents, so he didn't have to hear the yelling. The obscenities still lingered in the silence. There was nothing left to say.

Henry was going back to Nashville, and this time there was no return date. It would be an indefinite leave of absence from his family for an undefined purpose. Carrie continued to glare at Henry, who was doing his best to pretend he didn't see it. As he emerged with two pairs of Nikes from their closet, Carrie spoke in a voice made half hoarse from the fracas.

"Henry, stop. I need to tell you something. I didn't say anything before because I was bound by a promise. A promise I made to your grandfather right before he died. I have a feeling it has something to do with why you're so adamant about going back down there."

Henry dropped the shoes on the floor and turned to face her. "You knew? He told you? How could you . . . why would he . . . why didn't you tell me?"

"How could I have told you something like that? He was your idol, your hero. How could I explain that he was . . . was a killer? But you know now, don't you? You know a lot more than I do now. So we were both keeping secrets."

Oh, baby. If you only knew.

"I'm sorry I didn't tell you about Grandpa. From what I could gather, he was groomed by his dad, my great-grandfather, to be a part of his racist cult. They killed a lot of people, mostly black men, over a lot of years. But Grandpa got out. Somehow he managed to fake his own death, or something like that, and got back to the states. But he never went home. He left everything behind and started over in Indiana because he didn't want to be that person anymore. He changed. He created an entirely new life and lived it as best he could. It doesn't make up for what he did, but it shows his character. He was a good man after all." Henry sat down next to Carrie.

"Okay, so then why do you need to go back? You've solved the mystery, now you should have the closure you wanted. I get wanting to see your friend Ty. I'm glad you met him. But I don't see what's so pressing that you have to stay down there for weeks, maybe *months*? There's more you're not telling me, I know it! What is it? What?" She was starting to shout again.

"Look, you're right. There is more, a lot more to the story. I'm still not sure about everything, and that's why I need to go back. I have a lot more . . . research to do. More clues to follow. I'm – "

"Then why don't we come with you? I could take a couple of weeks off from work and we could make it kind of like a vacation. You could do your research, and we could try to have a little fun here and there."

"No, that wouldn't work. I could end up doing a lot of driving, maybe all over Tennessee like last time. Plus, you need to save those vacation days for our trip to Myrtle Beach in August."

"Dammit, Henry. You're not being honest. I know there's more that you're not telling me. Just tell me the truth!"

The mild throb in the back of his head now grew into waves of shrapnel that rolled through his entire brain. Over the past two months since his return from Tennessee, Henry had lost fifteen pounds and spotted more than a few new gray hairs on the sides of his head. He had used more sick days in those two months than in the previous five years combined. His sleep pattern had devolved into fitful spurts of rest in between long stretches of staring at a dark ceiling.

Also in the two months since spring break, Henry finally accepted a terrible truth. If he tried to ignore what he knew about Kaiser and those new rings, the guilt and stress would eat him alive. He could look in the mirror and see what it was doing to him. The last eight weeks had been hell. If he was going to have a life, a future, he had to make the trip south.

There was also the matter of his family's legacy. For David, and for every future Bowersox that might come into this world, he would set things right. It was this confluence of emotion and duty, of past, present, and future that was making his skull feel as if it could burst before he could make it to the bathroom.

"Carrie, I'm sorry. You're just going to have to trust me. I *have* to do this. It isn't a choice."

"There's always a choice, Henry. And you're choosing to leave us. You go do what you need to do. Just know I'm going to do what's best for David and me. Remember your son? He's looking forward to spending the summer with you! You're just going to abandon him . . . and me?"

"David is exactly why I'm doing this! This is his family history as well. He's tied to those murders just like I am! Someone has to clear the name – our name! I'm not going to let my son live under this cloud. I'd rather die than know I could have done something and didn't!" Henry stopped before he said too much.

Carrie looked into his eyes for a moment longer, then she left Henry alone to finish his work.

He continued sitting on the bed for a few minutes, searching for any way to exit gracefully. He found none. Packing complete, he rolled the suitcase to the garage and loaded his car. As Henry reversed down the driveway, he stopped and gazed at his house. He wondered when and if he would see it again.

***

At nearly the same moment, in a lavish two-bedroom townhome on the west side of Vicarstown, Phillip Kaiser sat staring at his laptop. He had spent most of the morning in the same spot, seated on a cushioned bar stool and resting his forearms on the dark speckled marble countertop of his kitchen island. His second cup of dark roast sat cooling beside the computer.

On the screen were numerous windows showing email accounts, Twitter pages, and Facebook groups. Kaiser's slender fingers danced as he bounced effortlessly from one task to the next. His eyes darted around the screen, unfazed from over three hours of online activity. If anything, his pace was quickening as the morning progressed. He knew this was only the beginning, an opening move in what would become an all-out offensive.

After a few more minutes of shuffling windows, creating accounts, and posting updates, Kaiser finally sat back and began to take stock of what he'd accomplished. A slight grin appeared on his pale face. He couldn't help it. This was progressing even faster than he could have imagined.

Since the night of Aleah Mattingly's death, which he still mulled over occasionally, knowing how close they had come to disaster, Kaiser had created over a hundred unique accounts on various social media platforms. He congratulated himself for his creativity as he scrolled through the names of the fictional organizations that were adding new followers by the second.

The Front for Black Justice

Alliance of African-Americans for Equality

Fight for Ferguson

Black Americans United

The names had poured from his fingertips, as had the provocative messages that he added in order to gain a maximum of new followers. Under the handle of Black Hand of Vengeance, Kaiser set the tone with his initial Twitter post:

"We are committed to one purpose: making the white capitalist bigots pay for centuries of injustice. Join us."

Similar messages, some more aggressive than others, were sent out from all of Kaiser's accounts. The response was nothing short of incredible. Some of the accounts, though less than two hours old, already had over a thousand followers. People were responding with overwhelming eagerness and excitement.

Never underestimate the ignorance of the masses.

He took a few sips of his coffee while still examining some of the newest replies to his provocative statements. This was going to take time to develop, but

Kaiser was now more confident than ever that this prong of his plan was going to succeed.

Kaiser had spent thousands of dollars on new equipment, including a private server that would protect his output from tracing by authorities. Money wasn't an issue for the man who was a millionaire by age thirty, but secrecy was. The Ravens would one day step from the shadows to lead a revolution, but that was dependent upon the success of this morning's labor.

Another more crucial aspect of his plan was still lagging: the recruitment of new members. The four men of their brotherhood had come together organically. There was no precedent for a purposeful and large scale addition to The Ravens. It was the one portion of the plan that still had Kaiser concerned and even a bit flummoxed. Bringing new men into their circle would be a delicate procedure. Whatever the barriers, Kaiser knew there was no other way. Without a significant influx of new soldiers, there could be no escalation of the fight and no ultimate victory.

Still, this morning had been a positive step forward for Kaiser's cause: the cause of supremacy for the white race in America. For so many years the fight seemed futile. The culture too saturated with black influences, the law too skewed in favor of "social justice." He had nearly given up a few years ago, until he found a handful of others who shared his passion. They faithfully carried on the Ravens' traditions, even though the greater war was being lost on TV, the Internet, and in real life. Black and white cultures were now permanently intertwined, or so it seemed.

This morning, more than at any point in Kaiser's life, the mission of destroying the menace of black culture seemed achievable. The dream of his beloved mentor might finally be realized. Kaiser envisioned a new America, racially divided in a way that not even southerners in the Jim Crow era could have hoped for. With any luck, Kaiser would play the pivotal role in creating this new-old America and live to see it flourish.

"Where are you, men? Show yourselves and let us build this army," Kaiser said out loud to the laptop's screen. He took another sip of coffee, then closed the computer. If the master plan were successful, Kaiser would look back and acknowledge that this quiet Saturday morning was when it all began to turn.

He stood up and stretched, then headed out to get a five-mile run in before lunch.

***

"You wanna do what?"

"I want to meet Phillip Kaiser face-to-face, get to know him," Henry said, hoping he could make Ty see his side.

"Kaiser? Okay, so you think this guy could be a stone cold racist killer, and you wanna sit down and have a latte with him? Are you crazy, son?"

"I know how it sounds, but what else can I do? You've done all the research and what do we really know about him? He has a good job, drives a nice car, and lives in a really nice house. That about cover it? We need more. A lot more!"

"I get it, you're just . . . you show up here out of the blue and suddenly you want to get up close with him. I think you need to think this through, that's all."

"Ty, trust me. I've pretty much done nothing but think about this since I last saw you. I mean, look at me. I'm a wreck. My marriage is on the verge of collapse, I'm losing weight and hair. I barely made it through the school year with my job status intact. This thing is taking over my life. I have to do this. I have to get close to Kaiser and see if there's anything there. Find out why he has that ring, and what, if anything, he's got planned. We could be talking about saving lives here!"

Henry stopped and sat down on Ty's couch. In the tension of the morning's events with Carrie, he had forgotten to call ahead and let Ty know he was coming down. Thankfully, Ty was home and not unhappy to see old Hank.

"Alright, dude. I can see. The struggle is most definitely real! And, you're right. I've tried everything. Kaiser's life is sewn up tight. I've never seen anything like it, really. That could be a red flag, or it could just mean he likes his privacy."

"Ty, the man wears the ring of a racist cult and also just happens to be super private? I can't believe he's not up to something. We have to find out. I've already decided. I'm not leaving town until we figure this thing out. I don't care what it costs, and I don't care how long it takes. It's pretty apparent that I'm not going to get my life back until I figure all this out."

"Hey, I respect that, man. And I'm with you. Whatever you need. I've never met anyone with a passion like you. I mean, I've been around a lot of tough guys in the Army. But you, my friend, you might have the biggest balls of them all! And it's not just your family legacy on the line, it's mine too!"

Henry smiled and held out his hand to Ty. Their eyes met as they shook hands, and any hesitancy about their mission was instantly swept away.

"Come on, man. Let's get some food in you and then figure out how to play this. We need to beef you up before you shake hands with the devil."

Chapter Fifteen

Monday, May 23; Vicarstown

Nauseous. Henry stared into the smeared bathroom mirror, attempting to keep the contents of his stomach from filling the sink. This was D-Day. The day he had been both dreading and relishing for months.

The steam of an early morning shower still hung in the air. Henry tried to savor the warmth and safety of that moment, knowing how rare that would be after today. He toweled off in a haze, trying his best to focus on the game plan that he and Ty had pieced together the night before. It was critical that he stay "in character" when facing Kaiser. There were certain facts, like that of his great-grandfather's affiliation with the Ravens, which must be divulged. Others, such as his real name and backstory, must be kept hidden.

Over the last two months, flashes from the morning when he first saw Kaiser intruded on Henry's mind almost every day. His pale face, his slicked back golden hair, and most of all, those eyes. Steely blue, serious, and determined. Even while seemingly relaxed in a coffee shop, Kaiser looked like a man on a mission.

Henry dressed and continued to gird himself. He could not allow Kaiser, or the things he could possibly be involved in, to intimidate him. There would only be one shot at making an impression and getting into Kaiser's life. On this day, of all days, Henry couldn't afford to be scared.

Fully dressed in business casual attire including his best navy blue button-down shirt, Henry decided to go back to the sink. He stared into his own eyes again and felt his bowels churning.

Bending over, he stuck two fingers down his throat and gagged until vomit hit the sink. Today was not a day for a nervous stomach.

On his drive to the coffee shop, where he knew he would find his man sitting in the same spot and probably reading the *Wall Street Journal*, Henry struggled to keep his focus on the road. He switched on the radio and found Air Supply raving about lost love. He flipped to ESPN's *Mike and Mike*, then to Dave Ramsey, then finally decided no radio would be best. He began a discussion with himself in order to keep his nerves in check. He hadn't felt this much anxiety on a drive since his first day of student teaching. He vomited that day, too.

"Just be direct, don't hesitate. Show him the ring and tell the story without blabbing too many details. Look him in the eyes, but don't stare. Act interested in his cause, but not too interested. You have to play this just right." He continued until the car reached its destination. He closed his eyes. "Please God, I hope I'm doing the right thing here. Please give me the strength."

Moments later, Henry found himself standing on the curb in front of McVee's Coffee Hut, the aroma of roasting beans wafting through the air.

He paused, took one deep breath, and then strolled inside. He resisted the urge to look directly where he thought Kaiser would be. He walked toward the counter and concentrated on the overhanging chalkboard where the Hut's offerings were listed. Though putting anything back into his stomach was the last thing he wanted to do, he had to order something.

Latte in hand, Henry turned toward the seating area and felt a surge of energy rise from his groin and ooze through his midsection. There, in the same seat and wearing a light beige suit, was Phillip Kaiser. It was surreal and sickening to see the man again, and in exactly the same situation.

Kaiser was staring off to his right, looking like a man victorious. He looked like a champion, someone who had accomplished something impressive and who was now replaying the event in his mind.

Henry's first urge was to turn and leave. Somehow he managed to navigate to a seat, purposely different from the first time he'd been there, and plant himself.

He knew Kaiser wouldn't hang around long, so there was no time for last minute self-motivational speeches. Henry patted his shirt pocket, assuring himself his grandfather's ring was still there. The ring would serve as his gateway into Kaiser's world.

Taking another deep breath, Henry stood on less than sturdy legs, and slowly made his way toward Kaiser. A sudden clarity descended on him. A clarity of purpose. He wasn't walking into a faculty meeting, parent conference, or some department meeting where he and his colleagues would bitch for an hour about the kids; he was literally walking into an entirely new and foreign experience. It was thrilling and terrifying in equal parts.

He was now standing over Kaiser, who was engrossed in an article on the *Journal's* front page. Sensing a presence, Kaiser looked up and met Henry's eyes with his own. With a force of will, Henry kept his gaze and did not blink or look away. Kaiser's blue eyes were almost shimmering up close, and even more piercing than he remembered.

"Excuse me, sir. My name is Henry Bryant. I'm sorry to intrude on you like this, but I didn't know how else to contact you. Would you mind if we talked for a minute?" Henry's voice was strong, and the nervous energy had transformed into confident decisiveness.

Kaiser eyed him suspiciously for what seemed like a full minute. Finally, he glanced at his watch and responded.

"What is this in reference to, Mr. Bryant? I'm afraid I'm due at a meeting quite soon."

"Well, it's of a very personal nature. I would greatly appreciate a little of your time to explain."

Kaiser considered this for a moment. "Yes, I believe I have a minute to spare. Please, sit down. Haven't I seen you in here before? Perhaps a few weeks ago?"

Incredible. I didn't even know he saw me when I was here in March. Not only did he see me, but he remembered me. Does he survey every environment he's in like that? Impressive.

"Yes, you're very observant. That was the first time I had been in here, and that's when I noticed you. After you left, I asked the clerk if you were a regular and they said you were. I hope you don't mind."

Kaiser grinned, which sent another surge down Henry's legs. "Checking up on me, eh? Well then, Mr. Bryant, what can I do for you on this fine morning?" He folded the newspaper and put it aside, indicating his total focus on Henry.

"Well, you see, I noticed your ring. It's very . . . unique. I spotted it even from where I was sitting last time and, well, I was hoping you would allow me to see it up close."

Kaiser showed no facial reaction. He simply raised his right hand from below and placed it palm down on the table. "You mean this ring? Yes, I will admit it is unique. Nearly one of a kind, in fact. But tell me, why was my ring so eye-catching? From that distance, it must have resembled a thousand other class rings you've seen in your life."

Henry stared down at the ring and, though he knew it was a replica of his grandfather's, the sight of it still stirred a mix of dread and anger inside of him. His stomach gurgled again.

"I recognized it for only one reason. This," Henry said as he pulled Herman's ring from his pocket. He laid it on the table.

Henry watched as Kaiser picked up the ring and examined it with complete fascination. Compared to Kaiser's ring, it was tarnished and rough. After a minute of intense study and comparison to his own ring, Kaiser looked up at Henry. Henry thought his expression was like that of a man who had just discovered he had a twin brother.

Kaiser cleared his throat and attempted to regain his stoic pose. "Where did you get that?"

"It was handed down in my family. It goes back several generations. I was going to ask you the same question about your ring."

Kaiser's gaze continued to flow back and forth between Herman's ring and Henry's face. The shock was still apparent. "You say your name is Bryant? I can only assume that means you are related to James Bryant. Am I correct?"

The fact that Kaiser knew his great-grandfather's name was both stunning and telling.

He knows his history. Of course he would know the history of The Ravens. He's trying to recreate it. Jesus, Big Jim Bryant must be some kind of hero to this guy.

"Yes. He was my great-grandfather. They called him 'Big Jim.' I never knew him personally, though."

"Was this *his* ring?" Kaiser asked, still caressing it. Henry thought if he said yes, Kaiser might fall to his knees in reverence.

"I can't be sure, but it might have been. As you can see, it's been around a long time."

"It certainly has. This is . . . this is extraordinary. You walk in here out of the blue and . . ." Kaiser halted and looked up again at Henry. His eyes were inquisitive and suspicious. "How much do you know about this? About what it stands for, about what you great-grandfather was involved in."

This is it! This is your chance...your way in!

"I know a great deal. In fact, that's the main reason I approached you. You see, I'm hoping to follow in my great-grandfather's footsteps. When I saw your ring, I was shocked but also encouraged. I was excited to see that the . . . tradition was being carried on. I wonder if we might talk sometime in a more private setting about that." Henry said this with such conviction that he surprised himself. He could see from Kaiser's face that he was more than a little curious.

"My goodness! This is a revelation! I must admit, I'm a bit taken off guard. But I believe you are correct. We should discuss this in a more appropriate setting. And soon. Would you be available tomorrow evening?"

"Uh, yes. That should be fine. Where should we meet?"

"My house, eight o'clock. Here's my card. I'll write the address on the back for you." Kaiser produced an obviously expensive gold pen from his suit pocket and wrote the address hurriedly. It was clear that Kaiser was a man unused to being taken by surprise.

"I'll be there. Should I bring anything?"

"Just yourself and that ring! This is . . . well, I might as well say it. You've thrown a wrench into my day in a way I could never have imagined. However, I'm glad you had the courage to approach me. I'm afraid I must be on my way now. Please call me if you need directions or anything else." Kaiser rose and extended his hand to Henry. Henry gave it a firm grasp. Kaiser's hand was cold, but the handshake was warm with feeling. Henry had accomplished the important first step: he had piqued Kaiser's interest and made a strong first impression.

He allowed Kaiser to leave and sat back down at the table. He replayed the conversation several times and determined that he could not have done a better acting job. Kaiser appeared to be ready to welcome Henry into his dark world with open arms.

* * *

Kaiser spent the majority of his day back at home, unable to focus on work after the bombshell at the coffee shop. This was either a disaster in the making, or perhaps the biggest break their burgeoning cult could have hoped for. A *legacy* recruit. It didn't seem possible, except there was that ring. He had examined it thoroughly and it was obviously an original.

And what to make of this Henry? He didn't appear to have a predatory nature like the others. And his relationship to *the* Big Jim Bryant? If Henry was telling the truth about that, it would mean . . .

Kaiser paced the cherry wood floors of his living room and ran his fingers through his now ruffled blond mane. He wanted to remain skeptical. Logic dictated that he must be careful. Vet this man properly. Verify his story. And yet . . .

Big Jim's great-grandson! If Henry's story checked out, this could be the partner he'd been waiting for. A man motivated by blood and family and tradition. A brother in the purest form. A *soldier* who would help in lifting The Ravens beyond any accomplishment his great-grandfather could have imagined!

Kaiser's initial shock melted into doubt, then bounced back to excitement, and finally to euphoria. Logical reasoning and careful analysis were quickly giving way. Besides, there was almost no chance this was a set-up. No one would dredge up a name from so far in the past – especially *that* name.

"This could be the next step in our evolution. If there is a God, I'd swear He is on our side right now," Kaiser said to the walls. He found himself glancing up at the clock every couple of minutes, unable to force time to move faster. Their meeting could very well decide the fate of his entire plan.

    With his mind unable to slow itself, Kaiser decided to go for a run. Five miles later, in spite of his best efforts, Kaiser still found it impossible to subdue his anticipation.

***

Henry spent the afternoon at Ty's apartment, where he was living temporarily thanks to his new friend's generosity. Despite trying again, both men had found no further information on Mr. Phillip Kaiser.

    "I don't like this, man. There should be more to this guy. He's like a blank slate, and that only makes me believe he's dangerous. Are you sure you want to go through with this meeting? Why not push it back, take time to prep some more?"

    "No way, Ty. I'm perfectly aware of the fact he's dangerous. Now that we've met, I'm absolutely convinced. He's a Raven. It was in his eyes, I can't explain it. He looks like . . . I don't know. Have you ever met someone and found it hard to maintain eye contact? That's how this was. Like he was examining me from the inside out."

    "That's it. I'm coming with you!"

    "Right. That's what I need. A black dude riding shotgun to my interview to join a racist terror cell. No thanks, pal!"

    Ty stood up and fought a smile. "Fine, I'll ride separate and follow you. You go in there and keep your phone turned on. If things go south and you need an exit, give me a call or text and I'll get in there quick."

    Henry considered this plan for a moment. "You're right. It's stupid for me to go alone. I'm telling you, though, he's more than a little intrigued. I could see it in his face. He wants to believe I'm real. I almost felt like he had been waiting for this to happen. If I stay in character, I think I'm in."

    "Yeah, then what?"

Again, Henry pondered before responding. "Then I figure out what they're up to. I win their trust, I get involved, and then, if necessary, we go to the cops with the evidence."

"And you think it'll just be that simple?"

"I don't know, Ty. Maybe we'll get lucky and they turn out to be just some racist memorabilia enthusiasts. You know, like the skinheads who collect old Nazi crap."

"And maybe you get yourself killed. Or worse."

"What do you mean worse?"

"Nothing, just don't get caught up, okay? I've seen guys go into combat and come back a shell. You know, they look and sound the same, but something inside is just gone. If these guys are as hardcore as we think, you'll have to start acting, talking, and even thinking like they do. It's like you're a detective doing deep cover, except you've never had any training. Shit could get confusing, that's all I'm saying. Just don't forget who you are, man. Leave some bread crumbs."

Henry stood up, marveling at the depth of genuine concern for a man whose grandfather had killed his.

"I hear you, really I do. And I definitely will. I can't forget. I've got too much to lose."

Chapter Sixteen

Tuesday, May 24; Vicarstown

What the fuck are you doing here, Logan? Just turn the fucking car around and leave! You need to be at Phillip's house in less than an hour!

Logan Feury sat in his silver BMW M3 sedan, thinking and smoking his third Lucky Strike in a row. He had left the dealership over an hour ago, yet somehow hadn't made it home for dinner. Instead, he found himself parked on DeTalente Avenue on the south end of town. This was the "ghetto" portion of Vicarstown, where the welfare-fed hordes lived in seventy-year-old shotgun houses and where cops regularly patrolled. His car would stand out like a Black Panther at a Trump rally.

To his left and across the street sat Martin Luther King, Jr. Elementary School. The playground, which featured a huge, rusted climbing dome, still crawled with kids and parents even as dusk began to descend. It was this scene, as Feury aimlessly drove around, that made him stop the car. To his right and beyond the sidewalk, a row of those shitty houses stood moldering in the humidity of an early evening.

The tinted glass kept Feury's face mostly hidden as he peered out and examined the people of DeTalente Avenue as if they were bacteria under a microscope. He was fascinated. No, sickened by the rot of ghetto culture. He viewed the people on this street not as humans, but as roaches whose colony he had infiltrated.

Fucking animals. Look at this fat piece of shit picking up her kid. No doubt a bastard. I'm guessing none of these little shits has a father. Disgusting.

The overweight black woman he was studying was crossing the street directly in front of Feury's car. She wore a loose black tank top that screamed "I LOVE SUNDAYS" in bright pink letters. She looked to be at least two hundred and fifty pounds, and her arms and chest were covered with numerous green tattoos.

Jesus, what a pig. Who the fuck would impregnate that?

The woman yelled at one of the boys running around the playground. He changed direction mid-stride and darted toward his mother. His lack of hesitation made it obvious she had trained him well.

Feury noted that the boy looked to be around ten years old. He wore a stained Kevin Durant jersey and baggy black shorts. He and his rotund mother made their way back across the street and down the sidewalk with their backs to Feury and his fancy ride. A few folks had turned their heads when he first rolled up in the Beemer, but since then he hadn't attracted any attention.

He watched them turn right and disappear into one of the shoeboxes they called houses in this neighborhood. After a few more minutes, darkness settled in and the party on the playground quickly broke up. Most of the kids were unattended, and they began to disperse in all directions without supervision.

Though he knew he had to leave – Kaiser didn't like anyone to be late to Ravens' meetings – Feury's thoughts kept returning to the large woman and her kid.

That bitch is everything that's wrong with this country. Probably living off my taxes. Smoking weed and watching reality TV all fucking day. The kid probably can't read and causes more problems than he's worth. Future drug dealer...coming soon to a tax-funded state penitentiary near you!

Feury put the sedan in drive, but he wasn't leaving DeTalente Avenue yet. He rolled past their house and found a turn-off just up the street. He turned the car again down the gravel alley running behind the row of houses on DeTalente. Once again, he sat in silence and waited. He looked around and saw no movement, just beaten up trash cans and even more beaten up garage doors.

What the fuck, Logan? If you leave now, you can still make it to Phillip's on time. This isn't necessary and she's definitely not worth it!

And yet, he was opening the glove compartment and removing a black nine millimeter along with a detached silencer. He'd never had need of the silencer before. In fact, he'd only ever used the gun at a shooting range. He'd gotten pretty accurate with it from fifty feet. Tonight, he figured, he might only need to cover ten or fifteen feet at most.

Their killing of the little mixed girl the other night hadn't satisfied him the way it usually did. He'd been present for the kill, as always, but he didn't get to do the honors. He hadn't been able to feel the knife entering her flesh, to know he was the one causing her pain. The "itch," far from being scratched, had instead spread into a full-blown infection in his brain. He hadn't been able to concentrate all day at the dealership. He needed to calm it before he lost his handle on it altogether.

In and out, quick and easy, no problem. But I want to see them. I want to watch the bullets go in and see their ugly fucking peasant faces when they die. I get some peace, plus score two more for the good guys. Phillip won't be happy, but he'll understand. He has to.

This wasn't the first time Feury had "gone rogue" by killing outside of the Ravens' ritual. Kaiser strictly forbade such killings, as they could lead authorities to close in on their clandestine activities. Feury knew this but did it anyway, because he had to. Their rituals were simply too few and far between to satisfy his cravings for bloodshed.

The problem this time was the lack of planning. Normally he would scout a place, pick the person, observe them off and on for days or even weeks, then strike. This one was spontaneous. More fun, yes. But also more dangerous.

Feury took his time getting out of the car, making sure he had the keys before locking it. He walked past the sagging one-car garage, opened the gate on the chain-link fence, and strolled into the backyard with confidence. Like nearly all the houses on this block, the kitchen was at the back of the house. The light was on, and Feury saw movement. Dinner time. Perfect.

He remembered that he hadn't eaten since his tuna sandwich at lunch, and his stomach growled as a reminder. He climbed up two steps and onto a sad, cracking concrete porch. A long-neglected grill sat to the far right next to a frayed lawn chair.

Feury re-checked his weapon, cocked it, and then tapped the end of the silencer on the window of the back door. He stepped to the side so that no one could see him just by looking out the window. He heard someone come to the door, but after a few moments there was still no sign of them opening it. He waited a few more ticks, then tapped the window again with more force this time.

After a moment, he heard the woman's voice shouting and the door being unbolted. Feury readied himself as she pulled the door open and showed her head and torso to him. Three quick bursts, and she was back-pedaling into the kitchen. Three bloody holes appeared in her upper chest, near the throat. She collapsed backward, sprawling over a chair and landing face-first on the linoleum floor. Her blood immediately began covering the ugly beige flooring.

Feury entered the house and smiled as his prey hit the floor. He heard a gasp and snapped his head to the right. There, still sitting at a small table wedged against the back wall of the house, was the boy from the playground. He was still wearing that blue jersey, and holding a fork full of cheeseburger macaroni Hamburger Helper in his right hand.

The boy's eyes fixed on the killer's, then flashed to his lifeless mother, then back to the killer.

"Sorry, kid. Nothing personal," Feury said, then let loose with three more bursts from his silenced weapon. The boy flipped backward out of the chair. The fork flew from his hand and smacked the ceiling, leaving yellow and brown stains on the drywall.

Feury quickly shut the door behind him and searched the rest of the house. No one else was around, just as he had suspected. He walked back into the kitchen, admiring his work. For him, the moments after a kill were better than sex. He moved to the door and looked out on the backyard. No one stirring; no one had heard or seen.

He went to the stove and turned off the burner. The skillet was still full of the pasta and meat concoction. Feury looked around for a plate and dipped out a generous portion. He sat in silence at the kitchen table, eating heaping forkfuls and looking at the blood sprays on the cabinets and refrigerator.

They'll probably chalk this up to gang activity. Or, maybe she has a piece of shit boyfriend who deals meth or something. They'll probably pin it on him! God, this tastes good. I haven't had Hamburger Helper since I was a kid. Well done, lady!

Feury looked at his watch and grimaced. No doubt, he was going to be late to Kaiser's meeting. He'd have to endure a dirty look maybe, but this was worth it. He eyed his shoes and clothing. No signs of blood. Taking the fork with him (wouldn't want to leave a DNA sample), Feury took a last look around the splattered kitchen and then left. He was pleased to see that no one had disturbed his beautiful car, and no one was milling around in the alley.

Speeding away toward the more respectable parts of Vicarstown, Feury turned up the radio and starting singing along to Christopher Cross' "Sailing." The "itch" was gone, replaced by a serene feeling of balance and satisfaction. He was a good soldier for the cause, and God, it felt good to be on the right side of the fight.

***

Henry arrived outside Kaiser's townhouse ten minutes early. He felt the same gurgle in his stomach that had plagued him before their first meeting. There was so much to remember. Ty had cooked up a quick fake identity for "Henry Bryant," complete with Facebook and LinkedIn pages. They hoped it would be just enough to throw someone off the scent if they went snooping into his background.

But that was only part of the flotsam floating about in Henry's mind as he sat in his car. He also had to remember his most important fake character traits: his racist opinions. He not only had to say the right things, he had to say them in the right way. If he didn't come off as genuine, these guys would sense it immediately. Henry remembered Kaiser's eyes, and how they seemed to sense everything in a given environment.

He's a lot more like a wolf than a raven.

Exiting the vehicle, Henry noticed two sharp-looking foreign cars near Kaiser's Audi--one a silver Jaguar X-type, the other a dark-colored Volvo sedan. It immediately struck Henry that these probably belonged to the other members of the Ravens. This was now a group interview, or perhaps an interrogation.

What if they already know who I am? I could be walking right into a trap. These guys are smart and obviously have resources. This doesn't feel right.

The sirens in Henry's mind were blaring, but before he could turn and get back to his car, the used Accord that was laughably out of place among this collection, he heard a voice calling his name. Phillip had emerged from the front door of his townhouse and was beckoning Henry inside with a welcoming tone.

"Henry! Eight minutes early . . . well done! Tardiness is among the few behaviors that I truly abhor. Please, come inside. The others are very excited to meet you!"

The eagle-eyed stoicism which Kaiser had exhibited in the coffee shop had been replaced with a markedly more jovial and relaxed attitude. He ushered Henry into the townhouse with a hand planted on his back. Henry was thrown by the change in Kaiser's tone, but also relieved. It was clear the welcome was genuine, and that his cover, at least thus far, had not been blown.

Henry was ushered into a living room that featured several large, framed classic reproductions. He recognized one as *The Birth of Venus* by Botticelli, and another as *The School of Athens* by Raphael. They were the sort of paintings Henry wished he could hang up around his classroom when teaching the Renaissance. They gave him a further sense of comfort, even as he approached two other men whom he assumed were also killers.

A man wearing a slim-cut gray suit with a narrow black tie, held out his hand first. He gave him a warm smile and an equally warm and firm handshake.

"You must be Henry! Great to meet you! My name is Michael Nix. Allow me to introduce another member of our little group. This is Grant Kessler."

Henry recognized the name from his reading of the local newspapers' coverage of the missing girl. "Grant Kessler the sheriff?"

"Why, yes! Evidently you saw my ads. Hopefully I got your vote!"

"Unfortunately I'm not local, but I've seen your name around town. I hear good things," Henry said, still trying to wrap his mind around the word *sheriff*.

"Good to hear . . . and thanks! Oh, by the way, do you have a business card? I would like to get your contact information while we have you here. Would you like a drink?"

"Sure. Um, I'll have whatever you guys are having. I'm sorry I don't have any cards with me. I'm happy to write any information down that you may need."

Kessler passed a pen and a small pad of paper to Henry, then poured out two fingers' worth of Woodford Reserve and handed the glass to Henry. He wasn't used to drinking much, especially not a double shot of neat bourbon, but Henry knew this was important. He swirled the amber liquid around for a moment, then took a healthy swig and did his best not to show discomfort as it burned every inch of his esophagus.

Nix spoke again to Henry. "I work in Nashville as a corporate lawyer. Pretty boring stuff really, but it pays the bills. So, Phillip never told us, what do you do for a living?"

Henry had gone over this part of his cover story with Ty in detail. They had settled on self-employment, since that would give him the flexibility to meet with the group whenever necessary. Ty had set up a couple of online storefronts that appeared just functional and legitimate enough to pass a cursory smell test.

"Oh, I run a couple of online businesses. I'm my own boss and it's great. I was never one for punching a clock forty hours a week."

"Good for you! I log a lot more than forty some weeks, and I can't say I particularly enjoy the work. But I like my toys too much to give it up," Nix replied and smiled.

Kaiser, who had left the room as soon as Henry entered, returned with a look of concern.

"I'm sorry, Henry. I had to make a call. We have one more among our ranks, and it seems that he is running late. I wasn't able to reach him." Kaiser shot a look at Nix.

Kessler spoke up. "That's not like him. Still, I don't want to wait. Shall we proceed with the meeting?"

"Absolutely. Mr. Feury will not ruin this occasion. Please . . ." Kaiser gestured for the men to follow him down a short hallway. Henry could tell that Kaiser was upset over Feury's absence, but he was doing his best to maintain a cheery posture.

Kaiser led them into a dimly lit room dominated by dark wood bookshelves. A study. A brown leather couch sat along one wall and faced two matching leather chairs. The bookshelves were packed with volumes, and many appeared to be antiques. A tinge of jealousy hit Henry as he scanned the titles. Most of them were histories or biographies. In another situation, Henry might have browsed for hours just pulling titles and marveling.

As they entered, Nix and Kessler took places on the couch, while Kaiser pointed at one of the chairs and invited Henry to sit. Next, Kaiser produced a small wooden box and opened the lid to reveal a row of cigars featuring Habana, Cuba on the label. Henry took one without hesitation and waited as Kaiser searched in his jacket pocket for a cigar cutter and an engraved silver lighter. He found them and offered both to Henry. His initials, P.A.K., were clearly visible in black cursive script. Each man took turns using the lighter, and for a few moments they sat enjoying their illegal treat in silence.

Kaiser glanced at his watch. For a split-second, Henry thought he saw a look of pure rage cross his face. Just as quickly, he recovered and turned his full attention to Henry.

"Well, Henry. I believe it's time for us to get down to business, as they say. Though I don't necessarily believe in a God, I do believe in fate. I believe that certain people are destined to make a major impact on society, while most never get the chance. Henry, I believe this group is destined for just such an impact. And when you approached me yesterday, I was stunned. It was as if you had been delivered to us on command. You see, I . . . we have recently made the decision to expand our ranks, and you would be our first and, perhaps, most important recruit.

"As you may know, we are in the midst of a great war. It is a war for the soul of our nation. It is being waged within every conceivable aspect of our culture. And we are losing. We've been losing for some time now. It seems that Negro culture and philosophy pervades every last portion of our society. We, the gentlemen you see before you, are warriors in this great fight. We are among the few who are willing to do what is necessary to beat back our enemy.

"Did you know that the death rate among whites in their twenties and thirties is increasing? They are the only demographic to see such increases. And why is this happening? Because they lack hope. They lack a viable way forward. They turn to drugs and alcohol because jobs and a real future are not feasible anymore.

"We have a president who serves only one portion of our society. The rest are left to fend for themselves, and the results are devastating. Rome burns while our leaders fiddle. Black Lives Matter protesters riot in the streets over a single incident of police brutality. Meanwhile, black youths in Chicago kill each other at rates higher than most Old West towns.

"But I digress. Before I get ahead of myself, there are a few questions we would like to ask. Please be honest, and please allow yourself to speak freely. You are among friends. No need for political correctness here! Would either of you like to start?" Kaiser looked up at Nix and Kessler, both of whom were eyeing Henry with fascination.

They all believe I'm the real deal! They almost look giddy. Now, just nail the questions and you're in!

"I will," said Nix. "Phillip has told us your story. You're the great-grandson of our founder. You sought us out in order to join his cause. Assuming that's all true, I need to know one thing. Have you ever killed someone?"

The question froze Henry. He had expected some light "tell us about yourself" questions before they delved into the heavy stuff. He collected himself and answered quickly.

"To be honest, no. I've had thoughts about it from time to time. I'm not opposed to killing if it's for the right reasons. I mean, in a war there's going to be casualties, right? I sought out Phillip because I assume that you guys, like my great-grandfather, are soldiers in this war."

Oh, well done. You can see in his face that he liked that answer!

"So, you acknowledge that there is a war going on. Just what exactly is your perspective on this war?" Nix seemed pleased with the first answer, but still pushing for more details. Henry thought back to some of the musings that Big Jim had recorded in his journal.

"I mean, our rightful place in society has been upended. We have to fight to get it back or we're facing a pretty bleak future. The mixing of the races has corrupted all of us. Now we're looking at a society that is not only racially weakened, but morally corrupt. All of the pillars of our society are now under attack. I mean, even the gays can sense it. They're pushing harder than ever for more rights and the country is just laying down for them. In another generation, this country could be unrecognizable. So yes, I would say we are in the midst of a war without any doubt."

The look on Kaiser's face as Henry finished his answer bordered on lust. It was becoming clear to Henry that these men, especially their leader, had been waiting for someone like him to come along for years. Showing Kaiser the ring had been a gamble, but it was paying off. It gave his every word immeasurable credibility.

Kessler leaned forward. "What exactly do you think we do?"

Henry took a breath before answering. "I'm not going to pretend I know the details of this group's activities. I know that my great-grandfather was willing to do whatever it took, including spilling blood at times, to right what he perceived as wrongs. I know that his group was a brotherhood. They stood for each other no matter what. They were unified in their belief in racial purity and the greatness of America. I figure if you guys are anything like what their group was, that's exactly what I want to be a part of."

Kaiser was unable to resist a grin. He took a long drag off of his cigar and released the smoke into the space between them.

"I wasn't going to tell you this tonight, Henry. But your words have inspired me. In my youth, I knew James Bryant. He was a mentor to me in my teenage years. I credit him for opening my eyes and sending me on the path that I currently tread today. Hearing you speak, it's as if he's been reincarnated into your body! I must admit I was intrigued but still skeptical after our encounter yesterday. A part of me simply couldn't believe that the Bryant bloodline was not only alive but seeking to follow in his footsteps. And while we still have some things to discover about you, I feel quite confident that you will make a fine addition to what you aptly described as a brotherhood."

Henry sat stunned, still processing the knowledge that Kaiser had known Big Jim. Was that possible? He didn't believe Kaiser was lying.

"You knew my great-grandfather? That's . . . incredible. How did you meet him?"

"Through my father. He had a great deal of respect for Mr. Bryant and made sure that I was exposed to his philosophies. It was, as you might imagine, life-changing."

Henry nodded and flicked his cigar's ashes into an ornate, free-standing receptacle. He decided it was best to say no more on the subject. Clearly, there was more research to be done on Phillip Kaiser.

As if to bookend this portion of the conversation, a frazzled man appeared in the doorway of the study. Kaiser sensed him and turned, his expression transforming from delight to anger in a split-second.

"Hey guys! Sorry I'm late. Hey, is this the new guy? Hi, I'm Logan. What have I missed?"

"Everything. You've missed everything. Henry, I'm afraid we're going to have to cut this short. I believe I've seen and heard all I need, but we will do our due diligence as a group and be in touch soon enough," Kaiser said, quickly rising to his feet and ushering Henry past the man and into the hallway.

As they approached the front door, Kaiser continued. "I do apologize for the abrupt conclusion to our meeting. It has been truly enlightening, Henry." He pulled out his cellphone. "May I have your phone number?" Henry told him and Kaiser entered it in his cell. "You should expect a call from me in a day or two. We will discuss next steps then. How does that sound?"

"I'm with you if you'll have me. Thank you for your hospitality, especially the Cuban! I look forward to hearing from you. I have to say, after hearing you knew my great-grandfather, this feels kind of meant to be." Henry extended his hand.

"Indeed it does."

***

Kaiser gave the hand a firm grasp and then opened the door for him. As the door closed behind Henry, Kaiser's face melted into a disgusted grimace. He turned and found Feury standing at the entrance to the hallway.

"I'm sorry, boss. I know this was an important meeting. I just lost track of – "

The explanation was cut short as Kaiser darted across the room and wrapped his right hand around Feury's throat. He slammed Feury against a wall and tightened his grip. Feury gasped and struggled for breath, but made no effort to fight off Kaiser's attack.

"You will not speak again until you are instructed, is that clear?" Kaiser asked in a calm and measured tone. Feury nodded, his face a light shade of purple. Kaiser's grip loosened just enough for Feury to fill his lungs.

"I know exactly what you've been doing tonight. I can see it in your eyes. You've engaged in an unsanctioned and unplanned hunt. You've risked the life and freedom of every man in this room, so that you can fulfill your selfish urges. Am I correct?"

Again, Feury only nodded. Kaiser let out a huff and looked down at the floor, then slowly brought his eyes back up to meet Feury's.

"You swore an oath. A *blood* oath to all of us. You are part of a fraternity that would gladly die to save you. That being said, I cannot allow you to continue to jeopardize our plans. We are on the cusp of delivering a crushing blow to the inferior elements whom we all know have co-opted our society. I want all of you to hear me, and hear me well. Don't make me revoke both your membership and your life. A cancer must be removed quickly if the body is to survive, and I will not hesitate to act if necessary. Have I communicated my feelings clearly enough?"

Feury nodded once more, and Nix and Kessler both indicated their understanding with an emphatic "Yes."

Kaiser released his grip on Feury's throat, but continued glaring into his eyes.

"Excellent. Now, Mr. Nix and Mr. Kessler, please give us your appraisal of Mr. Bryant and his potential as it pertains to this group."

Nix spoke first. "I thought he was nervous at first. But his answers were spot on. They felt sincere. He clearly has an admiration for his great-grandfather. Could be a game-changer for us. Grant?"

"Yeah, agreed. My only question is will he be able to kill when the time comes? You just don't know how someone is going to react until they sink the knife in."

Kaiser responded. "I believe we are unanimous, save for Mr. Feury who will receive no vote in this matter. I haven't had a chance to fully vet him, but I don't believe anyone could produce a vintage Ravens ring and speak as if he were channeling Jim Bryant unless he were genuine. And as for his lack of experience vis-à-vis the spilling of impure blood, we will address that situation in due time."

Kaiser turned again toward Logan, who still had not moved away from the wall where Kaiser had planted him.

"Mr. Feury, we will need your services. I want you to procure a subject for us, and as soon as you can manage it. Not too young. We don't want to spook Mr. Bryant on his first kill. I will allow you to use your discretion. This weekend would be ideal. Gentlemen, any objections?"

There were none. The meeting adjourned and Kaiser was left alone to ponder the results. The addition of a new Raven was imminent, and he felt more confident than ever their destiny would be fulfilled.

Chapter Seventeen

Thursday, May 26, 2016; Vicarstown

Henry sat alone in the driver's seat, staring at his phone. This was the longest he and Carrie had ever gone without speaking. Normally he would bend over backwards to make her forget whatever he'd done to anger or hurt her, but this time his priorities were different. This mission, this *calling*, was bigger than anything he'd ever been involved in. Even his marriage.

Still, he needed to hear her voice. Needed to know she would be waiting for him at the end of what lay ahead. He'd left her back in Indiana with their son and a lot of unanswered questions. Perhaps it was finally time to come clean about why he was really down here.

He pressed the call button and waited through several tones. His car sat in the parking lot of a CVS on the main strip running through town. He peered out through the windshield at the increasing lunchtime traffic.

"Henry?"

"Yeah, hon. How are you doing?"

She huffed audibly. "I've been better. I'm guessing this isn't a call to tell me you've come to your senses and you're on your way home."

"Uh, no. I'm sorry . . . not yet. How is David?"

"He's asking a lot of questions about you, and I'm running out of excuses. He needs his father, Henry."

"You know I would be there if –"

"Don't, Henry! Don't. You're not here. You've made it very clear where your priorities lie. You can't possibly still be doing 'research' on your grandfather. So, what is this? A break? A vacation? Did you meet someone? What is this?"

Henry took a moment before answering. He could hear the hurt in her voice and it turned his stomach. This was getting harder by the day.

"Baby, I need to tell you something. And no, it's not another woman or anything like that. It's way worse. I'm mixed up in something down here. Dangerous. I don't know how it's going to turn out. I just know that if I don't see it through, I'll never be able to come back home. I won't be able to live with myself. I'm sorry I didn't tell you before. I just didn't know how to explain."

"Does this have anything to do with what happened when your grandpa was young? When he was with those men, those killers?"

Henry closed his eyes and pictured the scene: his grandfather lying in bed, confessing to her the sins that must have poisoned his entire life.

They stayed silent for a long time. Henry could tell Carrie was on the verge of crying, though she was trying her best to hide it. His eyes began to well up. He didn't blame Herman for seeking out someone else as a confessor. His image of Herman Bowersox as hero and saint would have made that conversation nearly impossible.

"Henry, you have to be honest with me right now. What is going on down there? What kind of danger are you talking about?"

"I've stumbled onto something big. Something I'm not sure I can handle. But I have help. I've made some new friends who are going to do everything they can for me. Carrie, the Ravens aren't dead. Grandpa's group has reformed somehow. There's a whole new group of guys doing the same thing. I don't have any proof yet, but this is real. And I'm going to bring them down. From the inside. I'm joining their group and I'm going to make sure the killing stops for good."

"Jesus, Henry! No! You can't get involved with those kinds of people! You're not a cop! You're a teacher!

You're a high school history teacher with a wife and a son! Remember that, Henry? Just go to the police!"

"I can't, Carrie. Like I said, there's no proof. I only found out about these guys by a fluke. But it's real. And I can stop them, I know it. I've got a plan. I'm going to get in good with them and find some evidence. Then I'll go to the cops. Then I'll come home. Okay?"

Another silence. He knew there was no way she could support his risking his life, but he no longer needed her permission. For the first time, he was putting something ahead of Carrie and David.

He continued, "Carrie, I know what this sounds like. I need you to understand. This is what I'm meant to do. I know it. Please . . . "

"Just come home, Henry. Just come home. Do what you have to do, and get home to your family. We love you so much. If something happens . . . just come home." She started sobbing. Henry leaned forward and rested his forehead on the steering wheel, trying to imagine what she must be feeling.

"I will," he whispered. "I love you."

"I love you, too."

The call ended and Henry sat motionless. It felt good to have the truth out and to know that Carrie was still his wife, at least for the moment. Now he could focus on the task at hand: becoming a trusted member of the Ravens and finding a way to bring them down.

***

Sheriff Grant Kessler walked into headquarters and greeted his fellow officers with the smile that had become his trademark since taking the reigns as boss. His easygoing management style made him approachable and well-liked, even as he was beginning the process of cleaning up some of the lax procedures that marked the previous sheriff's term.

He had spent the morning on patrol, something he got to do less and less since taking the head job. Kessler had underestimated the load of paperwork and political tasks that go into being the face of the Sheriff's Department.

He sat down at his desk, which was neatly organized with a three-tier tray and an oversized desk calendar with reminders scribbled all over it. He pulled out the bottom right drawer and produced a lunchbox. Today's menu included a chicken salad sandwich, a small bag of Doritos and a granola bar for dessert.

While enjoying a bite of the sandwich, Kessler leafed through the paperwork from last night's arrests. Nothing out of the ordinary. A drunk and disorderly down at Buck's Tavern. A single-pot meth lab. A domestic assault and battery.

Kessler pulled the details on the assault and battery. Kelondre Moxon. Thirty-one years old. Arrested after he slapped his girlfriend and her fifteen-year-old daughter around in her apartment. He did the quick math in his head. The girlfriend must have been sixteen when she got pregnant with her daughter. Typical.

He turned to his computer and quickly searched Moxon's name in the police database. Moxon had two previous convictions, both drug-related. He had only been out of prison for nine months before last night's activities. Again, typical.

Kessler continued to munch on his sandwich as he scanned Moxon's arrest and incarceration history. He had spent six months in juvie at sixteen. No doubt he was a high school dropout with three or four kids from three or four different women.

No doubt he's still using drugs. No doubt he's not holding down any kind of gainful employment.

He stood up and walked around his desk. Closing the office door, Kessler pulled out his cellphone and dialed Logan Feury.

"Hello, Sheriff! What can I do for you?"

"Hey, have you found anyone yet for this weekend?"

"No. In fact, I was going to contact you pretty soon to see if you had any candidates. Been a while since we've . . . collaborated," Feury said.

"Well, I think I've got a solid candidate here. His bond is set at five thousand. Will that be a problem?"

"Shouldn't be. I'll pull it from petty cash here at the dealership. I like to keep a little extra on hand for these sorts of projects." Feury chuckled at his own perceived wit.

"Good. This guy should fit the bill perfectly. A worthless repeat offender. No one's going to miss him. How does tonight work?"

"Not a problem. I'll roll in after sundown. After I pick him up, I'll take him back to HQ and get him settled."

"Sounds good. Let me know when he's ready and I'll contact Phillip. He'll want to move fast," Kessler said and then hung up. He wasn't totally comfortable using his new office as a means of finding prey for the Ravens, but in this case he saw no risk. In fact, his winning the Sheriff's title was a part of their overall strategy.

He assumed his original position at the desk and tore open the bag of Doritos, satisfied that Mr. Moxon had committed his last crime.

***

Henry spent much of the afternoon driving around and trying to remember what his life was like before finding the ring and photos in Herman's garage. A time when his biggest problem was figuring out a workable seating chart for his unruly freshmen. A time when he and Carrie loved and laughed and mostly made marriage look easy. Those days felt distant and, worse, irretrievable.

He tried to figure any possible way he could approach the authorities about the Ravens. He knew he couldn't go to the local guys, since their boss was one of the killers. The state police or the feds might listen, but without actual proof they would quickly usher him out of the building.

Every time his mind drifted to thoughts of Carrie and David and home, it was quickly jolted back into focus with the image of his dying grandfather. Lying in his coffin, Herman opened his eyes and extended his withered hand toward his grandson.

You've got to do this, Henry. I know you're scared, but it's the only way. The only way I can rest. The only way you can face your son. You've got to...

Tears filled Henry's eyes as he snapped back to his view of the road stretching out in front of him. He'd been operating the car on mental autopilot for God knew how long. He was lucky to still be between the lines.

With no desire to think or drive anymore, he navigated back to Ty's apartment. He needed the good humor of his friend to bring him back from the creeping despair. He found Ty in nearly the same spot where he'd last seen him that morning: sitting on the couch, hunched over his laptop.

"What's up, slick? Man, you look like I felt when I heard Prince died," Ty remarked.

"I talked with Carrie. We're still married. That's the good news."

"And the bad news?"

"Everything else in my life. I need a drink or ten. What do you think?"

Ty took one last look at his laptop and slammed the lid shut. "I feel that!"

Thirty minutes later they arrived at a less-than-respectable establishment known as Gummo's. Though Henry hadn't been drunk since college – and even then only a handful of times if he were being honest – he badly needed to let loose.

Ty, who had chosen a maroon T-shirt with the phrase *I'm What Willis Was Talking About* boldly splashed across the chest in yellow lettering, sat across from Henry at a small wooden table. He drank a Red Stripe as he surveyed the small saloon.

"Dude, I don't know why I brought us here. I don't think there's a woman under forty in this whole place!"

"We didn't come here to pick up chicks, Ty." Henry took a gulp of his Captain and Coke. "We came here to drown our sorrows and, how would you put it? Kick it?"

"Yes, my man! We are kicking it . . . sort of."

"Good. Anyway, thanks for taking me out. And I apologize in advance for anything I may say or do under the influence."

"Don't worry. I won't let you get too far gone. I'm driving, so feel free to get a little crazy."

After three mixed drinks and two Buds, Henry was beyond buzzed. At some point, a John Mellencamp cover band took the slightly elevated stage at the back of the bar. They were halfway through an off-key version of "Pink Houses" when Henry spoke.

"Ty, what's it like to be black?"

Ty nearly choked on a sip from his second bottle. "What?"

"What's it like to be black? I wanna know."

"Well," Ty started with a grin, "it's a lot like being white, but without all the respect and advantages and rights and stuff."

Henry's eyes widened. "Seriously?"

"Yeah, man. I should be asking you what it's like to be white. You know that old Eddie Murphy SNL skit when he puts on makeup and pretends to be a white dude? And everybody just gives him money and treats him like a king?

That's kind of how I imagine it would be, but less exaggerated of course."

"I never really thought about it until recently. That's because I never had any black friends until recently. I mean, is there really a difference in the way you're treated? It's 2016. Aren't we past all that by now?"

Ty gave Henry a look that made him a little embarrassed. He took another pull from his Red Stripe and looked over at the band, which was now hitting its stride with "Hurts So Good."

"Take Ferguson, Missouri for example Michael Brown only knew the cops as enemies, as people who exist to make your life harder. That's what you've got to understand about being black. We don't see the police as being there to 'protect and serve,' we see them as the opposite. And I know they're not all like that, but when you've seen it and experienced it, you learn not to trust them."

The two men sat in silence, taking in the riffs and vocals of the Mellencamp trio.

"I think I understand what you're saying," Henry finally said.

"But hey, man. What you're doing down here . . . what you're doing here with the Ravens and your grandfather is . . . I just really respect you, man. You're restoring my faith. Seriously. It's pretty incredible when I think about what you're sacrificing. You're laying it all on the line. And I'm going to do everything I can to help you nail these guys, and get home safe to that beautiful family! Okay?"

"Ty, you're gonna make me cry. Can we hug it out?"

"Uh, not here pal. Maybe later, after it's over. Now, finish your drink and let's get out of here. I can't take this band anymore!"

That night, Henry slept better than he had in months. His hangover would be epic, but that was the least of his troubles. He woke up at eleven and looked at his phone. One text message. From Kaiser.

Tonight. Midnight. Will text coordinates one hour before. Regards, Phillip.

Chapter Eighteen

Friday, May 27; 11:45 PM; East of Vicarstown

Henry looked at his watch and sighed as he navigated his car through the hazy Tennessee night. Ty looked on in the passenger seat, dressed like a Navy SEAL and staring at his phone's GPS guidance. Only five more minutes to their destination.

Neither man spoke. They had already game-planned this mission from every conceivable angle. Henry knew he was most likely headed for an initiation. He had no idea what to expect, and that was the primary reason for Ty's presence. They'd had enough time after Kaiser's last text to figure out where they were going. A defunct factory outside of town. Seemed like a perfect place for a group of maniacs to hide their murderous activities. If this was indeed the Ravens' headquarters, Henry needed to see it.

With a half mile left before reaching the old plant, Ty exited the vehicle and began making his way toward it on foot. Henry had made fun of him for wearing the night vision goggles, but now they were coming in handy.

Ty's role was one of both reconnaissance and protection. He would case the perimeter of the plant and take note of ingress and egress points. He would also be Henry's backup in case things got out of hand inside. Neither of them knew what was in store for Henry once he walked in, but Ty insisted on being close by just in case. Henry carried his cell phone in his left front pocket. It was already set to send a text to Ty if necessary.

***

As he jogged toward his destination, Ty took out his phone and made sure it was on and silenced. He also double-checked his other essential items: an LED flashlight, a

Bowie camp knife strapped to his leg, and a .357 Magnum holstered on his right hip.

Though Ty was a former soldier, he had never seen combat and had only fired his gun on one occasion—at the gun range in Vicarstown. Beads of sweat began to form on Ty's forehead as he hoofed it through the thin layer of trees near the south end of the plant. He slowed down to take notice of his surroundings. He felt like Chuck Norris in that old *Delta Force* movie, though his confidence was tinged with anxiety as he thought of Henry walking into the lions' den. If something happened to his new best friend, Ty would never forgive himself.

***

Henry steered the rental down Hazelbaker Drive, a pothole-marred offshoot from the main highway that dead-ended at the abandoned plant. He spotted the hulking, dreary structure and initially saw no lights, but then noted a dimly lit entrance near where all the others' vehicles were already parked.

Just as when he had first met the group at Kaiser's house, the service door opened and Kaiser appeared with a look of pure satisfaction. He was wearing a black suit with a grey tie. Henry wondered if he slept in his formal wear.

"Henry! Good to see you once again! I see the coordinates were correct."

"Phillip . . . hi. Yes, they were perfect. I have to say you are the best dressed man I've ever met." Henry hoped the little joke would hide his growing unease.

Kaiser smiled and nodded in acknowledgement. As Henry entered, he first noticed the openness of the old factory. With the machinery removed, the building would easily hold two or three full basketball courts.

"Welcome to our new home, Henry. We adopted this old building with the hopes of making it our permanent base of operations. As you must have noticed on your way here, it is quite removed from the populated areas of town."

Henry took a long gaze around, and it was his turn to nod. "It's perfect!"

"We are agreed. Now, before we get started, would you like a drink?"

"Sure. A beer would be nice if you have it." *Best to play along.*

Kaiser led him up a set of metal stairs and onto the second level, where offices with glass enclosures allowed views of the factory floor below. One of the offices was fully furnished with a large oak desk, a couple of file cabinets, and a mini-fridge. Henry also noticed a laptop or tablet set up on the desk.

Kaiser produced two bottles of Heineken and a bottle opener. Henry realized that he hadn't seen any of the other Ravens yet.

"Aren't the others here? I assumed those were their vehicles out front."

"Oh, yes. They are all present. They're uh . . . making preparations at the moment. I told them I would take the honors of greeting and escorting you to the proper room," Kaiser said in between sips.

"I see. So, Phillip, would you mind shedding some light on why I'm here tonight? Can I assume that I'm being accepted into the group officially?"

Again, Kaiser grinned. His eyes widened slightly, exhibiting a rabid anticipation.

"You are, indeed, my friend. We have a little ritual that new members take part in. I have to admit that I've barely slept since our last encounter. Your words, your passion . . . I am beyond anxious to get you fully involved with our activities. And your bloodline . . ." Kaiser trailed off and looked into Henry's eyes. "I can see him now, in your face. You certainly are a Bryant."

"How well did you know Jim Bryant?"

"Unfortunately I can't say I knew him. I did meet him, more than once. My father insisted. I didn't realize at the time that I was communing with a legend. A true hero. He died before I was able to fully know him."

"I'm still stunned by the coincidence, or is it irony? Either way, it's incredible that you actually saw and spoke to my great-grandfather."

"Yes. Now you can understand my reaction when we first met. When you uttered his name. Unbelievable."

"So, your father was a Raven? That was why he wanted you to meet my great-grandfather?"

"Yes. Not a founding member, but among the first new recruits that they gained. In fact, he was the first second-generation member to join. Well, after your grandfather, of course."

"Of course." Henry gripped his beer so tightly he thought it might burst in his hand. If he lived through this night, he had even more information to process.

He doesn't know that Grandpa lived on after the war. That's why he trusts me so much. He thinks I'm like Big Jim Bryant reincarnated or something.

A moment of silence passed as they both reached the bottom of their bottles. Then a voice rang out from downstairs. "We're ready when you are, boss!"

"Ah, excellent! Henry, are you ready to become a Raven? In many ways, I feel as if you've been one your entire life. This part will simply be a formality."

"I'm ready," Henry said, and followed Kaiser out of the office and back down the metal stairs. His heart began racing, and he grabbed the railing to make sure he didn't fall down the steps.

Kaiser led him away from the door from which he had first entered, and into a rear area that was separate from the main factory floor. They passed through two doors, and then entered what appeared to be a large shower room. It was covered in grey tiling from floor to ceiling, with circular drains built into the floor throughout. There were no shower heads, but clearly this was a room where materials had either been cleaned or disposed of.

Once inside, Henry was quickly greeted by the other Ravens. They were also dressed like they were attending a board meeting. Suits and ties, with freshly buffed shoes and all. Henry took the opportunity to lighten the mood.

"Jeez, guys. I wish someone had told me I needed church attire tonight. I feel way underdressed here."

Got a couple of laughs. Good.

"It's just our way, Henry. You'll get used to it." Kessler held out his hand for a shake.

That's when Henry noticed the man chained near the far left corner of the room.

Henry was able to complete the handshake, but his attention was firmly planted on the struggling figure. He was a black man, perhaps in his thirties, shirtless with only a pair of black sweatpants covering his lower half. His hands were chained above his head, and Henry noted the chain was attached to a mobile hook that hung from the ceiling. It resembled a miniature crane which could be moved from one end of the room to the other along a track.

The man was conscious and whipping his head back and forth, surveying the five white men who stood before him. He was gagged with a washcloth. Henry looked away from him and toward Kaiser, who returned his gaze with force. Those eyes had a way of drawing Henry in and repelling him at the same time.

Kaiser spoke. "Henry, we are, as you know, engaged in a war. This war has raged for much longer than we have been alive, and surely it will continue after we are gone. American culture is rotting. Basic standards of morality and justice are being swept away with celebration. Behaviors once deemed taboo are now common. Conversely, behaviors once deemed noble are now cast aside and derided by the ignorant masses. We are but a small band, but I believe our part in this conflict will be quite large.

"Henry, you are, I believe, a key component in this battle. The warrior spirit flows through your veins, just as it did in your forefathers. Beginning tonight, we turn the tide in this war. We start to take back what has been ceded."

Kaiser concluded his speech by producing a long, notched knife with a blue handle. He led the men toward their captive, and the four Ravens quickly paired off on either side of him. Henry was left standing directly in front of the chained man.

Kaiser lifted the blade and offered the weapon to Henry. After a second's pause, he grabbed the handle with his right hand and took possession. His thoughts swirled into a blur of panic and reassurance. He was also conscious of another feeling: excitement.

What now, Henry? What are you going to do? Kill this guy? That's what they want. If you don't go through with this, they'll know you're a fraud. I should have known this was what they were planning. This was a mistake. Where is Ty?

Kaiser gently placed a hand on Henry's shoulder. The effect was surprisingly calming. He looked at his would-be victim, whose eyes were wide with terror, and then back to Kaiser.

There's no way out of this. I can't fake it. And there's no way I'm actually stabbing this guy. This is it. I'm done. Just run. Get out now and go back to Indiana. Call the police and hope they can find some evidence. Just run, now!

But Henry didn't move. He stayed perfectly still, feeling Kaiser's soothing hand on his shoulder. His heart should have been beating out of his chest, but it was calm. The knife felt comfortable in his hands, the way it had when his grandpa took him hunting as a child.

191 • Of Ravens and Lambs

"Henry, I know what you're feeling. We've all of us been in your shoes. Do you think any of us were born killers? Do you think we go around killing people for fun or sport?" Kaiser asked in a whisper. "No, we don't. We have to think of ourselves as soldiers. We are helping to rid the world of those who are corrupting our society. I want you to look at him. Really look at him. His life has been wasted running the streets, using drugs, beating women, stealing, and, worst of all, procreating. Yes, he has fathered several children with different women. His kind are like rodents. They will breed often and with anyone who happens to be around.

"What do you think those children are going to grow into, Henry? Upstanding citizens who vote and obey the law? Men and women who will pay their taxes and attend church on Sundays? Volunteer their time to help others? You and I both know that won't happen. Those kids will continue this man's legacy. They will multiply and spread their barbarous ways. Men like this have helped to ravage whole cities in this country. Detroit. Baltimore. St. Louis. There are large portions of those cities which are now wholly uninhabitable. Lawless ghettos where the stinking masses cling together in their wretched dwellings and reproduce so that a new generation may inflict even more damage.

"That's what I want you to see when you look into those dulled eyes. By any civilized definition, this is not a man. This is a plague. Do you understand me, Henry?"

Henry slowly nodded. His grip on the knife became tighter, and a new emotion began to fester in his mind: anger. He had been to St. Louis many times for Cardinals games. He had driven past the endless ruined projects of East St. Louis on his way to the safer regions of downtown.

Henry's feet began to shuffle him forward toward the prisoner. He felt the need to see the man's face close up, if only to confirm his humanity. He knew what Kaiser was saying was crazy. There was no justification for murder. Nonetheless, he was compelled. Henry had taught long enough to see the damage inflicted by generations of people who lacked even basic parenting or life skills. He trudged ever closer.

Without thinking, Henry took a corner of the washcloth and jerked it out of the man's mouth.

The man was breathing heavily but refrained from speaking. Henry's face was now just inches away from his. The knife remained firmly in his grip, held to Henry's side. Their eyes were locked on one another's. The inner voice that had reassured Henry since the beginning of this mission was silent.

"Please don't kill me, man! Please! I got kids! I . . . please don't!"

Without realizing it, Henry had lifted the blade from his side. It was now pointed at the left side of the man's rib cage. Kaiser and his men remained motionless. "I don't wanna die! Please, I swear I won't say anything! Just –"

The tip of the blade began to puncture the prisoner's skin between his ribs. Henry still stared into the man's eyes, smelling his foul breath and sweat that poured from his forehead. The man began to scream.

The knife continued to advance inward. Blood began to dribble out of the growing wound. As if awakened by the victim's shrieks, Henry's mind caught up with his actions.

Oh, Christ! What are you doing? You do this, you're no better than them! Stop it! Stop it now before there's no going back!

A loud buzzer interrupted his moment of panic. It sounded to Henry like an old-fashioned school bell denoting the end of a class period.

Henry pulled the knife from the man's ribs and saw that it had entered nearly two inches into his body. The

Ravens, led by Kessler, ran for the door and left Henry standing alone with his victim.

Henry, horrified by what he had allowed himself to do, threw the knife and ran to catch up with them. He now realized the alarm must be related to Ty. He didn't want to imagine what they would do to Ty if they caught him.

The group rushed upstairs and into Kaiser's office.

"The perimeter alarm was tripped. Could be someone snooping around, could be a deer or a bear. We need to search outside now," Kessler barked. Kaiser moved to a metal cabinet in the corner that Henry hadn't noticed before. He unlocked the padlock and opened it to reveal a small arsenal of guns. Kaiser reached in and began tossing handguns to each member, including Henry.

"Henry and I will take the southern end. You three start on the other side and we'll meet halfway around. If they heard the alarm, chances are they've already taken off."

They raced down the stairs and parted ways. The exterior of the building was devoid of lights. Kaiser and Henry slowly crept, guns drawn, past their cars and toward the darkness of the southwestern corner of the building. With forest all around, it would be nearly impossible to catch someone if they had taken cover. At least, that's what Henry hoped.

***

Ty sat in the woods about fifty yards from the entrance where Kaiser and Henry had just emerged. His night vision helped him to recognize Henry immediately. Relief flooded over him. He had heard the muffled screams from inside, and charged the door thinking Henry was in trouble. He thought, *If I make it out of here, I'm definitely giving him hell about how he's holding that gun! What an amateur!*

Ty remained still, confident the darkness would cover him. After several minutes of seeing no one, he began to stand up but quickly squatted again as he saw all five men converge on the service entrance.

"Nothing, boss. Like I said, it could have easily been a deer or something. I just put these motion sensors in the other day and they're pretty sensitive. I may have to test them out some more and adjust them," Kessler said, still looking into the black woods.

"If it was a person, what if they heard the screaming?" Nix asked, throwing a grudging look at Henry.

"That is also a possibility. We should wrap this up quickly and head out. Perhaps stay away for a few days. Grant, if we're able to return, I believe surveillance cameras should also be utilized," Kaiser said.

"Yeah, that's on my list. I'll keep an eye out in the meantime. You'll be the first to know if anything comes up."

The men walked back inside the facility, and Ty finally breathed. He stayed put, confident that Henry's life was not in danger.

***

Back inside the plant, the Ravens heard their victim yelling for help.

"Logan, finish him off quickly and let's get moving. Grant and Michael, procure the necessary materials for his removal. Henry, come with me, please," Kaiser said.

Kaiser led Henry into a side room on the first floor. "Henry, I'm sorry that you were interrupted. I'm proud of you."

"Proud?"

"Yes. You came face-to-face with the enemy and you did not hesitate to inflict a blow. Although you weren't able to finish, I have no doubt you would have. I saw it in your eyes, Henry. You have the killer instinct just as your grandfather and great-grandfather did. You truly are one of us. You are a Raven!"

Henry stood looking past Kaiser and onto the factory floor. The realization of just how close he had come to killing an innocent man was beginning to hit him.

"Thank you, Phillip. Thank you for this opportunity. I promise I'll do everything I can to help this group succeed in its mission," Henry blurted out, trying to stay in character.

They shook hands. "No, Henry. Thank you for seeking us out. You have no idea what you are yet capable of. I have great plans for you, and for us!"

Henry heard two gunshots ring out. The man he had almost killed was now dead.

"Come, Henry. See how we purify our prey and continue the tradition begun by your own flesh and blood."

They walked back into the tiled room to find their victim lying in a small pool of blood. Michael Nix was dousing the body with lighter fluid, while Grant Kessler turned on a large exhaust fan built into the ceiling. He also carried a fire extinguisher.

The five men gathered around the body. Henry tried his best not to look at it, though his eyes kept training back to the man's face. He now had a large, bloody hole in his right temple and another one in his chest. Henry felt the vomit begin to creep up, and he looked up at the exhaust fan until the feeling passed.

Kaiser announced, "Gentlemen, we purify society with our actions. We have struck another small blow tonight in that mission. We are as a searing flame, removing the impurities from all that it touches. And, most of all, we are brothers. Our bond can never be broken, even by death itself. Corvis Oculum Corvi Non Eruit!"

The Latin phrase was spoken by all in the group, save for Henry who stood motionless and numb. He now understood exactly what his grandfather had experienced, and why he had to find a way out.

Kessler struck a match and tossed it on the corpse. The flames shot up immediately, sending Henry back a step. The smell of burning flesh filled the room, and Henry once again fought the urge to wretch. The group watched the body burn in silence for over a minute, only to be halted by Kessler's use of the extinguisher.

Minutes later, the evidence of that night's murder was gone. The charred remains were dumped down a chute that, Kaiser explained to him, led to a room in the basement which had been sealed off with concrete blocks. The chute, which was accessed via a section of pull-up tile that made it nearly invisible, was the only way into the room.

The ashes on the tiled floor were promptly vacuumed up and also dumped into the chute. The blood was bleached and the towels were also thrown into the chute. Aside from some warping of the tiles from the heat, the room appeared to be unused. Henry wondered how many times they had performed this ritual before tonight. They proceeded with their duties as if working on an assembly line.

After one more sweep of the perimeter, the Ravens departed from the plant. Henry doubled back in his car and picked Ty up after he was sure the others were long gone.

"What the hell happened in there, Henry? I heard the screaming and I thought for sure you were toast." Ty removed his night vision goggles.

"I don't . . . I can't talk about it right now."

"Did they kill a guy in there? Oh my God! They killed a guy! Were you there?"

"Ty, I said I don't want to talk about it right now. Okay? I mean, I'm in over my head. I'm really in over my head now."

"Are you okay, though? Did they . . . did they try to initiate you or something?"

"Yeah, I'm a Raven now I guess. And, no. I'm not okay. I'm really fucking far from okay. Please just let it go for now, man. I need some time to think."

"Right, okay. I'm just glad they didn't hurt you. And bonus, now we know where their hideout is. So that's something."

Henry said no more. He drove Ty back to his apartment and continued to drive around until dawn. He knew he had seen and done things that couldn't be undone. The tame and easygoing Henry Bowersox wasn't coming back. Not after this. There was only the new Henry.

As the sun arose to color his pallid face, Henry kept asking himself the same questions: Who am I now? Am I really a Raven? Am I a murderer? Is there any way back? Kaiser's voice boomed in his head with an answer: *You are a Bryant. You are a soldier!*

Part III

The Wages of Sin

"Somewhere out there is a true and living prophet of destruction and I don't want to confront him. I know he's real. I have seen his work. I walked in front of those eyes once. I won't do it again. I won't push my chips forward and stand up and go out to meet him. It ain't just bein' older. I wish that it was . . . I think it is more like what you are willin' to become. And I think a man would have to put his soul at hazard. And I won't do that."

~Cormac McCarthy, *No Country for Old Men*

Chapter Nineteen

Saturday, May 28; Clarksville, Tennessee

Running on no sleep and ragged from the events of the previous evening, Henry drove toward Clarksville. No music or talk radio this morning. Just simple and comforting silence. Ty had called and texted numerous times, as had Deja. Henry wasn't ready to discuss with them or anyone what he had done. How could he?

As his Accord rolled down Interstate 24, Henry's mind stayed focused on his immediate future rather than his past. The entire night had been spent agonizing over his near-murder of a defenseless man. He still couldn't explain it. It was as if Kaiser had been able to roll back all of Henry's notions of morality and civility in order to tap into his deepest prejudices.

He finally understood how Kaiser was able to assemble this team and reactivate the long-dead traditions of the Ravens. Kaiser was nothing less than a master of manipulation, fueled by ambition on a scale unrivaled by anyone Henry had encountered before.

If the man ever went into politics, there'd be no stopping him. Like a superhuman version of Donald Trump.

He veered the Accord onto a familiar exit. It seemed as if he had just been here a couple of days ago. In fact, it had been two full months since his visit with Jacob Harrigan in that hellish nursing home. Henry came away from that meeting believing they would never see each other again. Harrigan had little to offer in terms of helping to discover where Kaiser came from. It was obvious now that Harrigan, along with being a murderer, was also a very good liar.

During their first encounter, Henry was surprised to find himself somewhat intimidated by the ninety-year-old. Though physically a shell of his younger self, Harrigan still maintained a killer's look and attitude. Henry remembered the way Harrigan had stared at him. It was as if he were saying, *If I weren't so broken down I'd kill you just to watch the life run out of your face. Just for five minutes' worth of entertainment.*

As he parked in the nursing home's lot, Henry knew this time would be different. He was different. And he wasn't leaving until Harrigan confessed. He'd already nearly killed one man, he wouldn't have any qualms about threatening an elderly bigot.

Henry glanced at himself in the rearview mirror. He was a mess. Large dark circles had appeared under his eyes, which themselves were dominated by tiny red streaks of lightning. No time for freshening up. He exited the car and marched into the nursing home.

It was barely nine o'clock, and Harrigan looked as if he had just risen from bed. Henry didn't knock. He swung the door open and closed it firmly behind him without a word. He stood staring at Harrigan, who was sitting on the side of his bed wearing heavy red flannel pajamas and fuzzy slippers.

Harrigan looked startled as he took in Henry. "Jesus, what's all the fuss, kid? Henry right? I remember you. You look like shit."

"Fuck you, Harrigan! I don't need your commentary right now. I've had a hell of night. And now you're gonna tell me some things. Things you should have told me the first time I was here. I'm not fucking around. Do you understand me, Harrigan?"

Harrigan maintained his demeanor. He rubbed his veiny, bald head with his troll-like hand while keeping his eyes fixed to Henry's. Even at ninety, he was going to be hard to intimidate.

"You're not the same guy, are you? You've changed. I'm guessing I know why, too! Well, I don't know what you think I can tell you that I didn't already, but let's give it a shot."

Henry moved quickly, darting in front of Harrigan and getting his face within inches of the old man's. He was immediately taken back to last night, when he was eye to eye with a broken man while sticking a knife in his ribs. The image quickly passed.

"You're right, old man. I'm not the same guy. The old Henry was willing to believe your bullshit. The new one knows better. Now, I've got one question for you. And by God, you'd better give me the truth. I know you know Phillip Kaiser. How do you know him?"

Harrigan smiled and exhaled, filling Henry's face with putrid morning breath.

"That's what you came here for? I suppose I shouldn't be surprised. Should have known you'd eventually connect the dots. Okay, I'll play along. How much do you know?"

"I know he met Big Jim Bryant on multiple occasions when he was young. I know he was indoctrinated into the Ravens by his father. I don't yet know who his father is or was. I need . . . " Henry tailed off as he read Harrigan's face. He continued, "Oh, my God. You're Kaiser's father, aren't you? You lied to my face when I was here before, told me you had no idea where he'd gotten the ring. It was your ring, wasn't it? It was you pushing him into it. Tell me."

Harrigan's smile faded, and what remained was a look of pain and disbelief.

"Yes, Henry. Phillip is my boy. I wasn't lying about my other son, Kevin. I tried to bring him into the group and it ended up killing him. A couple of years before Kevin died, I learned that I was going to be a father again. The girl's name was LeeAnn Kaiser. She was a waitress at the downtown diner there in Vicarstown. About as sweet and pretty as you'd ever want, but very poor and uneducated. Her family was shit. She was doing well just to pay rent on a little trailer for herself on the outskirts.

"Anyway, I guess she took to the way I always treated her when I ate there. I started coming in every day, sometimes twice a day. Well, before long I started visiting her at the trailer. She had to be at least twenty years younger than me, but it didn't seem to bother her. I think she just liked having a man around who didn't beat her up or yell at her.

"I was married then, of course. But you know how it is. You get bored, things get stagnant. I guess I fell for LeeAnn because she really saw me and liked me without me having to try and impress her. God, she was a sweetheart! So, about a year or so into our little fling, she tells me she's pregnant. I wasn't too unhappy about it, but I needed to keep it a secret anyhow. I told her I'd do as much as I could, but she was to never speak of who the father was.

"That baby ended up being Phillip. I helped her out with money when I could, and I stayed in his life up until he was an adult. And yes, I brought him to Big Jim a few times near the end of Jim's life. Jim was the only one I ever told about Phillip. He was a good friend. He helped explain things to Phillip, about the war we're all in and how he could help. I could tell from an early age that Phillip was different from Kevin. Phillip had the killer instinct. He was very receptive to Jim's teaching and mine. By the time he got to be a teenager, he was ready."

Henry sat down in the recliner next to the bed as Harrigan told his story. Finally, Phillip Kaiser made sense. He'd been indoctrinated by the founder himself.

"When was the last time you saw Phillip?"

"Oh, it's been a long time. Hard to say for sure. He was probably getting ready to head off to college. I believe he had a scholarship to Vanderbilt. Sharp kid. LeeAnn moved away shortly after that and I lost touch with both of them. I believe LeeAnn died a few years back with lung cancer."

"So Phillip doesn't know you're in here? He hasn't tried to contact you at all since then?"

"No. Not once that I know of. I think when he went away to school he cut all ties with his old life. Maybe even his mother. When he put his mind to something, it was really amazing with him. It was like he could flip a switch and blot out everything except his target. A single-minded man to be sure."

"Do you want to see him?" Henry asked.

Harrigan raised his face and looked at Henry with fear.

"I don't know. If what you're saying is true, that he's put together a new group and they're carrying on the traditions like we did, then I'm proud of him. He's keeping the fight going. I guess I wouldn't mind seeing him again to tell him that."

Henry suddenly took Harrigan by the throat and threw him back onto the bed. Harrigan's hand furiously searched for the call button, but Henry used his other hand to block him. He was struck by the strength still left in the old man's body.

"Proud? Proud, you sick son of a bitch? Proud that your only living son is a homicidal cult leader? How is it that sick fucks like you can keep on living, but great men like my grandfather don't? Huh?" Henry loosened his grip on Harrigan's throat and let him breathe.

Henry continued in a more reasoned tone, "I want you to think about something after I leave. Think about it like you've never thought about anything in your life. Your son is a murderer. He's actively recruiting new members to kill more people. I could use your help in trying to stop him. And that's what I'm going to do. By God, I may die trying, but I'm going to stop him. Now, I'm going to call you sometime and ask if you're ready to help me. Please think about it. It could be the last good thing you do before you die."

***

Henry felt invigorated after leaving the nursing home. Harrigan's story made sense and he believed it. He also believed that Harrigan could still be useful in his fight to bring down Kaiser. Henry hoped that by appealing to what remained of Harrigan's conscience, he could convince him to help.

On the drive back to Vicarstown, Henry blasted Live's *Throwing Copper* CD most of the way, hoping to drown out the endless parade of images pervading his mind. While listening to "I Alone" for a third time, Henry decided that he would not tell Ty of what he had done the night before. There was no way to explain or excuse it. He worried that Ty wouldn't understand and cut him out of his life.

Already on the verge of losing his wife, he didn't want to lose his best friend as well. Yes, he considered Ty his best friend, which made him briefly reflect on his "former" life. And what about Carrie? Would he ever tell her? Probably, when this was all over and a distant memory. If they made it through this with their marriage intact. He thought about calling her to check in, but rejected that. What could he say?

By the time he made it back to Ty's apartment, he was still singing along to Live but was thoroughly exhausted. He'd been without sleep for over twenty-four hours. Ty opened the door before Henry could get his key out.

"Hank! Dude! Where have you been? I've been trying to reach you all night! Get in here. You look like hell, man."

"So I've been told. I'm sorry I didn't get back to you. I needed to decompress after last night. And I needed to make a stop this morning. I've got news to share, but I haven't slept and I'm beyond tired. Can you give me a few hours, and then we'll talk?"

"Sure. Get some rest. I'm just glad you're okay. I'll let Deja know, too." Ty pulled out his phone.

Henry looked at the clock as his head hit the pillow: almost noon. He didn't see it again until it read 5:17. The sleep had been necessary, but now he felt even worse than when he'd woke up hungover from his night out with Ty. His eyes still foggy, Henry looked at his phone and found only one new text message – from Kaiser. Every time he saw Kaiser's name on a notification, his heart jumped.

Henry . . . Phillip here. Please join me for dinner tonight at 7. Smitty's Steakhouse. Please confirm ASAP.

He quickly texted a confirmation and then jumped out of bed. He desperately needed a shower and a change of clothes. After that, he joined Ty in the living room feeling like he had regained some of his old self.

"Looks like I've got a date with Kaiser tonight. A fancy steakhouse, no less. How do I look?"

"White. That's how you look. Very white," Ty said, fighting a laugh.

"Good, that's what I was going for. So here's the scoop. The old man, Harrigan, that I visited in the nursing home back in March? He's Kaiser's dad! I kind of forced it out of him this morning."

"Holy shit! That's big! Do they keep in contact at all?"

"Apparently not. But here's the other crazy part: Harrigan is the one who introduced him to my great-grandfather when Kaiser was still a boy. They both helped to indoctrinate him and turn him into a Raven."

"Damn, that's crazy. That helps to explain Kaiser, though. Why he is the way he is."

"Right. It's all starting to fall together. But we've got more work to do. The final step: gathering evidence. I saw a laptop set up in the office inside the factory. I didn't see Phillip take it when we were leaving. Your intrusion had them more than a little rattled, so we may have caught a break. I think that's where Kaiser is doing a lot of his planning. I need to get inside and access that computer. If I find anything, I'll copy it and email it to you and put it on a flash drive. Then we send it to the cops and let them do the rest. How's that sound?"

"Risky, man. Very risky. Are you sure you want to do this? They catch you, and you're dead."

Henry stared at Ty for a moment. "Maybe there's a better way, I don't know. But these guys are monsters, and the longer this takes the more people they're going to kill. If I can get into that warehouse, this could all be over by tomorrow night."

"I hear you. Will you need help accessing the computer? You know that's my thing."

"You'll have to walk me through it over the phone. If they catch you in there, God knows what they'll try to do. If it's me, maybe I can talk my way out of it. Either way, best not to get caught."

"Okay. When are we doing this?"

"Tomorrow, for sure. I'm going to try to get Kaiser to open up about his bigger plans while we're at dinner. You got a good look at the outside of the factory. Do you think we can get in without setting off any alarms?"

Ty raised an eyebrow. "Are you doubting my skills? I'll find a way in. You just focus on buttering up ol' Phillip. See if you can get anything concrete out of him. And maybe bring back a New York strip for me? Medium rare."

Henry smiled. "Yeah, right."

A few minutes later, as Henry was preparing to leave, Ty's laptop began to ring with a familiar tone. It was

Deja calling on Skype. Ty answered and Deja's face filled the screen.

"Whoa, Dee! You getting ready for a date or something? You're all done up."

"Not that it's any of your concern, but yes. And no, I'm not telling you who it is! Hey, is Hank there? I need both of you."

"Dude, get over here. Dee's got something."

Henry strode toward the couch, struggling with the Windsor knot he was attempting with a paisley tie.

"Hi, Hank! I got Ty's text just now. This just keeps getting crazier, huh?"

"You said it, Deja. I'm still struggling to digest it all. I'm supposed to be meeting Kaiser for dinner in just a few minutes."

"Good. Keep him busy for a couple of hours. Ty, I've got an errand for you. I finished researching that old factory you guys were at, and I found some interesting things. First, Kaiser's name doesn't appear on the title. The factory is owned by a fake-sounding company named Black Flock Industries. An obvious reference to the Ravens. That company also owns five other properties in and around Vicarstown, and two in Nashville. All of them appear to be old warehouses. All purchased by Black Flock within the last five years.

"Ty, I'm going to send you the addresses of those buildings. I want you to go check them out and find out what's inside. I have a feeling this could be the next piece of the puzzle."

"Nice work, Dee! I'd say you've earned a night on the town after all that work."

"Thank you, Deja. This is exactly what we needed. Ty, be careful if you go out there tonight. There's no telling what you may find."

"No sweat, Sherlock. You know I'm a smooth operator."

Deja snickered. "Yeah, he's so smooth he fell off the stage during homecoming! Yep, you're a ninja, Ty."

"Hey, I was pushed. I was still elected king, wasn't I? You want to trade stories? 'Cause you know I've got some beauties."

"Sorry, you're breaking up. Gotta go! Love you, bro!"

The connection ended before Ty could launch into a counter-story. He turned to Henry. "You keep Kaiser in your sights for as long as you can tonight. I'll text you with updates when I have some info. See you back here in a few hours. Yeah?"

"Yeah, Ty. Just keep an eye out. Be smart."

"You, too, my friend. You, too."

* * *

Henry arrived at Smitty's at precisely seven, only to find Kaiser already seated and perusing the menu. As usual, Kaiser was dressed impeccably, wearing a periwinkle sport coat over a white shirt and a yellow tie. A more festive ensemble than usual.

"Ah, Henry! I arrived earlier than expected, I hope you don't find it rude that I went ahead and got seated."

"No, not at all. This seems like a very nice restaurant. What do you recommend?"

"The filet is exquisite. But, my personal favorite is the orange duck. Succulent and tangy. An absolute masterpiece! That's what I'll be having." Kaiser scanned the laminated menu as if he were undecided.

They discussed the menu, favorite restaurants, and cocktails, as if last night's group murder scene never happened. Henry was stunned by how cultured Kaiser could be in one setting, and so completely bloodthirsty in another. It was fascinating and unsettling.

It was only after their meal – Henry also had the duck and it was the best meal of his life – while sipping their Irish coffees, that Kaiser turned the conversation toward serious business.

"Henry, I'm so sorry that your initiation was cut short last night. We'll be beefing up security soon enough, just in case. But I believe I saw what I needed to see. You allowed yourself to become something you probably never thought you could be. You became the predator. There exists only a small portion of the human race that can do that at this late stage of our development. Technology and modern convenience has robbed us of our most basic instincts. It was good to see that it still resides inside of you."

"Thank you. I have to tell you that I was pretty shocked at myself! I didn't think I could go through with it, but I was wrong," Henry said with perfect honesty.

"I could see the doubt and the hesitation. But the predator overcame those feelings. You, my friend, are truly a Raven. And I believe it is time to make it official!"

Kaiser produced a small, black ring box and handed it to Henry. He already knew what was inside. He opened it to reveal the same gold ring that Kaiser and the others wore proudly. He held it up between his fingers and gazed at his prize.

"I realize you already possess Jim Bryant's ring, but I thought it fitting that you have one of your own. It is beautiful, is it not? The symbol of our brotherhood. The tradition created by your own great-grandfather, now resting in your hand so many years later! The irony is delicious."

Henry slid the ring onto his right ring finger and found that it fit very well.

"I had to guess on the sizing. I see that I was spot on," Kaiser said, admiring his work.

"It fits great! Phillip, I'm overwhelmed. Thank you so much for accepting me into your . . . our brotherhood."

"No need to thank me. You've earned it. I'm excited to have you on board. Your addition is especially fortuitous, considering we are on the cusp of such a major expansion."

"Expansion? You mean we're going to be recruiting other new members?"

"Yes, that is part of what I mean. Our numbers must continue to grow, for that is the mark of all healthy organizations. But much more than that. We're expanding our mission. Beyond the ritual, beyond individual targets. We're going to strike a major blow in this war, and it's going to happen soon!"

"Oh, that is exciting Phillip! Please, tell me more," Henry said, trying not to seem too eager for details.

"I would love to, but I'm afraid our current venue is not conducive to such open talk. We must be sure to keep this kind of conversation private and secure at all costs. But trust me, Henry, you're going to be heavily involved. And it may only be a matter of weeks now. Things are progressing much faster than anticipated."

"I see." Henry tried not to show his disappointment.

"Let me give you a glimpse of what I have in mind. As I'm sure you're aware, the KGB was extremely active within the United States during the entire Cold War period."

The Cold War was one of Henry's favorite topics to teach about. Still, he was puzzled by this statement.

"Yes, go on."

"But what most people aren't aware of is the KGB's influence upon the Civil Rights Movement. They were deeply involved in aiding the movement, but not because they were concerned about equal rights. The Soviets saw an opportunity to destroy America from the inside using race as the trigger. They even went so far as to plan bombings at black colleges and then lay the blame on groups such as the

Jewish Defense League. Playing one group off the other to stir hatred and violence.

"Those bombings never occurred and, as you know, the United States never experienced the second Civil War that the Soviets longed for. The passions died down over the years and people found ways to live and let live. But Henry, those passions are arising once again! People are allowing their hatred of the other side to drive them to do and say things we haven't seen in decades. I believe the time is ripe. We have a renewed sense of purpose among our race. All they need is a clarifying event. Something that will open their eyes and finally convince them to join the war they've been losing for years and didn't even know it!

"I would love to share details, but I've said too much already. Soon, Henry. Soon you'll know it all because you're a part of the linchpin that will set it all in motion." Kaiser clapped his hand on Henry's shoulder. Henry, unable to respond intelligently, simply nodded and feigned agreement.

***

Only blocks away from Smitty's, Ty was staking out a darkened warehouse from across the street. He saw no lights on inside, and had witnessed no activity for the past fifteen minutes. The warehouse sat several blocks off the main drag of Vicarstown. It was bordered on either side by other industrial buildings, with a small abandoned park located across the street.

Ty had checked two of Black Flock's buildings off the list easily. He simply shined his flashlight into a window and verified they were completely empty. He was beginning to believe this errand was a dead end.

After another idle minute, Ty got out of the car and walked nonchalantly across the street toward the warehouse. He recognized quickly that the first floor windows had been blacked out with paint on all sides.

There was no way to see inside. He also noticed a new-looking keypad next to one of the doors. Scouring the perimeter, he saw no sign of security cameras or motion detectors.

Satisfied it was safe to proceed, Ty found the remotest part of the building and produced a heavy wrench from his backpack. After peering around to be sure no one was watching, he smashed one of the painted-over windows with one swing. He quickly ducked down and scampered away, waiting to see if an alarm would sound as it had in the factory the night before. He heard and saw nothing. .

He waited longer just to be sure, then ran back toward the opening and climbed through it.

Ty flipped on his flashlight and understood immediately he had finally uncovered something. Dozens of large wooden crates lay scattered across the warehouse's concrete floor in stacks.

Ty estimated there were at least two hundred boxes. He made his way to the far side of the building so his light couldn't be seen from the street. Then he produced a small crowbar and hammer from his backpack.

Selecting one box at random, Ty used his tools to loosen the lid. He slid it aside and shined the flashlight on the contents. Bullet-proof vests. Navy blue. Kevlar. There appeared to be at least ten of them in this box, and there were several identical boxes all around it.

Ty moved a few feet away to another grouping of boxes and opened one at random. This one contained a dozen Benelli shotguns, the type used by many police forces around the country. He silently whistled to himself and he pulled one out and examined it. He knew, somewhere in here, there would be crates filled with the proper shells.

Another grouping of crates, another chosen at random. This one had cases of bullets for nine millimeter handguns, which were also most likely sitting in a box near him. He continued to look around with the flashlight, trying to identify anything on the crates which might give away their contents. They all seemed to be blank, with only long numerical codes stamped on the outside to set them apart.

He noticed a series of boxes sitting along a wall that were set apart from the rest. He jogged over and quickly pulled the lid from one.

"Holy shit," he reacted involuntarily.

He reached in and pulled out an M26 fragmentation grenade. He turned it over and over, reading the markings and filling with dread. The remaining boxes contained other forms of high explosives, including rocket propelled grenades and C4.

Ty began to sweat and his breathing became heavy as he comprehended what all of this meant. The Ravens were serious about going to war, and now they had the supplies to start it.

Before replacing the lids carefully, Ty took two of the grenades and threw them into his backpack. Then he thought of something else and went back to a previous crate he'd opened.

This might come in handy.

He climbed back out of the same opening, knowing they would surely notice there was a window missing. No matter. The mission was a success. He decided to skip the remaining warehouses on his list. There was no longer any doubt about their purpose.

Chapter Twenty

Sunday, May 29, Vicarstown

"This is bad, Hank. I mean, real bad. They've got an arsenal in there. He's gearing up for something major," Ty yelled, pacing around his living room. It was seven on a Sunday morning, much earlier than his usual waking time.

Henry sat on the couch, twirling the newly minted Raven ring around his finger. He wasn't surprised. Ty's findings matched Kaiser's words perfectly. He hadn't been lying: Kaiser was very close to launching something much larger than they had imagined.

"What do you think we should do?" Henry asked.

"I think we go to the cops now, dude. We've finally got something to show them. There's no way all of that stuff was obtained legally. We feed the cops the address and let them do their thing."

"Okay, but what cops? We already know Kaiser's got the Sheriff's Department under his thumb with Kessler in charge. There are no city cops, only the county sheriffs. So, what, we call the State Police? What do they do? They'll call the Vicarstown authorities and talk to guess who – Sheriff Psycho himself! He'll tell them, 'We're already investigating it and we've got it under control' or some shit. I guarantee you it leads nowhere if we call them now. Plus, then we've probably blown any chance we had of figuring out what they're up to and stopping it."

Ty huffed and sat down on the other end of the couch. "You're probably right. If we can show the state cops Kaiser's plan *and* give them the warehouse full of weapons, then they would listen to us. I just feel like you've had to do too much already. I feel like you've, well, you've changed a little. I think this whole thing hanging over you has been a lot to handle. You need a break, dude. Seriously."

Henry struggled to look Ty in the eyes. *I am different. And it's way worse than you think.*

"I appreciate that, man. I do. But we're close now. And we don't have much time left. You should have seen the way Kaiser looked when he was talking about the next phase of his plan. He's not only crazy, but probably the most ambitious fucking guy I've ever seen. No, I can't stop now. No way. If all goes well, by the end of today, we'll be pulling the plug on the Ravens permanently. Are you with me, brother?" Henry extended his hand.

"Yeah, Hank. You know I'm with you. Let's do this." They clasped hands and regrouped.

They spent the next hour going over their plan for the morning. The objective was to gain access into the old rubber extrusion plant, and then into Kaiser's computer. Ty would help Henry get inside the building, but then would hang back at his car and they would communicate via their phones. If someone pulled up, Ty could use the excuse that he was lost and calling someone for directions.

By nine that morning they were rolling down Hazelbaker Lane toward the old plant in Ty's black Jeep Wrangler. After a few minutes of claustrophobic driving through the trees, the vacant and haunting structure came into view. It seemed taller and more ominous in the light of day. Its rusting metal roof cast a shadow over the Jeep as they approached.

No other vehicles were present, so they proceeded on foot toward the building. They first made a pass around the entire structure, looking for new cameras or other security devices. They saw none, though that didn't mean they weren't there. Henry knew they were taking an awful risk by breaking in, but he saw no other way.

Ty decided their best bet for getting in quietly was through one of the three large garage-style doors located on three different walls. They chose the one on the back side of the building, and Ty dropped his backpack and began searching for tools. A large metal handle at the center of the door was Ty's target. It contained a keyhole which Ty was attempting to pick.

Henry grew nervous as Ty fiddled for what seemed like five minutes, until they finally heard the click. Ty looked up and gave Henry a devilish smile.

"How in the hell did you know how to do that?"

"YouTubed it."

Henry shook his head as Ty twisted the handle and pulled the door up. They waited with breaths held, expecting to hear the siren that had blasted Henry out of his murderous stupor during their last visit. Nothing happened.

"Damn, I'm good. Okay, I'm going to get back to my car. Call me when you find the computer. You cool?"

"Uh, yeah. I'm fine. I'll call you in a minute."

Henry crept inside and was immersed in the post-industrial, musty smell. The plant was quiet and illuminated by the hazy sunlight coming through a few second floor windows. He did his best to stay along the walls in case of motion detectors. He saw none, but couldn't be sure.

He moved quickly up the stairs and immediately found the office that Kaiser had brought him into seemingly hours ago. The door had been left open, and the Windows Surface Pro with the keyboard attached sat exactly where he'd seen it before. His phone pinged: a text from Ty.

All clear so far. How does it look?

Henry sat down and powered up the tablet. After the initial start-up, he was met with a password screen. He texted back: *Just hit password screen. Have a few ideas. Hang on.*

Henry thought back to his conversations with Kaiser. What would a man like Phillip Kaiser use as his personal password? He wasn't sure how many tries he would get before it locked him out. Kaiser hadn't mentioned any family. It seemed that the Ravens *were* his family. Henry typed RAVENS and hit enter. Incorrect.

"Shit," Henry moaned. He stared at the screen for a few more moments. The Latin phrase they always use? Too long. Jim Bryant? His idol? Maybe. He typed JIMBRYANT and pressed enter. Wrong again. He called Ty.

"I'm getting nowhere with this password and this is taking too long. You got any ideas?"

"Actually, yes. Meet me back at the garage door. Quick."

Henry was confused but followed the order. He was afraid this operation would end before even having a chance to succeed. He scurried back to the garage door and found Ty waiting with a flash drive in his hand.

"I forgot I had this. I downloaded a program called Windows Password Genius a while back. Plug this in to the tablet and I'll walk you through it. Pretty easy, actually."

"I'll call back in a minute." Henry grabbed the flash drive and ran back inside and up to the office. Within three minutes, the tablet's password had been reset and he was looking at Kaiser's files. He found files titled Phase One, Phase Two, and Phase Three. He also found files named for each of the Ravens' members, including Henry. He was tempted to open his, but instead focused on copying the files as they had planned. There would be time for studying later.

First, he copied each file to the flash drive. Then, just to be sure, he emailed the files to Ty and Deja, as well as uploading them to his Dropbox account. One way or the other, the files would be accessible

***

Outside, Ty continued his lookout duty. It had been twenty minutes since Henry first entered the building. Ty sent him another text: *Almost done? We need to get going!*

Henry sent a quick answer: *Almost done. Two minutes tops.*

"Freeze, motherfucker!" Ty dropped his phone and looked up to see Sheriff Kessler, in uniform, aiming his nine millimeter at him from around twenty feet away.

"Get on your knees, now! What the fuck do you think you're doing here, nigger? This is the last place you want to be, boy. Answer me," Kessler roared, edging closer.

"I . . . I got lost, sir. I was just calling my friend for directions. That's it, I swear!"

Kessler noticed the cellphone lying on the ground a few feet in front of Ty, who was now on his knees with his hands behind his head. Kessler approached quickly, never taking his aim from Ty's chest. He picked up the phone with his left hand and backed up a few steps. Kessler's eyes narrowed as he scrolled through the recent texts. Henry's name jumped off the screen.

"What the fuck is this? Huh? What are you two trying to pull here?"

Ty couldn't answer. This was what he had feared most: that he would be overpowered or taken by surprise. But how had Kessler gotten here so fast? This couldn't be a coincidence. Somehow, they must have tripped a silent alarm or a motion sensor. His eyes filled with tears at the thought of what might come next.

Kessler looked again at the phone, then to Ty, then over his shoulder at the plant. Ty could see the indecision in his face. He wanted to investigate what was happening inside, but he also didn't want to leave Ty alone. It was obvious that Kessler had come without backup.

"I'm gonna ask you again, nigger. What the fuck are you and that imposter doing here?"

Ty's just-in-case precaution emboldened him. "I'm sorry, Officer Whitey. I'm not at liberty to answer that question. I suggest you go fuck yourself," Ty said with a smirk.

***

Enraged, Kessler's indecision left him instantly. He fired three shots into Ty's chest, sending him flailing backwards and into a patch of high grass. Kessler stood in his shooting pose, letting the sweet feeling of inflicting death rush over him. He slowly turned and faced the plant, knowing Henry was somewhere inside.

Kaiser had been so sure about Henry, they'd done almost no background research on him as they had planned. What little they had done had checked out, but it seemed from the beginning that Kaiser was determined to bring Henry in based solely on his bloodline. Kessler had been impressed with Henry at their first meeting, and everyone was convinced of his commitment when he stabbed that piece of shit breeder in the ribs. It appeared now that all of it had been one very convincing acting performance by a man they didn't know at all.

Kessler made a sweep of the building's perimeter and noticed the partially open garage door. He now felt justified in having spent a few hundred extra dollars on the silent alarm system that covered all the exit points and sent a warning to his phone when triggered.

He peeked inside and immediately spotted Henry making his way down the stairs.

***

Henry had heard the gunshots and was desperate to get to Ty. Seeing Kessler approaching with his gun drawn, Henry felt the strength run out of his legs.

Oh, Jesus. Ty is dead and it's my fault. He's gone and it's all my fault. Oh, Jesus. Oh . . .

"Get your fucking hands in the air, traitor! I should have known. We all should have known. This was all too fast and convenient. I should have smelled the nigger on you the second we met," Kessler barked, approaching Henry in long strides.

"Kessler, this isn't what it looks like. You're jumping to conclusions here. Just wait!"

"Oh, am I? Because to me it looks like you're cavorting with niggers and breaking into our headquarters. Am I wrong on those two counts?"

"Look, man. I don't have any idea who you're talking about. I came here alone. Phillip gave me a key to get in here, but it must have tripped the alarm anyway by accident." Henry prayed his mission could still somehow be salvaged.

"You lying cocksucker. I saw your friend's texts. Lucky for you Phillip has to approve punishment of members, or you'd be dead already. Turn around."

Henry slowly put his back to Kessler, fearing what was to come. A sudden excruciating pain on the top of head mercifully ended a millisecond later as Henry fell to the floor, all senses gone.

***

Ty jerked awake after briefly losing consciousness. He was lying on the ground, feeling the tall weeds brushing his body. He quickly felt the area in the middle of his chest where Kessler's bullets surely would have ripped through his heart and ended his life.

Man, I knew it was a good idea to take one of those bulletproof vests from the warehouse! And Dee says I never think things through! Wait 'til she and Henry hear about . . . shit, Henry! Ty rose to his feet slowly.

His chest felt like it had been crushed in a monstrous vice, and he staggered when he tried to run. He stopped and put his hands on his knees for a moment. He tried to think through his options. Was Henry already dead? Should he go inside right away or hang back?

In either case, he needed the gun he'd brought with him in his backpack. He slinked to the rear passenger side of his Jeep and pulled out the black bag. With chest throbbing, he tried to stay low as he made his way around the Jeep and toward the plant.

He pulled out the silver .357 and then slung the backpack over his shoulder.

He was nearing the entrance that Kessler had passed through just minutes before when he heard a car rumbling down the road to the plant. Ty knew it had to be more Ravens approaching. He ducked down and scrambled on his knees toward the edge of the forest.

Two cars, a silver Jaguar and a royal blue Volvo S60, rolled in and fanned out around Ty's Jeep.

A man emerged from the Jaguar, wearing an expensive navy blue suit and even more expensive looking sunglasses. He looked over at the man exiting his Volvo.

"What the fuck is this about, anyway," the man from the Volvo said. "Did you get the same crazy text from Kessler as I did? And whose piece of shit Jeep is this?"

Hey, now! I love that Jeep.

"I have no idea," the Jaguar man said. "If Kessler says it's an emergency, then it is. He doesn't fuck around."

They both entered and Ty was left to contemplate his next move. He knew three of them were now inside the facility, but still no sign of Kaiser, whose photo he'd seen on his LinkedIn search. Surely he would be on his way if Kessler had contacted the entire group. He rummaged through the backpack and tried not to think about what they could be doing to Henry inside the plant.

They might be waiting on Kaiser before they do anything. No time to hash out the details. Let's roll! Ty quickly formulated a risky plan. He moved among the trees and got as close to the door as possible without revealing himself. He tried to work through the probabilities of his gambit, but there were too many variables. Henry needed help now and no one else was coming. Ty felt a sensation he hadn't experienced since his time in Afghanistan: the willingness to die for a fellow soldier.

Ty froze as he heard the door open. He stayed low and saw Kessler walking back toward his beige Sheriff's vehicle. Kessler stopped and looked around.

"Where the fuck did he go?" Kessler bellowed. He spent another minute in his futile search, then he approached Ty's Jeep and examined it.

To Ty's surprise and relief, Kessler moved to the Sheriff's vehicle and got in. He inched the car along the road, looking all around for his victim.

Kessler slowly rolled out of sight, and Ty allowed himself to breathe again, feeling the pain in his chest erupt as his lungs expanded, and then made his way out of the woods. In his right hand, Ty held an M26 grenade he had pilfered from the Ravens' warehouse stockpile. Still moving toward the door, Ty pulled the pin using his left hand. He waited two more seconds, then tossed the grenade underhand toward the door. He turned and moved as quickly as he could in the opposite direction, not watching it take two hops on its way toward impact.

The explosion rocked the quiet wilderness. Ty felt the heat from the small fireball that now engulfed the entrance to the plant. His hearing muted, Ty crouched with the .357 cradled in both hands. He waited to see if either of the remaining Ravens would take the bait and venture outside to investigate.

After a few seconds of waiting and watching the flames licking the scorched wall above the service entrance, Ty heard the unmistakable sound of a fire extinguisher in use. That was one of the many variables that Ty hadn't considered: what if he burned the plant down with Henry still inside?

The flames and smoke began to subside, and Ty struggled to catch a glimpse of the two men. He began to believe his plan had failed, and that he might have to go with plan B, which involved charging in the door like a fool and probably getting himself killed.

A figure appeared in the doorway holding what looked like an assault rifle. Ty didn't wait to find out. He fired three shots at the figure from his crouched position, feeling the reverberation flow through his arms and into his bruised torso.

Shot in the arm, the man let the weapon fall from his hands to the pavement in front of the doorway before he, too, fell to the ground.

Ty, seeing that one of his three shots had connected, ran forward but kept the gun's barrel level in case the other Raven decided to show his face. He saw no one else as he approached the man who was lying in a heap and groaning. Ty ignored him and focused on the doorway and the location of the man's weapon.

He found the rifle lying a few feet away. Ty shoved the .357 into the back of his pants and picked up the AR-15. *Nice upgrade!*

He ducked his upper half into the doorway for a split-second, hoping his head wouldn't be blown off. He took a second quick look and was satisfied he hadn't seen anyone. He stepped inside the charred framework of the doorway, unsure of how or where to proceed. He knew he needed to get to Henry, assuming he was still alive, and get him out before Kaiser and possibly others arrived.

He searched the few open rooms along the far side of the plant without success. He proceeded up the metal stairs as quietly as he could, knowing the other man had to have been alerted by the gunfire.

Ty quickly found the office where Henry had been furiously downloading information just minutes before. It was quiet and dark, the same as all the rest of the offices. He went to the next one, keeping the rifle at his hip and ready to fire. He saw nothing in this office either, and thought perhaps he should venture back downstairs.

Before Ty could take another step, he was slammed into from behind. The ferocity of the attack shocked Ty, who dropped the rifle and began groping for any part of his attacker. The man punched at Ty's head and upper torso like a maniac, sending him reeling backwards toward the stairs. With a second to recover, Ty leapt to his feet and met the man's next wave of attack with swinging strikes of his own.

The two men, both bloodied and gasping for breath, wrestled and tugged at each other until they were both on the floor. A searing pain hit Ty as his attacker bit into his left earlobe. Ty screamed and instinctively elbowed the man in the face. A small piece of Ty's ear stayed in the man's mouth as he recoiled from the elbow strike. Ty understood this was real mortal combat. Only one of them would emerge from this brawl alive.

Somehow, in the midst of the struggle, the man produced a switchblade and was attempting to force the blade into Ty's chest. Ty caught the knife with both hands and slowly moved the hand backward. With a final effort that made his chest scream from the strain, Ty smashed the hand against a wall, causing a howl of pain. The switchblade dropped to the floor.

Instead of reaching for the knife, Ty put his hands around his opponent's neck and began squeezing. The man responded with wild gouges to Ty's face in an attempt to blind him.

Ty could feel the blood dribbling out of the gash where his upper earlobe had been. It sent out seismic shocks throughout his head every time his heart pumped. Still, he could feel he was winning the battle.

But the man scissored his legs and created enough momentum to roll himself on top of Ty, loosening Ty's grip on his neck. After sending a blow to the side of Ty's head, he started choking him. The two men stayed locked together, rolling steadily toward the top of the stairs, then over. With Ty now above the attacker on the second step down, he released his grip on the man's neck, grasped a railing spindle with his left hand, and shoved his right foot into the man's belly. This broke the hold on his neck and sent the Raven tumbling down the stairs. Though the downward force nearly separated his shoulder, Ty held on and watched his attacker hit the concrete floor, his body lying sprawled, unmoving, the head at an unnatural angle.

Ty rested as he watched for signs of movement from his victim. Then he wobbled one step at a time toward the bottom. As he got closer if became obvious that the man wouldn't ever be getting up.

His neck is broken for sure.

Ty checked and it was just as he expected: no pulse. He didn't stop to ponder about the first man – but perhaps not the only one if the man outside continued to bleed – he had ever killed. That would come later. He hadn't experienced Post-Traumatic Stress Disorder while in the military, but he likely would after this episode.

It took only another minute for Ty to locate Henry, who was weakly calling out for help. Ty discovered the tiled room at the back of the plant.

Henry lay on the floor, covered in his own blood but conscious.

Ty saw that Henry had taken a severe beating from Kessler, and perhaps the other two as well. His face would be swollen and he most likely had a concussion, but Henry was going to live. Ty ran to him, still woozy from his own battles. He knelt and looked over Henry's injuries.

"Oh, Jesus, Hank, you're okay. I mean, you're not okay, you're beat to shit. But, you're alive!"

Henry smiled and winced as the cuts on his lips spread open. "Thanks to you, brother. Thanks to you. Let's get out of here."

"Can you stand?"

"Yeah, here, just give me a boost. Okay, okay, let me get my bearings for a second."

The two men shuffled out of the room and stumbled like drunkards out of the plant. The man Ty shot had dragged himself a few feet away from where Ty left him, but was unconscious. There was still no sign of Kaiser or a returning Kessler.

"Hank, my boy, we may live to tell this story to our grand-kiddies yet," Ty remarked as they limped toward his Jeep.

He got Henry situated, then thought twice and ran back into the plant. He didn't want to leave his backpack full of goodies behind. He also snagged the AR-15. Ty thought about searching around for his phone, but knew they didn't have time to waste. He got back to the Jeep with his supplies and they drove away knowing how close they had both come to death.

Chapter Twenty-One

Sunday, May 29

Kaiser surveyed the damage to his lair and his troops in disbelief. His thoughts traveled to ancient Carthage and the defeat of Hannibal at the Battle of Zama. In one swift and sudden twist, all of his great plans appeared to be destroyed. He paced around the first floor of the plant while Feury's corpse still littered the bottom of the stairs.

Nix sat with his left arm lying limp across a rickety card table. Kessler was doing his best to patch him up while keeping Nix from freaking out again.

"Jesus, stay still Mike. The bullet passed all the way through. You got lucky. We'll get you some antibiotics and you'll be fine," Kessler said as he wrapped Nix's bloodied bicep in gauze.

"That fucker killed Logan. I can't believe this. How the fuck can one nigger do so much damage . . . to *us*? We're the fucking Ravens! We're the ones that are supposed to –"

Kessler ended Nix's rant with punch to his jaw. It wasn't full force, but just enough to get his attention and, more importantly, to shut him up.

Kaiser continued to stalk the premises without a hint of emotion. His thoughts moved from Hannibal to Napoleon, whose Grand Army of over six hundred thousand troops swooped into Russia in 1812 like a plague of locusts. Napoleon's dream of a conquered and obedient Europe was nearly in sight. But then Moscow burned and the winter came, and Napoleon's men fell like corn stalks at harvest. Their defeat seemed impossible, just as this scenario had seemed impossible to Kaiser only hours before.

Kessler stood up and approached Kaiser with caution. Their faith in him was shaken for the first time, but they still looked to him for answers and direction.

"Phillip, what's our next move?"

Kaiser's slow march halted, his eyes still fixed on Feury's twisted form.

"First, I must apologize to you both. It seems apparent that my faith in Henry was misplaced. I made dangerous assumptions about him based solely on his bloodline. I wanted to believe in him so much that I didn't take the proper precautions. My foolish judgment has cost us much today." His grim stare still locked on Feury, though Kaiser no longer saw him.

Kaiser continued, "We need time and manpower – two things which are now in short supply. We need information, first and foremost. I believe I know why Henry and his friend came here today. More importantly, I believe I know why Henry went to the trouble of gaining our trust and access to our activities. It was a clandestine coup d'état by a man intent on gaining some sort of revenge or perhaps even redemption. I'll give him credit. He played the part well. He used my eagerness against me. No one has ever taken advantage of me in such a way. Most impressive."

He broke into a jog toward the stairs, easily vaulting over Feury's body and onto the third step. Seconds later, he was in his office intent on finding out what Henry had seen and with whom he had shared the information. He returned to the first floor with tablet in hand, looking as if some of his old confidence had returned.

"We have new targets. I believe we still have time to salvage our plan, but we must act immediately and without hesitation. Michael, you must find Ty and Deja Lockwood and eliminate them post haste. Henry sent our files to both of them via email. My guess would be Ty was the one that Grant shot and presumed dead. Deja would most likely be a sister or perhaps wife.

"We have Henry's phone, so I will attempt to garner some insight from it regarding his true identity. I prefer to capture him alive, along with any close family he may be hiding. Each second that passes draws us nearer to our final demise. Those files must not be made public. Our entire plan for Phases Two and Three depend on it.

"Speaking of Phase Two, Grant, we cannot wait any longer. I realize we are wildly accelerating our plans, but there is no alternative. If we're successful in procuring Ty, Henry, and our other targets, our vision can still become reality. Do you agree?"

Kessler hesitated for a moment. "I know you're right. It's just going to be tricky. I thought I'd have more time to sort out some logistics. When does it need to happen?"

"Tonight at the latest. The timing could still work if a few variables fall into place. Questions?"

"What do we do with Logan," Nix asked.

"Leave him. He was a fool who deserved the ending he received. Anything else?" Kaiser asked, shifting his glare toward Kessler.

"What is the rendezvous point? And what if our shit gets spilled all over the media sometime today?" Kessler asked.

"If necessary, we will meet at the warehouse on Fifth Street. I suggest we immediately switch to our alternate phones and stay away from our homes for a while. Don't start worrying about everything all at once. We have contingency plans for every scenario," Kaiser noted with a hint of the arrogance that had become his trademark.

The three men marched from the plant with a new sense of purpose. Kaiser's internal mourning gave way to the more familiar feeling of imminent immortality.

* * *

"Stay with me, man. Don't fall asleep. You've got a concussion," Ty shouted at Henry, who was slumping in the passenger seat of Ty's Jeep. He turned into the parking lot of the Vicars County Hospital emergency room.

Ty slid out of the driver's seat and limped around the front of the vehicle toward Henry's side. Henry was still conscious but hadn't spoken a word since they left the plant. The passenger door opened, and Henry looked at his friend as if he'd just been awakened from a satisfying nap.

"What are we doing?" Henry asked.

"We're both getting some quick treatment, then we're heading out of town. How are you feeling?"

"Like Lincoln after the play ended. How do I look?"

"I'd say you nailed it. What about me? Still gorgeous?" Ty grinned.

"Yeah, like Apollo at the end of *Rocky*. What happened at the plant?"

"I duked it out with a couple of your Klan boys and lived to tell about it. Come on, let's get you in there." Ty grunted as he helped Henry out of the Jeep.

They barely cleared the doors when a young nurse took notice and gasped.

"Oh my God, what happened to you guys?" she asked.

Ty responded, "Uh, bar fight. A bad one. He got it worse than I did. Check him out first, please."

***

Henry was given a CT scan to rule out brain injuries, as well as twelve stitches on the top of his head where Kessler's gun butt landed. He got five more stitches above his right eye, where Kessler's fist had repeatedly made contact. Then he was admitted for observation.

Ty's bitten earlobe was bandaged. His chest glowed red and purple from the impact of Kessler's bullets, but his injuries weren't sufficient to keep him in the hospital.

"Deja Renee, where the hell are you? Shit is real! We need to talk! Call me yesterday," Ty shouted into the hospital phone. He slammed it down on the adjustable table hovering over Henry's bed.

"That girl never answers her phone! Mom always told her, 'What if there's a real emergency?' And look at us now."

"Ty, I blew it. I thought I could outsmart Kaiser. I'm so sorry, man. I fucked it up for everyone."

"Don't say that, Hank. It was a good plan, it just wasn't perfect. Think about it, dude. You conned your way into a secret terror cell like a boss! They really trusted you. I don't think many people could have pulled that off."

"Maybe so, but where are we now? They have our phones. They probably know I sent you and Deja those files. They might be going after your sister right now. Hell, maybe even Carrie and . . ." Hank stopped, unable to finish the thought. He grabbed the phone and dialed his home number in Evansville. No answer. He tried Carrie's cell. Voicemail.

"Baby, it's me. Please listen carefully. It may not be safe for you to be home now. Don't ask me why, just trust me. Get David and get out. Go to your mom's, or better yet, get to a hotel. Please call me. I love you, Car. And I'm sorry," Henry finished through a haze of tears.

The two sat in silence after that, wondering if they would ever hear from their loved ones again. Henry attempted to stand, thinking that he could push through his injuries. He sat up too quickly, and the room swirled around him crazily until he lay back down. He hammered the bed with his right fist.

"Son of a bitch! We don't have time for this. Kaiser's probably already got guys headed to Evansville, and I'm lying here useless." He closed his eyes and waited for the room to come to a standstill.

Ty began pacing the room, unsure of their next move and unable to keep the worst case scenarios at bay. Both men felt defeated and defenseless in the face of the inevitable retaliation. Ty grabbed the hospital phone and dialed Deja's number again. Miraculously, she picked up after the first ring.

"Oh my God, Dee! You answered! Okay, okay, I need you to listen. First, where are you?"

"I just got out of the shower. What's going on?"

"No time for all the details. Long story short, you might be in danger. The Ravens caught us and almost killed us this morning. We're at the hospital now getting patched up. They have our phones, Dee. They probably know who you are and they'll find you. You need to leave ASAP and get out of town." He looked at Henry, who was gesturing frantically. "Hank wants to talk to you." Ty handed the phone off.

"Deja, I hate to ask this of you, but I need your help. Could you please drive to Evansville and stay with my wife and son? You need to lay low anyway, and they're going to need someone who knows what's going on in case I can't get there."

"Sure, Henry. Jesus. Yeah, like you said, I shouldn't stay here anyway. Of course. Are you sure you guys are okay?

"A little banged up, but we're fine. Close call, but your brother bailed me out. I owe both of you big!"

"Just remember that when this is all over. What's the address?"

"721 Red Bank Road. They might be headed to her mom's, I'm not sure. I can't reach her. Here's her cell." Henry read off the digits, then handed the phone back to Ty.

"Dee, you're the best, girl. There's one other major favor we need from you. You should have an email waiting for you from Hank. It contains all of the Ravens' files and we're hoping they contain evidence of what they've been doing and what they're up to next. And trust me, they're up to something big. They've got enough weapons stored to restart the Civil War. We don't have access to a computer right now, so look over those files and see what's in there. Now, you're getting dressed and out the door soon, right? Don't mess around. These guys are going to be pissed like none other."

"I got it, I got it. I'm out the door in fifteen minutes. Now you listen. You both sound terrible. You need to stay at the hospital and rest for a bit. I'll call soon. I love you, bro."

"Love you too, sis. Please be careful," Ty said, choking up a little as he hung up the phone.

"Remind me to give your sister a big hug and kiss when I see her again," Henry said with his eyes still closed.

"You looking to get fresh with my sister, Hank?"

"Don't worry, I'll be hugging and kissing you too if we survive this."

"Gross. Okay, cowboy, here's what I'm thinking . . ."

* * *

The next six hours were the longest of Henry's life. He had never felt more helpless. He stayed in bed at the hospital while everyone who mattered in his life faced imminent danger.

Ty was on a mission to secure some of their belongings, especially Ty's laptop, before the Ravens showed up and destroyed everything. Deja was on a three-hour road trip to Henry's hometown, hoping to find them alive and well before hiding them some place where the bad guys would never look.

He took a moment to reflect on all that had transpired over the last few months. His discovery in Herman's garage felt like a lifetime ago. Even his initial meeting with Kaiser seemed far off in his memory. Those were fragments from his old life. He could barely remember a time when he didn't know Kaiser's name. He'd scarcely thought of anyone or anything else in months.

Somehow he already knew this nightmare would only end after a face-to-face confrontation. He also understood there was little chance of surviving such a meeting. The old Henry would have shivered at such a thought. The old Henry was weak and scared and sheltered. The new Henry smiled at the thought of seeing his old "leader" again. On some level, he looked forward to confronting Kaiser even more than seeing his wife and child.

Henry dozed and fought to stay awake, not bothering to turn on the small flat screen TV that hung near the ceiling on the wall facing him. The quiet was a welcome respite from the chaos of the past few days. Only the occasional visit from a nurse or aid, asking him if he wanted more water or checking his vital signs, broke the peace.

He knew he needed to stay and rest up, but the waiting was killing him. There would be no true rest until this entire adventure was behind him. Still, he closed his eyes and tried. Just as he began to get comfortable, the phone whined. His eyes flew open, and his hands scrambled to find the phone.

"Hello? Carrie?"

"Henry, it's me. I got your message. What's happened? Are you all right?"

"Yeah, I'm . . . I'm not fine but I'm okay. Just had a close call. Look, where are you?"

"I'm at home. I took David to church. That's when I heard from your friend Deja. She said she's coming here, but I don't understand. What's going on, Henry? Please tell me everything."

"I don't want to go into details, but just know that it's best that you stay hidden for a while. The Ravens found out I'm a fraud and now I'm pretty sure they're going to be coming after us. The good news is I think we have enough evidence now to put them away. But until the police can round them up, we're all in danger. How long until Deja gets there?"

"I'm not sure, probably another hour. Oh God, Henry. I'm really scared. When am I going to see you again? Tell me you're coming home," Carrie said, her voice shaking.

"As soon as Ty gets back, I'm going to try to get out of here and on the road. Hopefully by tonight, the Ravens will be locked up and we'll be heading back to our house together. We just have to hold steady for another few hours. Okay, baby?"

"Okay. I'm going to stay calm for David. I don't want him to know what's going on."

"Agreed. You go ahead and get your stuff ready. I want you out the door the second that Deja pulls up. And call me as soon as you get to the hotel. Stay somewhere outside of Evansville. Got it?"

"Got it. Henry? I love you, and I'll see you soon. Right? I'll see you soon?"

"I promise, baby. I love you, too." Henry shut off the phone and laid his head back. A wave of anger rolled through him, but not anger at Kaiser or the other Ravens.

"Goddamn you, Grandpa. Goddamn all the Bryants," he muttered to no one. He gritted his teeth and slammed his foot down onto the thin mattress.

After a minute of silent meditation, he opened his eyes and grabbed the phone again. He dialed zero and waited, hoping this call would pay dividends in the near future.

Chapter Twenty-Two

Sunday, May 29, Vicarstown Sheriff's Department; 11:25 AM

Sheriff Grant Kessler, elected with eighty percent of the vote in Vicars County, strolled into the main lobby of the Sheriff's Department with a duffle bag full of explosives. He smiled at Leah at the front counter and passed by without a word. He swiped an ID badge – another Kessler initiative to improve safety – and stepped into the department's main offices.

Either from the weight of the bag, or the weight of his impending errand, he could feel sweat dripping under his uniform. This task had always been a part of the Ravens' long-term plans, but Kessler never fully believed this moment would arrive.

Not that he wasn't ready or willing.

Kessler's loyalty to Kaiser far surpassed the oath he took as the county's sheriff. In his view, and Kaiser's, his election was simply another step toward fulfilling their goal of reversing the decades-long deterioration of American society. Such a monumental mission would require sacrifices, both from within the Ravens and without. As Kaiser was fond of saying, they were playing chess in a nation full of Angry Birds players.

Today, Kessler thought, they would cash in a few pawns.

"Hey, Grant. Don't normally see you in here on a Sunday." Deputy Tim Barker said with a grin. "Thought you'd be at the gym."

"Yeah, that paperwork has piled up on me so I figured I'd take the afternoon and knock it out. Then, yes, it's gym time. Gotta get this body ready for thong season!"

Barker laughed a little too hard, showing himself to be the kiss-ass Kessler knew him to be. He continued walking toward the door of his office, feeling the weight of the bag bearing down on his right shoulder. Luckily, the trip from the main lobby to his office was a short one.

Even more fortunate was the location of Kessler's office. It was situated directly in the heart of the two-story complex. It would provide an ideal ground zero, not to mention hiding place for the explosion, which with any luck would cripple the substructure and destroy both floors. The more carnage and casualties, the better.

Kessler unlocked his door without further interaction, and immediately closed and locked it behind him. His office door's window was frosted, so no one would catch a glimpse of their sheriff in the act of committing domestic terrorism.

He gingerly placed the bag on his bare desk, knowing the bricks of C-4 inside were stable but not taking any chances. Kaiser hadn't told him how he had managed to procure some of the weapons and explosives they were planning to utilize, and he didn't care.

He slowly unzipped the bag, already imagining the headlines and cable news coverage that were soon to follow. He reached in and wrapped his fingers around the first brick of plastic explosive. Two raps sounded on the door's opaque glass.

"Sheriff, have you got a minute?" He froze. The paranoid portion of his brain immediately believed it was a federal agent at the door, ready to bust him. After a second, he realized it was just Susan Morris, their newest deputy.

"Uh, yeah Suze. Give me like five minutes, okay?"

"Sure, no rush. Just had a question, but it can wait."

The interruption forced Kessler to remember all of the friendships he had developed over the years as a deputy and then sheriff of their office. He was a natural at making friends, and most folks in the department were thrilled when he won the head job. He'd spent thousands of hours among these people, discussing their work and personal lives as well as protecting their fair county from crime. Was this act really worth destroying their lives as well as his own career and legal standing?

Unequivocally, yes. Though he found it dismaying that he was about to end the lives of dozens of law-abiding white Americans, he understood and agreed with the reasoning. They might be nice, innocent people, but they would be much more valuable to their race and nation as victims rather than survivors. In death, they would become martyrs and heroes.

Once again, he began the process of setting the explosives. He laid out all twelve bricks in two rows on the desk. Next, he pulled out the wires and connectors which would allow him to set off all the explosives with one remote detonator. Thanks to the wonders of the Internet, Kessler had learned much about plastic explosives over the past year. With Kaiser as tutor, he had practiced until he could correctly set the charges without hesitation.

Still, he felt his heart beating faster than usual. He looked down and realized he also had a full erection. He considered jerking off right on the C-4, but time was critical. There were other priorities to attend to as soon as this part was finished.

His hands set to work, pushing the thin metal rods into each of the bricks. Though he worked fast, he felt the minutes slipping by. This was taking too long. On a normal day, he would keep his door wide open and people would constantly be stepping in to ask a question or update him on a case. It was a minor miracle that only one person had knocked so far.

He wiped the sweat from his face and surveyed the room, double checking his work and gearing up for the finish. When he was satisfied, Kessler collected the duffle bag and exited the office. He was quick to lock the door before anyone could approach. He turned and found Deputy Morris eagerly awaiting him.

"Hey, Sheriff, are you all right? You're sweating like a pig."

"Huh? Yeah, Suze. I'm good. What did you need?"

"Oh, it's nothing really. Barker and I need you to settle a bet for us, that's all."

He wanted to slap her. On the verge of taking the boldest step toward racial purity in this century, and he had to deal with this stupid shit. *They probably want me to say if I think Barker really looks like Christian Bale, like he always says he does. Asinine and fucking stupid.*

"Tell you what, Suze. I need to run back out to my car. I'll meet you back at your desk in a couple of minutes. Deal?"

"Deal, Sheriff. Like I said, no biggie." She strutted back toward the collection of cubicles that formed much of the east wing of the building. Kessler craned his neck to check for any others approaching, but saw none.

A minute later, Kessler was in his car two blocks from the station. He sat facing the building, but his focus was on the goings on in peaceful Vicarstown. He watched a man with a guide dog jaywalk across Third Street toward the station. He spotted a teenage boy smoking at the corner of Third and Walnut. Their world was about to change, and they had no idea.

He pulled the detonator from the duffle bag and laid it in his lap near the steering wheel. It was attached to an old flip phone, which would activate the explosives when the correct code was punched in, followed by pushing SEND. The device made him think of the movie *The Hurt Locker*, when that Iraqi guy blew up Guy Pearce with the help of an old Nokia phone.

But this wasn't a movie, and the people who were about to die weren't actors. He brushed those thoughts away. This was no time to get sentimental. This was a war, and the turning point was only seconds away.

He powered up the detonator and flipped open the phone. His thumb pressed down on the number pad six times, realizing for the first time that the numbers spelled out RAVENS. A clever touch by Kaiser. Kessler's thumb hovered over the SEND button for several seconds. There was still time to abort. Still time to find another way.

He pressed SEND.

He immediately felt the vibration of the asphalt under the sheriff's cruiser. Then came the visual confirmation. All of the station's first floor windows exploded outward in a shower of flame and glass. Several good citizens standing near the building were incinerated, along with, Kessler assumed, nearly all who were caught inside.

The second floor crumbled in a second, collapsing among the fire and chaos. Shrieks of terror came from all directions. Pedestrians dropped to the ground, then began running from the blast site after their senses returned. Some folks seemed to be running around in the street with no purpose other than to add to the surrealism of the moment.

The sound was like nothing Kessler could have prepared for. Even knowing the blast was coming, he instinctively ducked down in the seat when the roar struck him. He recovered quickly and threw the car into drive. In the immediate aftermath, no one would remember seeing a sheriff's car driving away from the vicinity. He needed to get out of town and regroup with the others.

Kessler felt nothing as he drove. The remorse or regret he thought he might feel did not come. There was only the mission. Kaiser had succeeded in draining the humanity from his protégé long ago.

***

Phillip Kaiser drove his Audi northwest on I-24, keeping an ear to the news talk radio station for any word about the

Sheriff's Department explosion. He grew tenser with each passing minute, checking his phone and cursing Kessler for not updating him on the status. This had been a hell of a morning, and if Kessler botched this part, their plans would completely unravel.

He kept seeing Henry's face. Henry *Bowersox*, not Bryant, as Nix had quickly uncovered after rifling through his phone and performing some quick online searches. Again, he cursed himself for not having seen through Henry's thin ruse. He saw what he wanted to see in Henry, and now he was on his way to ensure that Henry wouldn't completely derail the ongoing righteous mission of The Ravens.

Then he thought about Logan Feury. The man was an undisciplined lunatic and, by his own admission, not that bright. But he was a loyal soldier, and a valuable one. He was the kind who was willing to do the dirty work, because he liked the dirty work. He would have shot his own mother in the face if Kaiser asked him to. Now, he lay sprawled in the floor of an abandoned rubber extrusion plant. That was something else Henry would pay for.

The faint voice of Rush Limbaugh was replaced by a new one, representing the local radio station's news department.

"We here at WBLZ apologize for the interruption, but we have a major news announcement. According to multiple reports, an explosion this morning destroyed the Sheriff's Office in Vicarstown. It is believed nearly everyone inside the building was killed by the blast, as well as others who were nearby. At this time the cause of the explosion in unclear, but terrorism has not been ruled out. Please stay tuned to News Talk WBLZ for more updates."

"Well done, my friend," Kaiser muttered. He immediately swerved the car off the interstate and stopped in the emergency lane. Using a mobile wi-fi hotspot, Kaiser powered up his Surface Pro tablet and accessed first

Twitter, then Facebook. He began updating all of the pro-black Twitter accounts that he had created only days before.

His first and favorite account, Black Hand of Vengeance, had acquired a stunning half million followers in just over a week. Kaiser made sure to post numerous times a day to all of his accounts, but he reserved his most virulent language for this one. Staying just shy of openly advocating violence, the Black Hand of Vengeance was a constant source of outrage and a sounding board for angry racists of all varieties.

Kaiser decided early on that the Black Hand would take credit for the explosion in Vicarstown. He typed, "The Black Hand has struck its first blow for justice against the white pig. Expect much more to follow! #VicarstownBombing" He pressed "tweet" and didn't wait to read any reactions.

On his other pro-black Twitter accounts, Kaiser promoted the same hashtag with slogans and phrases that supported the bombing and laid the real blame on white police brutality. Within minutes, #VicarstownBombing was the number one trending topic in America on all major social media sites. Kaiser felt like a proud father, but only half of his task was complete.

He flipped over the master sheet with the login information for all of his accounts. On this side, he had an equally robust list of pro-white social media accounts of his creation. Many of these involved a direct link to supporting local police forces against charges of racism and brutality. The first account he pulled up was named Whites for Police Rights. The rhyme was unintentional, but he'd kept the name for amusement.

It was a source for vicious anti-black rhetoric as well as supportive slogans for white police officers. This account, also created just eight days prior, had nearly three hundred and fifty thousand followers.

Under @WhitesforPoliceRights Kaiser tweeted, "The #VicarstownBombing shows that blacks have declared war against our police officers. The time for talk is over. Get armed and get ready for battle!"

After nearly twenty minutes of updating accounts with conflicting messages, Kaiser pulled the Audi back onto the interstate and pegged the speedometer at ninety. As instructed by the mediocre local announcer, he stayed tuned for any update they would give. Apparently the fire had spread to an adjacent building, but the count on dead and injured was still to be determined.

The female voice on his phone's GPS guided him onto the exit for Interstate 69 North. At present speed, it would take him straight into Evansville within an hour. Kaiser glanced at his watch, satisfied with the time he was making. The plan that seemed ruined only three hours ago was now very much alive.

***

Fifteen blocks away from the Sheriff's Department offices, Ty crept into his apartment and prayed there would be no Ravens present. Relieved to be alone, he began hurriedly gathering their essentials. A thunderclap stopped him cold. He had heard similar noises before, but only in certain regions of Afghanistan. He recognized it instantly as an explosion, though he didn't yet know where it had come from. No matter, he was certain that Kaiser and his men were responsible.

Minutes later, Ty heard the wails of ambulance and fire truck sirens as he locked up the apartment and sprinted to his Jeep. He remembered the warehouse full of weapons, and felt a pang of guilt for not having at least tried to warn the authorities. He heard the reports on the radio and realized the uniformed sheriff who shot him earlier that morning must have been involved in the bombing.

"Oh, Jesus. Oh, Jesus," Ty continued to mutter as he continued driving and listening. He remembered to stop at a Walmart and pick up two cheap "burner" phones to replace the ones the Ravens had taken.

Back at the hospital, every face Ty encountered displayed a blank and distant look. The ER would soon be a nightmare of yelling and movement. The rest of the hospital was quiet as a tomb, with most entranced by the nearest television. Ty walked in to find Henry looking the same way as Fox News blared its coverage nationwide. The banner at the bottom read: TERROR STRIKES IN TENNESSEE. They were already citing Kaiser's Twitter account as the culprit, though no one knew anything about the mysterious Black Hand.

"Good God, dude. This is beyond crazy. Your boy Kaiser is a flat-out terrorist. I can't believe this. Henry, you okay?"

"No, I'm not. But, you're right. This is way bigger than we could have imagined. And I think I know why Kessler bombed his own building. Jesus, I just wish we would have moved a little faster. Maybe we could have . . ." Henry trailed off, his eyes never leaving the TV.

"I know man, I know. But maybe we can stop their next steps. Remember, we've got their files downloaded." Ty produced his laptop and opened the lid on his lap.

"Yeah, I hope there's something useful in there. If not, we've got nothing. And bonus, I'm now officially part of a fucking domestic terror cell." Henry shook his head.

The aerial coverage of the smoldering building continued unabated on the TV, while Ty logged into his email and found the message from Henry. He began opening files and reading as fast as he was capable.

"I know we need to get going, but I don't know if we can wait for Deja to pour over all this information. If their plans are spelled out somewhere in here, maybe there's a chance we can prevent it," Ty said, still scrolling and reading.

Henry stayed silent, trying to allow Ty a few minutes of research. He was anxious to get on the road toward Evansville, but equally anxious to know Kaiser's next move. The Fox News banner was now stating at least twenty were dead and dozens more were injured in the blast.

After what felt like an hour to Henry, Ty finally spoke. "Holy shit, Hank. It's all here. I mean, it's not well organized and it's wordy as hell. He's got bios on all of the Ravens, including you. A lot of this is like Kaiser's journals where he's just rambling about what he wants to do. But here it is, right here! He wants to blow up a police headquarters and blame blacks for it. He wants to start a war between whites and blacks based off this one event. Shit, that's what all those guns were for. He wants to get both sides riled up into a frenzy, and then arm them to the teeth! This is bad, man. This is really bad."

Henry was already working his way out of bed as Ty read on. The wooziness had mostly subsided, but his head still pounded from the impact of Kessler's gun butt. Still, the time for recovery was over. He couldn't keep himself in bed any longer.

"Pack it up. We're leaving. I'll drive. You go ahead and send all of that information to the state police and, I don't know, every fucking federal agency you can think of. Start with the FBI and work your way down."

"Wait. If I do that, you'll be implicated along with Kaiser and all the others. They'll be hunting you just as hard as they do the real killers. Maybe we should think about going straight to the cops first before we head north."

The words *real killers* stopped Henry halfway out of the hospital bed. *I am a real killer, and maybe I deserve to be hunted.*

"What cops? The Vicarstown cops? They're all dead except for Kessler. Somehow I'm sure he escaped the blast. I know these guys. Once they put the pieces together, they're coming for my family. I want to make sure they're safe, then we talk to the police. As for them hunting me, I can't worry about that. Let's go."

"We could go to the Tennessee Highway Patrol. I'm sure they have an office in Nashville. Hank, you've –"

"There's no time! They'll keep us there for hours asking questions, meanwhile Kaiser is chasing down my wife and son. No way, Ty. They'll get the information in the files, and that's all they need right now. Can we go now, please?"

"I get it, Hank. I just don't want you running into something again without proper backup. I mean, look at us! We're both lucky to be alive. We need help, man."

Henry thought for a moment and realized Ty was right. They would need a small army to defeat Kaiser. Besides, Deja was already en route to Evansville and would help Carrie and David to stay hidden.

"I see your point. But I don't want us both tied up at the police station. You . . . no, I should be the one. I started this and I should explain it. Drop me off in Nashville, then get to Indiana as fast as you can. Meet up with Deja, Carrie, and David, and keep them under wraps until this all blows over. How's that?" Henry's tone was low and brooding.

"I know it's going to hurt, but this is the right way. The sooner you get everything laid out for the authorities, the better for everyone. This violence is only going to get worse."

For the first time since the revelation that a new group of Ravens existed, Henry felt no fear for himself. He was no longer afraid to die, only afraid of losing his family, his friends, and the chance to stop Kaiser permanently. Grandpa Herman often spoke of determination and grit. As they left the hospital, Henry finally understood what those words meant.

Chapter Twenty-Three

Sunday, May 29, Mount Vernon, Indiana; 3:15 PM

The Economy Inn on Fourth Street, the main strip running through the small farming town that sat ten miles west of Evansville, lived up to its name. Deja and Carrie noted the 1980s décor and the box television that offered free HBO but no remote control. The double beds were of sketchy cleanliness, and Carrie lifted the covers and mattress to check for bedbugs.

Their hope was that they would only be here for one night, and that their families would be reunited in a matter of hours. After a short settling in period, David sat on one bed playing with a Star Wars Lego set while the two women sat on the edge of the other bed and watched horrified as the Vicarsown Bombing dominated national news.

The tweets sent by Kaiser from his ghost accounts were getting plenty of coverage, but there was also talk that those could be a cover for other malevolent suspects such as ISIS. The carnage on social media had boiled over, leading Facebook and Twitter to begin suspending accounts and issuing warnings to all users about racist and/or violent content.

Kaiser had succeeded in pouring gasoline on America's smoldering and never-ending race war. By mid-afternoon, the Black Panthers, the KKK, and other groups were mobilizing and planning next steps. Mixed neighborhoods fell silent as neighbors loaded their weapons and locked up their homes in a mix of fear and indignation.

The violent backlash that Kaiser craved had already started in his home state. CNN reported a bar outside of

Knoxville had burned down after a brawl began inside and someone lit a Molotov cocktail amidst the clamor. One person was dead and several others were hurt in the melee. In Memphis, a known KKK leader was attacked in his home and beaten to death by two black teenagers. In Little Rock, Arkansas, a black college student carrying a backpack was shot and killed by a white officer outside the police station.

Deja looked at Carrie and tried to comfort her with a smile. "You okay? You haven't said anything for a while."

"Just trying not to think about what Henry has been through these past few weeks. I should have never let him go down there. I should have fought him harder from the start. I should have . . . " Carrie stopped herself and shook her head. "Can't think that way. I have to stay positive. He and Ty will be here soon and the police will catch this Kaiser guy. They have to."

"They will, honey. I know Ty and I'd like to think I know Henry a little bit by now. Ty can annoy you like none other, but he's also smart and strong. So is Henry. They'll come through this. We all will."

"Mommy, I'm hungry. Can we eat, please," David asked with a whine. Carrie realized they had skipped lunch in their rush to get away from the house with Deja.

"Yes, sweetie. Just a minute and we'll get something. I thought I saw a little diner just a block down from here. You want to join us for a late lunch?" Carrie asked Deja.

"Um, no, you go ahead. I'll hang back and see if I can get any updates from Ty. He hasn't checked in in over an hour. Just be quick. Don't be doing any window shopping."

"That's the last thing on my mind. Okay, we'll be back in an hour or less. Come on, David." Carrie took her son's hand and guided him out the door.

Deja tapped Ty's name on her contact list and waited through several tones. No answer. She tapped Henry's name next and got the same result. Maybe they were driving through a zone with a weak cell signal. *Or maybe they're dead.* Deja forced that thought out of her mind and typed out a text to both of them. "We have arrived at the hotel. All are safe. Call me ASAP."

She turned her attention back to the TV, where a blonde news anchor was chatting up two "experts" about the situation in Vicarstown and beyond. Remembering Ty's call from this morning, she pulled out her Lenovo laptop and brought up the email from Henry.

One by one, Deja perused the files with the skill of a law student who was accustomed to reading hundreds of textbook pages per night. As Kaiser's plan became apparent, and as the results of that plan played on mute on the TV, Deja opened a Word document and began writing a synopsis of the information from the files. It would take hours for media or law enforcement to dig through this dense material. Her summary, written by a woman who sometimes saw legal briefs in her sleep, would clarify Kaiser's motives, actions, and future plans. It would also explain Henry and Ty's involvement.

Within a half-hour, Deja had a full sense of what Kaiser wanted to accomplish. She had transformed nearly a hundred pages of wordy, dislocated files into a succinct and easy to read one-page document. She began sending the full slate of files, along with her summary, to numerous state and federal law enforcement and government agencies. She also sent them to every media source she could think of. Still, she felt it wasn't enough. The violence and paranoia was spreading by the minute.

Before she could finish her thought, two knocks sounded at the door. Surprised, Deja looked at the bottom right of her screen and realized it had been forty minutes since Carrie and David left for lunch. She set the laptop down on the bed and walked to the door.

"You weren't kidding about being quick! I thought you'd at least take an hour."

She opened the door and encountered a tall, blond man in a sharp grey suit. In his left hand, he held an expensive-looking black leather briefcase. In his right, he held a silenced nine-millimeter.

"Hello, Deja. Such a pleasure to make your acquaintance."

***

Ninety minutes earlier, Phillip Kaiser's Audi rolled into the driveway of the Bowersox residence in Evansville. Flustered by lane restrictions on I-69 due to construction, he hadn't arrived as early as he wanted. He approached the front door with his briefcase in hand, but kept the gun out of sight. If Henry's lovely wife and young son were home, they would find Mr. Kaiser to be a friendly guest.

Knocking and ringing the doorbell brought no one to the front door. Kaiser began circling the house, looking for an entry point. He found it on the side of their attached garage. A side door with windows and a limited view from any neighbors' houses. Using his silenced weapon, Kaiser put two bullets through the deadbolt and kicked the door open with ease.

Inside the house, Kaiser took a brief tour and realized Henry had already gotten the message to them to flee. This would make his work more complicated, but no less important. He needed Henry's family alive and in his possession. They could be extremely valuable in the coming hours and days as bargaining chips. And if the situation called for it, Kaiser would extract an enormous amount of pleasure in destroying the lives of those whom Henry loved the most.

He walked around from room to room, aimless at first. He was torn between needing to locate Henry's wife and son and learning more about Henry's life. Picking up trinkets, examining photos hanging on the walls, Kaiser absorbed the information and a picture of Henry as a teacher and family man began to form. The guy was a fucking boy scout.

But that image conflicted sharply with Kaiser's own experiences with Henry. He had seen the look in Henry's eyes when he was sticking the knife into his victim's ribcage. The Bryant blood, the Bryant legacy, was alive and well inside of Henry. He was born a soldier, but had been formed into a weak and feckless do-gooder instead. What a waste.

In the living room, Kaiser scanned the walls and stopped on a collage of photographs. He approached the grouping and was struck by one image featuring Henry with his arm around a grey-haired man wearing a Cardinals jacket and an Evansville Otters baseball cap. Kaiser's face came within an inch of the photo as he studied the old man.

There again was the face of a Bryant. It was unquestionably the face of James "Junior" Bryant, the son of the man whom Kaiser so revered. But how was that possible? Junior never came home from the battlefields of Europe during World War II. With no remains to bury, his father and mother had held a funeral for their lost war hero son in Vicarstown in late 1945. Big Jim personally told Kaiser the story on multiple occasions.

And yet, there he was. Alive and well many years after the war, and with a family of his own. Kaiser began ripping open drawers and cabinets, desperate to find more information about Junior's mysterious hidden life. Was he still alive? What happened to him during the war? And, most importantly, why did he abandon his family and the brotherhood of The Ravens?

He found Herman's obituary lying on a stack of bills inside a kitchen drawer. Kaiser read it three times, allowing the truth of Junior's existence to wash over him.

The story began to coalesce in Kaiser's mind. Junior had somehow either faked his death or survived a mortal wound and decided to start a new life elsewhere when he got back to the states.

Henry's betrayal now finally made sense. He was raised by a race traitor, so it was only appropriate that Henry would grow into one as well. A legacy of weakness, passed down from grandfather to grandson. Pathetic.

Kaiser snatched the photo of the two Bowersox men, folded it, and stuffed it in his suit jacket pocket. The newfound anger gave him a jolt of energy and a new sense of purpose. Henry's death must be achieved, as well as that of his son. The Ravens of both past and present owed him that much.

Ten minutes later, in the spare bedroom Henry and Carrie used as an office, Kaiser found the clue he was searching for. In the corner, atop an L-shaped wooden desk, sat an old-looking Dell monitor and keyboard. Next to the keyboard, Carrie had conveniently taped a piece of lined paper to the desk which contained the Bowersox family's usernames and passwords for an assortment of email accounts, websites, and online banking.

Kaiser perused the list and found their login information for myaccountaccess.com, a website used to track their Visa card activity. He accessed the site and read through the Bowersox family's most recent transactions. A devious smile overtook Kaiser's face as he read the two entries from Sunday, May 29th.

Economy Inn, Mount Vernon, IN...........$47.55
Duke's Diner, Mount Vernon, IN...........$18.50

Without logging off, Kaiser reached for his phone and dialed Kessler. "Grant, I found out where Henry's wife and son are hiding out. They're at a motel in Mt. Vernon. I'm on my way to retrieve them now. How long until you make the rendezvous point?"

"Uh, probably three hours. I'm still in Tennessee. After the explosion I kind of lost my bearings for a little bit. I'm okay now, though. I'm on my way."

"Grant, listen to me. I know what you did today wasn't easy. But I hope you understand how important it was. Not just for us, for the entire country. Have you seen the news coverage? The plan is working, It's just as we hoped. But we have loose ends here and I need your help one last time. Are you with me, brother?"

"Of course, Phillip. I'm always with you. You know that. Have you talked to Nix?"

"He has his instructions and is proceeding. Mt. Vernon is only a few miles west of the rendezvous point, so I should be able to meet you both on schedule." Kaiser told him the address of the Economy Inn. "Stay strong, brother. We're so close now," Kaiser said and then hung up.

He pulled out the folded photo of Henry and Herman. The resemblance to each other and to Big Jim Bryant was unmistakable. It was also heartbreaking. Two men, in two different eras, choosing to betray their race and their brothers in arms.

Kaiser crumpled the photo and tossed it onto the keyboard. He left the house and drove west toward Mount Vernon, still marveling over the image of the two Bowersox men. One recently deceased, the other surely soon to follow.

***

Henry sat at a rectangular metal table in a cramped room with four men from the Tennessee Highway Patrol. In his former life, Henry would have been intimidated by this scene. Not today. He calmly explained the events of the previous three months, noting repeatedly why he and Ty had elected not to approach authorities sooner.

The detectives sat around Henry at the table and took in his story without comment, their faces grim and intent. They had obviously been shaken by the bombing in

Vicarstown, and their thirst for justice in this case was apparent. After Henry finished, Lieutenant Sam Weinzapfel, seated directly across from Henry, spoke first.

"Mr. Bowersox, I can't imagine the amount of guts it took for you to walk into that nest of vipers. I think it's safe to say that you're going to save a lot of lives with what you've done. That being said, you should have come to us much sooner, especially after your friend discovered the weapons cache. Perhaps today's events could have been avoided."

Henry nodded slowly. He knew they had made mistakes, and the bombing weighed heavily on him as he considered the lieutenant's remarks.

Weinzapfel continued, "Still, you couldn't have known what these men were capable of. Or even when or where they meant to use those weapons. The files you retrieved this morning are going to prove crucial in stopping further attacks, and, ultimately, bringing The Ravens in dead or alive. I suspect they won't give themselves up quietly. Now, is there anything else we need to know?"

"Yes. I'm certain that Kaiser is going to come after my family in Indiana. They're probably on their way right now. Ty is headed up there as we speak, but I need help to make sure my family is safe. Please, what can you guys do for them?" Henry fought back a sob.

Weinzapfel addressed one of the other officers. "Charlie, get on the horn to the Evansville police and ISP. Mark, I want you to coordinate with the feds. See what resources they have in or around southern Indiana." He turned back to Henry. "We're on it, Mr. Bowersox. You've been carrying this load for a long time with only a little help. You can relax now. The cavalry is coming."

"Thank you so much, Lieutenant. But I won't be able to breathe until I know they're safe and The Ravens are done for good."

The detectives quickly scattered to their respective assignments. Henry stepped out into a fluorescent-lighted hallway along with Weinzapfel. He led Henry to his office, where he offered him coffee and a place to rest. Still weary from the morning's events, Henry agreed.

Henry stretched out on a small, uncomfortable sofa in the office. He was near to dozing within a few minutes, but jumped back to full consciousness when his replacement cell phone began ringing. With no contacts programmed in, he had no idea who was calling.

"Hello?"

"Hank! Is that you, my man? I'm in the Bluegrass State and making good time. How are things there?"

"Ty! Good to hear. It went well. They're all being very helpful and responsive. I think this may all be over very soon. They're pulling in pretty much everyone to help." Henry rubbed his eyes and tried to re-focus.

"They better be treating you well. You're a freaking folk hero for God's sake! Any word from Deja or Carrie?"

Henry checked the clock and realized it had been more than two hours since he had last talked with his wife.

"No, and that worries me. I just got out of the meeting with all the state officers. Have you tried to call them lately?" Henry asked.

"Yeah, twice in the last twenty minutes. Nothing from either of them. I . . . wait. What? I have a missed call on here from a few minutes ago. How did that happen? These cheap phones suck, dude."

"You bought 'em, pal. Call whoever that was back. Then get back to me as quick as you can."

"Sure thing. Back to you in a minute," Ty said and ended the call.

Henry leaned back on the sofa and tried not to count the seconds until Ty's call-back. He hadn't wanted to spend the time spilling everything to the cops, but he was glad to be here among allies. Finally, he felt the balance of power had shifted to the good side in this fight. He looked at his phone and realized he also had a missed call.

Jesus, Ty. What bargain bin did you buy these phones in?

Before he could check the voicemail, Henry's phone rang again. He answered on the first ring.

"Ty?"

"Uh, Hank? You better . . . you need to write this number down. You got a pen?"

"Yeah, just a second." Henry searched the top of Weinzapfel's desk and found a pen and a yellow inter-office envelope to write on. "Okay, ready. What's going on, Ty? Is everyone still safe?"

Ty breathed heavily into the receiver and took a second to respond.

"It's Kaiser, Hank. He called my phone. He got the number from Deja's phone. He . . . he's there, man. He's there with them, at the hotel in Mount Vernon. He said he wants to talk to you directly. He said they're all alive and well, but . . . I'm sorry, Hank. Just call this number."

Ty read off the digits, but Henry wrote nothing. A cold sensation started in his feet, ran into his balls, and then flowed through his guts. Ty's voice was lost in the whirlwind as Henry's fear turned to panic, and then panic turned to resignation.

My family is going to die, and it's my fault. I knew it from the beginning. Somehow I would bring harm to them. Oh, Jesus, please . . .

"Henry? Henry! Listen, man. I know this is our worst fear come true, but they're still alive. He wants to talk to you. There's still a chance for them, but you have to stay strong. Are you still with me, partner?"

Another few seconds of silence, then Henry was back. "Yeah, you're right. They'd be dead already unless he wants something. Give me those numbers again."

Henry ended the call and nearly crushed the light plastic phone with the intensity of his grip. Without stopping to inform the state officers first, he placed the call to Kaiser. With each buzz of the call tone, Henry's rage and fear spiked to new levels.

"Ah, Mr. Bowersox! That is your real name, isn't it Henry? Thank you for calling me back. I was afraid I would never get a chance to thank you for your service to our cause." Kaiser spoke in the same reserved, arrogant tone Henry had grown accustomed to.

"Thank me? I seriously doubt it. Let me talk to my wife and son. Please, Phillip. Let me know they're all right."

"Oh, but I have so much to thank you for, Henry. Your actions this morning, inconvenient as they were, served as a necessary spur. You have motivated us to move our plans along at a much more accelerated rate than any of us could have anticipated. I must say, I haven't enjoyed a day, or learned as much in a day for that matter, as I have today. So, please, accept my sincere thanks.

"Now, onto your next query. Yes, your precious family is fine for the moment. They, along with your Negro companion's sister, are resting comfortably. And, I might add, in much more desirable conditions than that dreadful motel they were holed up inside. It really is shameful what teachers are paid these days."

Henry mustered the strength not to spike the phone like a football in his anger. Then, his mind seized on something Kaiser said. He had never learned as much in a day. What did that mean?

He's been in my house. The fucker has been inside my house. He knows everything . . . knows about Grandpa Herman.

"So you know the truth about 'Junior' Bryant? He turned away from his father and built a new life without The Ravens in it. Now you know why I did what I did. I didn't have a choice. Once I found out you and the others were carrying on their ways, I knew what I had to do."

"So you did. I was quite taken aback when I saw the photo of you and him together. I suppose you see yourself as some sort of hero for what you've done. Let me assure you, you are not a hero. You and your grandfather are the worst kind of traitors. Not only traitors to your country, but traitors to your own race. You both refused to participate in the fight for the very soul of our society. Quite honestly, it makes me ill just thinking about it.

"But I digress. The reason for this interaction is as follows: you will come back to your hometown tonight and face me, alone. The location shall be none other than the residence of your former role model and grandfather, Herman 'Bowersox.' Be there at nine this evening. That should give you plenty of time. Do not arrive early, and if any police or help of any kind are detected, your family and Ty's sister will die. You've seen what we're capable of. I will gladly watch your offspring suffer, but I would rather watch you." Kaiser finished and cut off the call.

Henry sat in Lieutenant Weinzapfel's office and wept like a child for several minutes. His premonition was now reality. He would face Kaiser alone, with his family's lives and legacy hanging in the balance.

Chapter Twenty-Four

Sunday, May 29, Interstate 69 near Madisonville, Kentucky; 4:30 PM

Henry sat fidgeting in the back of a Tennessee Highway Patrol car when he heard about a church shooting in Vicarstown. According to the report received from the dispatcher back in Nashville, it was a tragic situation that could have been far worse. A white teenager opened fire during a prayer vigil, killing one black man and wounding two others. Fortunately, a resident in attendance was carrying a concealed pistol and killed the would-be mass shooter before he could do more damage.

It was another in a growing list of violent acts and clashes that had occurred throughout the day since the bombing of the Vicarstown Sheriff's Department hours before. The good news was that TV and online news sources had effectively communicated the message about Phillip Kaiser and The Ravens being the real culprits behind the terror.

Kaiser and Michael Nix – along with Henry, according to some media outlets who hadn't yet gotten word of his innocence from the police – were now the most wanted criminals in America. Grant Kessler was also on the list, but it was still unclear as to whether he was dead or alive. Some believed Kessler died as a suicide bomber, others thought he could still be at large.

Slowly and painfully, the nation was getting the message that this was not the act of a crazed pro-black organization bent on starting a race war. It was, in fact, a carefully staged ruse by a small group of white racists who intended to tear the country apart.

Though the death toll from reprisal attacks and spontaneous street riots was still growing, it was clear by early evening that the worst case scenario Kaiser had envisioned was not happening. Most people were staying home, or trying to support each other in vigils like the one at Church of the Cross where the shooting had occurred. The nation had proven to be less racist, and less prone to violent over-reaction, than Kaiser was counting on.

As he rode in the back of the Highway Patrol car, somewhere in the middle of Kentucky on their way toward Evansville, the lives that he, Ty, and Deja had saved were furthest from his mind. He thought only of his own wife, whom he had virtually abandoned in favor of investigating his grandfather's past and his terrible legacy in the present. He thought of his son, only seven years old, and what he must be thinking and feeling. If David survived, would he have the emotional strength to move forward? Would this ordeal destroy any semblance of a normal life for him?

Henry also thought of Ty and Deja, his newest and best friends. Their willingness to trust him and their dedication to a common cause despite the danger was more than admirable. Alone in the backseat, it was hard not to get emotional. It was entirely possible that he could lose nearly every person he loved on the same day.

No time. They were only an hour away from the ultimate destination: the former home of Herman Bowersox. He took out the crappy phone and dialed Ty. Once again, he would have to lean heavily on his friend.

"Hey, where are you?" Henry asked.

"Uh, I'm on some gravel road. I think the sign back there said Uebelhack Road. Does that sound right? Am I close?"

"Yes. Have you come across a really nice white farm house that looks like it was recently renovated? It has a huge, old barn off to the side."

"Just passed it a minute ago. What now, chief?"

"You should be coming up on Norman Road. When you get there, take a right. You'll see an old oil well road on the right. Pull back there and park. If you walk that road for about a half mile, you'll dead end at an oil pump that hasn't run in years. Directly beyond that is Grandpa's property. There's some woods, then you'll see the house up ahead and a pond off to the left. You got all that?"

"Crystal clear. I'll find a good hiding spot and stake out the place. I'll be there when you arrive, so don't worry. You've got backup. Keep your phone on in case I catch anything major that you need to know about. Cool?"

"Yes. Thank you, Ty. Be sure to stay out of sight. Kaiser said he would kill them if I'm not alone, and I believe him."

"Got it. Right now I'd do anything to trade places with them. We've got to do this just right, or . . ."

"I know, but I still have faith. Plus, I've got a wild card up my sleeve that might pay off. Take care, brother. I'll see you on the other side." Henry didn't wait for a response. He laid the phone down and put his head in his hands. This was the longest car ride of his life, and it had nothing to do with distance. But as the miles dragged on, Henry's despair began to dissipate.

Though he had been too concerned with rescuing Carrie, David, and Deja to notice, a great weight had lifted from Henry's shoulders. Win or lose against Kaiser and his men, the blood that once so tainted the Bryant family legacy had been washed away. Henry exorcised those demons by saving the lives of countless victims that might have been claimed by Kaiser's insane plan for a national race war.

As he raced northward toward his final meeting with Kaiser, Henry's dread became confidence. His fear became strength. The killer instinct that Kaiser had awakened in him was brimming back to the surface

***

Phillip Kaiser checked his Longines watch and smiled. Henry Bowersox, the man who had wrecked his plans and outed him as a racist terrorist, was only minutes away from arriving. Kaiser had never taken special care to live a long life. He never wanted a wife or children. He had no political ambitions. He didn't even care to be famous. From an early age, the age when he first came in contact with Big Jim Bryant, Kaiser wanted to be a soldier in the culture war.

Reforming The Ravens had been a source of deep personal pride. He saw their killings as a small but meaningful blow in the ongoing war. When the plan to expand their mission using social media and one major event, perhaps the destruction of a police station, occurred to him, Kaiser maintained his patience and carefully crafted every detail over several years.

When Henry "Bryant" came into his life, Kaiser believed he had found his lieutenant. Someone he could rely on to carry on and expand their efforts for decades to come. Someone who would perhaps even take command of The Ravens one day.

Now, as he paced the grounds of Henry's dead grandfather, Kaiser came to the full realization of his failure. Though he harbored great anger toward Henry, and fully intended to destroy him and his family tonight, he blamed himself even more. Decades of planning undone by one fatal mistake: trusting his instincts instead of facts.

Kaiser prided himself on his lack of superstition and his reliance on logic. He was a man of science. A rational man who saw the world for what it was: a collection of tribes destined to fight over the finite resources of the planet. How, then, had he allowed everything he had worked for to unravel in the course of one day?

The answer was simple: he chose to trust Henry because he was a Bryant. He allowed himself to be caught up in an emotional response. He tried to drink the mirage, and now he was choking on the sand. No matter.

Kaiser had prepared himself for an abrupt end many years ago. The very nature of their work meant that The Ravens would always be in danger of being exposed. It was much more difficult to stay hidden in plain sight than it was in Big Jim's time. If this was to be the final act of his life, Kaiser would make it memorable for all involved. And, most importantly, he would make one final contribution to his tribe's ultimate victory. In the end, the triumph of the white race was much more valuable than his own life.

Kaiser casually strolled to the back of Herman's house. He approached the old red garage.

Michael Nix, armed with an Uzi, and Grant Kessler, holding a fully automatic AK-47, stood on either side of the garage's front door. Kaiser stood chatting with them, gauging their mood and reassuring them that all would work out in the end. In reality, Kaiser understood that most, if not all three of them, would be dead by dawn. He marveled at their continued allegiance to him, even after his blunder in judgment regarding the addition of Henry to their group.

Nix and Kessler were tasked with guarding the contents of the garage at all costs. Inside, sitting on the greasy floor with hands and feet bound, were Carrie, David, and Deja. They sat in silence, aware of the various ways their lives could end.

First among those was the large amount of C-4 plastic explosives which Kessler had rigged up around the garage in much the same way that he had at the Sheriff's Department. He made sure to use less of it this time, noting that it wouldn't take much to bring down the sixty-year-old garage and kill the three people inside.

The C-4 had been Kaiser's idea. It was both a dramatic gesture and a solid insurance policy. The plan was for Kaiser to set off the explosives while Henry watched, then for Henry himself to be put down after a sufficient amount of time for him to feel the grief of losing his family. If those plans somehow went awry, Kessler had set a timer on one of the C-4 bricks. One way or the other, the garage would be rubble at 9:30.

Nix and Kessler were both operating under the assumption that Kaiser had a plan for their escape and future. Their names and faces were now permanent fixtures on every newscast in the country. They could never return to their old lives. Like Kaiser, both men had accepted the risks involved in joining The Ravens. Unlike Kaiser, they believed their mission would still carry on beyond this night. They wanted revenge on Henry for betraying them and for killing Logan Feury. But more importantly, they wanted to live to fight another day.

Kaiser left them to their guard duty and walked across a squared concrete patio. He entered the open breezeway that connected a small, one-car garage with the main house. Taking a seat on a weathered white glider, he removed his silenced Glock .357 and grasped it in his right hand as he gently rocked. The creaking of the ancient chair masked the silent tension as he waited for their prey to arrive.

A minute later, at precisely 8:59, a brown sedan rolled down the long, paved driveway. Henry appeared a moment later, wearing a black sweatshirt and faded jeans. He looked to be unarmed. As Henry made the slow march toward the front of the breezeway, Kaiser greeted him.

"Welcome home, Henry. I'm sure you spent an evening or two on this porch in the past. Did you not?"

"Yes, many. Grandpa loved to listen to the Cardinals on the radio. We'd come out here after supper and listen to the ballgame. Sometimes we'd play cards." Henry looked around as if he could see it happening.

"Ah, treasured memories. After tonight, I'm afraid that may be all you have. You've cost us so much, Henry.

It's difficult to put into words just how much. I felt it necessary to even the score. Your family . . . they are here. Out there, in the red garage. They are alive and unharmed, for the moment. But, I'm afraid getting them out will take some doing. We have C-4 ready to detonate at my command. You know me, and you know I'm telling you the truth. So, what say you, Henry Bowersox?"

Henry gazed out toward the back garage where he saw Nix and Kessler holding their posts.

Kaiser approached Henry and motioned for him to turn around. He patted Henry down for weapons as Henry spoke. "Phillip, I know that you want me dead and I understand that. I've thrown a major wrench into your plans. I get it. But why my family? They're innocent, not to mention white. Why waste their lives when it's me you really want? Please, Phillip. Let them go and I'll give myself to you without a fight. You can torture me, do whatever you want. Just please don't make them pay the price for my actions."

"I'm afraid it's not that simple, my friend. Your bloodline is tainted. You and your grandfather, two different generations of Bryants, have betrayed us. What chance does David have of being a strong and loyal man? None, I'm afraid. And as for your wife, her death is purely for amusement. You will watch them die, naturally. That will be your torture, and my delight." Kaiser gestured toward the back garage with a flourish.

He rose from the glider and smoothed his suit jacket while keeping the gun pointed down at his right side. Kaiser studied Henry's face and noted a lack of fear, as well as something else. He noticed movement coming from behind Henry somewhere at the front of the house. Cocking his head, Kaiser observed a dark figure seated on the passenger side of Henry's car.

"I believe I was clear when I told you to come alone. Who is that?"

"You said no police and no help. I brought neither. I brought a guest. One that I thought you might want to speak to." Henry turned and waved toward the shadowy figure in the car. The passenger door opened, and an anguished gasp escaped from Kaiser's mouth.

***

Ty slithered through the tangled brush on the outskirts of the Bowersox property. He felt as if he were moving in slow motion, but it was necessary to keep from alerting the bad guys. Full dark had descended upon southern Indiana. An overcast sky meant no moon, and a better chance for Ty to stay hidden. The experience of snooping around the abandoned rubber extrusion plant gave him confidence. He made the mistake of getting too close last time, and now the stakes were even higher.

He spotted two Ravens at their post at the front of the red garage. A dusk-to-dawn light hung from a wooden post about twenty feet above the patio, illuminating the entire front portion of the garage. Still sitting in the woods nearly a hundred yards down the hill, Ty saw Kaiser walk out to them and discuss something.

He waited for Kaiser to leave them, then crawled out of the dark woods and up a slight slope toward the lake behind the garage. This act also seemed to take far too long, but if he were discovered, it would be a disaster because there was no other immediate backup. The Evansville Police along with the Posey County Sheriffs and some federal officers were all on stand-by just a half mile away at the Busler Truck Stop. They had agreed to allow Henry to meet with Kaiser, and were awaiting his signal or, if things went awry, gunfire.

Ty stayed low and scampered across an open plain of grass toward the back of the red garage. Here, Herman had stashed numerous items that escaped the notice of Henry and his family when they cleaned out the house. Among these were a rusted watering can, several panes of glass left over from a window replacement project of long ago, a broken down wheelbarrow, and a half-rotted wooden extension ladder.

The ladder lay propped against the flaking back wall of the garage, its rungs lost in the growth of weeds. Ty put his back to the wall as he tried to come up with a plan.

He had completed a thorough sweep of the property and seen no signs of anyone other than the three Ravens. Evidently, Kaiser didn't have any reserves to call in. Or maybe this errand was personal and he wanted it to be a more intimate affair.

Either way, Ty understood he had to find a way to neutralize the guards. He had a hunch that Deja and the others were being held inside, and that the building was probably booby trapped. He also knew Henry had something in mind for Kaiser, which might create enough of a distraction to pull this off.

After another minute of deliberation, Ty reached down for the ladder and pulled it from its resting place with agonizing slowness. The ladder tugged against the rustling overgrowth. Though he was being incredibly careful, Ty feared that the two maniacs on the other side of the garage would hear.

His head swiveled from side to side, expecting to face a hail of bullets at any moment. But no one came. They weren't even doing regular perimeter checks around the garage or taking turns walking around the house. Overconfidence. Ty liked that in an enemy.

After the longest and most vulnerable seconds of his life, Ty had the ladder free from the weeds and leaning gently against the garage's gutter. The next step would be equally terrifying: trusting a seventy-year-old wooden ladder to support his hundred-and-ninety-pound frame without snapping or creaking loudly.

With breath held, Ty began his climb. Fearing a break, which would virtually ensure his death, Ty kept his feet at the sides of the rungs. The wood let out a few moans and squeaks, but none that he felt could be heard from more than a few feet away. He swung his right foot over the gutter first, securing his balance before bringing his other one over. The garage's roof had a pitch of nearly six feet, which was enough to hide Ty as he crouched on the rear side. He exhaled, closed his eyes for a moment, then crawled toward the peak of the roof and felt the rough texture of the shingles on his fingertips. One slip of a hand or boot, and he was dead for sure. They would come running around the back, spot him in a second, and tear him in half with a clip's worth of ammo. Slowly, steadily, he reached the peak and peered over it. The entire back of the house, including the breezeway and patio, were visible. He could see Henry standing in the breezeway, facing the red garage and talking with Kaiser. Peering down a bit further, he spotted the top of the guards' heads.

Ty watched for over a minute, gauging their reactions and plotting his next moves. He dug into the small of his back and found another useful item that Herman had left behind. It was an ancient ball-peen hammer with a notched wooden handle and a noticeable chunk missing from the ball portion. Ty grasped it in his right hand and waited.

He noticed Kaiser reacting to something on the breezeway. Someone was walking up to the entrance from the front of the house. *A hell of a time for a visitor*, Ty thought. Then the stranger came into view, and Kaiser back-pedaled a step or two. The visitor was still covered in shadow, but he appeared to be walking with a cane.

Nix and Kessler both took a step toward the breezeway, bringing their guns up to firing positions. They stopped, knowing their leader would alert them if they needed to move. Ty realized this was the distraction he needed.

Launching himself from the rear side of the roof's peak, Ty took two giant steps down the slope toward the front of the garage. To his left was Nix, who turned after hearing the footfalls but was too late to react to the flying object that smashed the left side of his face. Nix let out a scream and dropped the Uzi, sending it sliding onto the patio.

Kessler, distracted by Nix's cry, lost sight of Ty as he leapt off the roof, careening into Kessler's body like a professional wrestler flying off the top rope. Both men crashed into the grass, with Kessler shrieking as his collarbone shattered. Ty landed on Kessler, then rolled away as momentum carried him several feet into the yard. His head bounced off the turf twice, leaving him momentarily dazed.

Ty rolled onto his back and found it impossible to get to his feet. He realized his gamble could have just failed. If he lost consciousness, Henry would be alone against this small army.

Chapter Twenty-Five

Sunday, May 29, Herman Bowersox residence

The craggy, leathery face of Jacob Harrigan appeared in the entrance to the breezeway. He was wearing his best Sunday suit without the jacket, determined to look good if this were to be the last night of his life. He supported himself with a thick, hickory wood cane which featured deep and bizarre carvings of human faces. He was sweating in spite of the unseasonably cool evening air, and his carefully slicked back white hair had already taken on a disheveled look.

Kaiser looked at the old man as if he had just descended from a spaceship. His shock was anticipated by Henry, who had pleaded with Jacob earlier that morning to find his way here for a reunion of sorts. Henry had no idea what, if anything, Jacob had to say to his son. He simply hoped his mere presence would unnerve Kaiser.

It was a calculated risk. There was a decent chance that Jacob would give Kaiser his blessing for all that he had "accomplished" and that they would joyfully finish off Henry and his family together. Henry had been eye-to-eye with Harrigan twice, and he did indeed possess the killer instinct that Kaiser liked to talk about. But Henry thought he saw something else in Harrigan. Maybe it was wishful thinking, but he thought he sensed remorse.

"Hello, Phillip. My God, you've changed," Harrigan croaked, his voice barely more than a whisper.

Kaiser continued to gape at his father. After a few seconds delay, he responded. "Jacob Harrigan. You'll forgive me for not calling you 'Dad.' You weren't sufficiently present to have earned that title. What business could you possibly have here and now?"

"As you know, it has been a long time. Something like twenty years. I just wanted to see my boy again, before it's too late. I saw your handiwork on the TV today. You're a celebrity now. Is that what you were aiming for? Fame? Recognition? I never pegged you as the attention-seeking type." Harrigan shuffled two steps closer toward his son.

Henry finally noticed what Kaiser was holding in his left hand: a flip phone. He had seen Kaiser's iPhone and knew that wasn't it. He thought of the bombing from that morning and understood immediately: the phone was a detonator. The back garage was rigged to blow up.

As the two Ravens conversed, Henry began to slink into the background along the side wall of the breezeway

"You know precisely nothing about me, Jacob. Nothing. Today's events were planned, but certain elements have complicated them. That is the purpose of our current location, to iron out some of those complications." Kaiser turned his head to look at Henry. He kept the silenced Glock drawn but still pointed at the floor. Henry froze.

"I know enough, Phillip. I know you've created a whole new version of The Ravens. I can see that you've advanced to levels that we never dreamed of in the old days. I have to give you credit for ambition. You've put on quite a show today."

"Introducing me to Jim Bryant and the philosophy of The Ravens was your single positive contribution to my life. I suppose I should thank you for that. You opened my eyes to the war, and to our clever ways of waging it. But as you said, I have progressed from those tired days. As we speak, all over this country men and women are taking up arms against the enemy they always knew, but refused to see. I have awakened them. The Ravens were once a clandestine group with minimal impact. Tonight, we come out of the shadows and lead the white race to the victory that is decades overdue."

Henry continued his furtive side-step as Kaiser made his speech. It was obvious Kaiser still craved his father's approval even after two decades of separation. Henry knew the feeling well, having constantly sought the approval and pride of Grandpa Herman.

Harrigan leaned heavily on the cane. "Phillip, there were a lot of years in my past when I would have been very impressed by that speech. Hell, I probably would have followed you even though you were my boy. You are passionate, driven, and very smart. Normally, a father couldn't help but be proud of a son with those attributes. But you're wrong, son. You're wrong about all of it.

"I've had a lot of years to think about what we did. To remember all of the people we killed. And what difference did we make? We didn't win any 'battles.' We didn't have a righteous cause. All we did was hurt people. Tore families apart. Terrified neighbors. We were no better than those assholes who put on the white robes or the idiots who shave their heads and get swastika tattoos. We were just plain, old murderers. That's all I am, son. And that's all you are, too. Just a sick person who enjoys hurting people.

"This has to stop, Phillip. Tonight . . . this has to be the end of The Ravens. For good. It's gone way too far." Harrigan moved closer to Kaiser.

Phillip's face twisted from a state of shocked amusement to genuine anger. He took a step toward Jacob, who was now within arm's length.

"No, you're not a killer, old man. Not anymore. Now you're a coward. Just like so many other white men who turn a blind eye to the destruction the Negroes have wrought. You're also a fool for having come here. Did you honestly believe you could have any impact on the outcome of our plans? You're already dead, Jacob. You –" Kaiser was interrupted by a torpedo smashing into his back.

Henry had slipped behind Kaiser's line of sight, and flung himself with all the force he possessed. The pistol dropped from Kaiser's right hand as he fell forward into a wicker chair in the corner of the breezeway. Henry heard commotion from behind on the patio, and hoped that it was Ty creating some problems as he blasted Kaiser with punches to the head and body.

A dazed Kaiser didn't stop Henry from prying the flip phone from his left hand and it smacked the concrete floor with a plastic clack.

***

Harrigan, stunned by the sudden dual brawls on the breezeway and patio, stood motionless in panic and indecision. His son was being assaulted by the same man who had threatened his own life very recently. He should be defending Phillip.

But the innermost sanctum of Jacob's mind and heart understood and even respected Henry's actions. He had spent a lifetime inflicting pain and suffering on innocent people. Now, in the final chapter of his life, Jacob Harrigan had a chance to be on the right side of history.

Still, as he watched Henry continue to have the advantage over Phillip in their struggle, Jacob's heart was heavy with sympathy for his son. He had introduced Phillip to Big Jim and to the lifestyle of murder and secretiveness that drove The Ravens. Ultimately, everything that Phillip had done, including the horror of that day's events, was really Harrigan's fault.

Harrigan turned and stood over the two men as they wrestled and pelted one another. He yelled at them to stop, but got no response. He raised the heavy cane as high as he could lift it. He felt the weight of the solid piece of wood that had been his own father's as it pulled against his long-unutilized bicep. He brought the cane down. He felt the thud as it landed, and heard the groan from the recipient. He saw the blood and thought, *What have I done?*

***

Ty saw stars after his leap off the back garage's roof. He tried to pull himself off the ground, but the swirling inside his head made him stop. He detected the muffled sound of scuffling from on the breezeway, but Henry was on his own. After a few more seconds, the stars subsided, and Ty took inventory of his surroundings. He was amazed by the results of his garage-leap stunt.

One of the guards lay sprawled with his back against a shabby white concrete patio table. Though fuzzy at first, his face finally came into view and Ty winced. Nix's left eye was gone, replaced by a bloody hole. Blood was pouring from the wound down his face and onto his gray tactical jacket. He wasn't moving.

Ty looked to his right and found Kessler, who had absorbed the brunt of Ty's flight. He had an open cut on his forehead, possibly from when it made contact with the patio. He wasn't moving either. He crawled toward Kessler and felt his chest explode in pain. The deep bruises from being shot earlier in the day were throbbing as if the bullets had just hit him. Struggling for breaths, Ty closed his eyes as he crawled and summoned calm from somewhere inside his brain. He checked Kessler's pulse and found it strong. Unconscious, but still dangerous.

Knowing he needed to get to his feet, Ty used Kessler's body once again. He pushed off against the sheriff's abdomen with both hands, steadying himself as he rose from the ground. Now he could see into the breezeway, and it looked like an old man was swinging a cane while Henry and Kaiser rolled around. He wanted to help, but his legs felt anything but sturdy.

He wobbled for a few moments, trying to block out the feeling that a baseball bat was landing blows on his chest every few seconds. Finally, he moved forward. At first clumsily, then with more of the athletic fluidity he was accustomed to. He moved toward the man with the crushed face and felt a gurgle in his stomach.

The mouth was still open as if in mid-scream, but no sound came from it. Ty felt for his pulse and detected a faint and slow beat. He might or might not wake up, and in his current state would probably bleed to death. Good . . . let him. Ty didn't like to feel that way toward any human, but this was a blood sport.

***

Henry looked up to find Harrigan's cane had smashed into the side of Kaiser's neck. It had missed its target by a few inches, which would have killed him if it had connected with his temple. Kaiser released his grip on Henry and emitted a groan. It must have felt like a tree branch coming down, even considering Harrigan's lack of strength.

Henry scanned the floor and located the Glock and the detonator. He scrambled to his feet and scooped up both items. He turned to see Kaiser scampering through the storm door.

Harrigan looked at Henry with a wild stare.

"Get your family out of here. I'm going after him. I'll do my best to keep him occupied."

"Right. Thanks for that. I'm sure it wasn't easy," Henry said.

"Thank you, Henry, for bringing me back. I don't think this makes me even with God, but at least I'm going to die doing something good." Harrigan moved toward the storm door with surprising speed.

Henry turned and found Ty, woozy but alive, standing on the patio with two Ravens laid out around him.

"Holy shit! How did you manage this?" Henry asked.

"Pure luck, pal. I couldn't hit this guy with that hammer from that angle again with a hundred tries. Guess you could say I'm clutch."

"I got the detonator from Kaiser, but I'll bet the door is booby trapped. I say we break one of the windows over there and bust them out."

Ty nodded. "Yeah, breaking down the door is probably a bad idea. What about calling in the cavalry? They'd surely have a bomb squad. Let the pros handle it."

"There's no time! Knowing Kaiser, he's probably got the whole goddamn place set on a timer. We've got to get them out now."

Ty handed him the AK-47. They both walked toward the garage with guarded optimism. So far, their mission had gone as well as they could have hoped.

The garage's windows were nearly door-sized and divided into nine smaller panes supported by rusted metal brackets. They would need to break out the middle row of panes, then unlatch it and raise the frame before the captives could escape. Henry smacked the middle pane and saw it crack but not shatter. Immediately, they heard shouts coming from inside. Henry and Ty shared a look of intense relief before taking another whack at the glass.

"Shit! Look out," Ty screamed, but too late. Kessler appeared behind Henry and bashed the back of Henry's head with a pistol. Henry had time to think, *Not again!* before he fell against the garage and slid to the ground unconscious.

"Looks like I get a chance to kill the same nigger twice today. And it's not even my birthday." Kessler sneered as he drew a bead on Ty's forehead.

***

Inside the dark and empty house, Harrigan crept along the walls searching for his prey. It had been decades since he had felt this kind of rush: the rush of a predator with his target cornered. He would never have believed this was how his life would end, but now it seemed fitting. His son was out of control, and he would expend his last breath, if necessary, to stop him.

***

Kaiser crouched in Herman's old bedroom, feeling the bloody welt rising on the right side of his neck. He was more stung from the knowledge that his father had just joined his enemy than from the wound. Though he had never felt anything greater than antipathy for his father, he never thought he would have to kill him. Now it was certain and Kaiser was at peace with the idea. Just another casualty of his ill-advised decision to accept Henry into The Ravens.

After retrieving the double-barreled shotgun he had stashed inside the house for just such an emergency, Kaiser waited. There seemed to be no likely scenario in which he would achieve both Henry and his family's deaths, not to mention his dark-skinned compatriots, and his own escape from the certain police deluge that would ultimately arrive. He had abandoned hope of continuing his plans on schedule, but they could still be completed with more time.

Kaiser extracted a gold cigarette lighter from his pocket and held the flame to the musty, stained carpet. The fire took hold slowly, but within a minute it began to spread. The hardwood floors underneath would provide plenty of fuel. Kaiser understood that chaos would be his best camouflage when the police arrived.

He moved away from the bedroom and into a large, rectangular living room. With no furniture, the room seemed cavernous. The glow from the burgeoning inferno provided enough light for Kaiser to spot Harrigan about twenty feet away in the dining room. He checked his watch: only five minutes until the charges would send Henry's family into oblivion.

As Harrigan approached, Kaiser brought the barrels of the shotgun up to aim at his chest. Harrigan didn't flinch as he continued toward his son.

"Jesus, Phillip. Of all the ways I thought I'd go out, this one never occurred to me. Go ahead, son. Kill me. As you can see, I'm ready to go."

"Oh, I intend to. You've been dead to me for a long time. Destroying your physical body won't be difficult.

Especially after you decided to join the ranks of the faithless and disloyal. Your death, much like your life, will be utterly meaningless."

The flames began to consume the walls of the bedroom and spill out into the living room. Harrigan's tired but determined face was illuminated by the glow. Kaiser looked upon that face and felt true rage. He dropped the shotgun and lunged at Harrigan, pushing him backwards onto the floor of the dining room.

Kaiser began choking the old man with a brutal force that sapped the rest of the energy from his father's body. Harrigan held his gaze with his son for as long as he could, feeling the breath and life slipping from him.

"Now, father, you die. Corvus Oculum Corvi Non Eruit!"

His eyes bulging, Harrigan let out one final groan. Kaiser continued to apply maximum pressure to his throat well after he knew it was over. Never in his life had taking a life been such an emotional experience. He removed his hands from Harrigan's neck as he stared at his face, relishing the conquest while ignoring the creeping flames.

Seconds later, his silent moment of homicidal meditation was rocked by what felt like an earthquake. The house shook violently with a blast of sound that reminded Kaiser of a locomotive. He rolled off of Harrigan and jumped to his feet. He looked down at his watch and smiled. The explosives had timed out at exactly 9:30.

Suddenly, a day in which so much of Kaiser's work had been ruined seemed destined to become his day of victory after all. He walked back into the living room, which was now half engulfed in flames, and retrieved the shotgun. Next, he turned toward the door to the breezeway, determined to wipe out any enemies still left alive outside.

Time to embrace the chaos.

Chapter Twenty-Six
9:23 PM

Ty, focused on the barrel of the pistol aimed at his head, noted movement out of the corner of his eye. Henry was alive. He knew he needed to keep Kessler talking, otherwise they were both dead.

"Look, man. This is crazy. Have you even thought this thing through? There are like a hundred cops just a few blocks away. They've got this place covered. There's no way you're getting out of here. Why do this? How is this worth it to you?"

"Even if that's true, this is still worth it. You two fucks messed with the wrong guys. We're the boogeymen. We're the fucking devil. You don't fuck with us, we fuck with you. It's worth it because I'm part of a brotherhood. I stand with them, no matter what. And you, a fucking worthless goddamn nigger, killed my friend. You killed Logan." Kessler wagged his pistol to emphasize the point.

Ty closed his eyes. *This is it, I'm dead. He'll make sure this time.*

"Hey, ass hat," someone bellowed from behind Kessler. He turned to see Deja standing ten feet away, drawing a bead on him with a nine millimeter. Ty sprinted forward and tackled Kessler from behind.

***

The men struggled for control of the weapon, and Kessler, remembering he had shot Ty three times only twelve hours before, rammed an elbow into his chest. Ty growled and rolled away, allowing Kessler to rise to his feet. His gun had been lost in the struggle, but there was no time. He thought he could already hear sirens approaching in the distance.

He turned to face Deja. He didn't believe she would shoot him. He could charge her, take the gun, and kill all of them. But that would take precious seconds. He looked left and noticed the far side of the Bowersox house was on fire. There was no sign of Kaiser. He also saw the limp body of Nix lying against the patio table. Still alive, but useless to them in his current state.

He turned back to Deja. She was holding the gun's aim steady, but her eyes told him she didn't really want to fire.

"Go ahead, bitch. Shoot me!" Kessler ran toward a line of trees at the edge of the yard. No shot came as he entered the cover of the woods.

***

Deja helped Ty to his feet and hugged him with a force that made his chest throb again. He groaned, but held the hug anyway.

"Dee . . . how? How did you get out of there? Where are Carrie and David? Are you guys okay?"

"I'll explain later. Yes, we're all kinda fine. Now grab Henry and let's go. We need to get away from this garage. It's going to blow any minute. I thought I heard something about 9:30. What time is it?"

Ty checked his Casio. "9:28. Shit! We need to roll now!"

***

Ty and Deja helped Henry, who was beginning to get his mind back into focus, to his feet and toward the front of the house. Carrie and David, who had been hiding behind an oak tree nearby, flew out and screamed as they latched on to Henry. The flood of relief and joy that engulfed Henry was unlike any in his life.

Still, he knew this wasn't over.

Once they reached a safe distance from the back garage, Henry forced himself to let go of his family. He asked Deja to hand over the gun she held, knowing Kaiser was lurking. They ducked down and waited for the explosion.

A deafening boom filled the night. The darkness became like mid-day in the light of the fireball that destroyed the garage. Chunks of concrete and wood rained down on the house. The smoke and dust from the explosion joined with the smoke from the house fire to create a haze around the entire property.

Henry, seemingly invigorated by the blast, rose to his feet and brandished the pistol.

"Ty, Deja, keep an eye on my family, please. I'm sure the cops will be here soon. If they hadn't seen the house on fire, they definitely heard that."

"Whoa, partner. Where are you going? The house is on fire. You're not thinking of going in there," Ty said, grasping Henry's shoulder.

"That's exactly what I'm going to do. This guy came after my family. I'm going to find him and end this now."

Carrie stood up. "Henry, you don't have to do this. Let the police handle it. They're coming now. Stay here with us, please. We're safe now."

"No, we're not. Kaiser isn't like anyone else. If he gets away tonight, he'll be back for us later with new followers. He won't forget, and he won't forgive. I'm sorry, Carrie. I hope you can understand. I'm doing this for us."

"You're doing this for yourself, Henry. It's a vendetta. Please don't do it."

Henry looked her in the eyes, then down at his shaken son. David was shivering and teary-eyed, gripping his mother's hand with all of his strength. The sight tore Henry's heart out, and bolstered his determination to finish the game alone. He turned and ran into the breezeway and through the storm door.

As soon as Henry entered the kitchen he saw Kaiser. He had never seen Phillip look so dreadful. His suit was blood-stained and torn from the struggle with Henry. His meticulously shaped blond hair was wrecked, with tufts hanging over his forehead in crazed patterns. The welt on his neck looked like a giant strawberry oozing thick, dark liquid. But the eyes . . . his eyes had the same intensity and magnetism as always. He was still on mission.

A ten-foot-long wooden bar separated the kitchen from the dining room, where Kaiser was still standing near his father's corpse. It appeared the entire portion of the house behind Kaiser was fully engulfed in yellow flame. The heat and smoke watered Henry's eyes and staggered him.

Without a word, Kaiser lifted his shotgun and unleashed a barrage into the kitchen. Henry dove to the worn tiled floor in time to dodge the pellets as they ripped through the cabinets and plaster walls. He kept the grip on his own gun, ready to reciprocate. Kaiser's shotgun roared again, this time destroying the facing of the refrigerator and shattering the storm door's glass.

Pieces of Henry's history lay all around him. He struggled to contain his emotions, which shifted moment to moment from anger to sadness to fear for his family, and back to anger. Realizing Kaiser would need time to reload after two shots, Henry bounced from the floor into the air and fired wildly several times in Kaiser's direction.

***

Kaiser hit the floor hard when one of Henry's missiles made an impact. His left shoulder burned and Kaiser grunted as he crawled to take cover behind the bar. The heat and smoke from the fire he created was growing unbearable. Soon he would lose consciousness, and all of his grand designs would be lost.

Kaiser managed to load in two new shells and lock the barrels back into place. He stopped and listened for a moment. Above the roar of the fire he could hear police sirens. They were moments from arriving.

Kaiser shouted, "Henry, my dear brother, I regret to say our time together is at an end. Bravo to you. I never believed I would meet my equal in this fight, but you have proven me wrong. Farewell!" He fired another shot into the kitchen, then jumped to his feet and sprinted down a flaming hallway toward the steps to the basement.

***

Henry, who had crawled to the side of the bar and was inches from successfully sneaking around the side, saw the move and fired two more shots as Kaiser fled. He knew this house better than anyone, and he immediately realized where Kaiser was heading.

He turned and exited through the storm door and back onto the breezeway. There was only one door leading outside from the basement, and Henry could have found it blindfolded. He stepped off the breezeway toward the backyard and marveled at the hole in the earth where the garage used to sit. The C-4 had ripped the structure off its foundation and sent it flying in all directions like a million tiny meteors.

Henry jogged right, down the hill toward the basement door. Kaiser presumably had not entered the basement until now, and it would take him some time to find the exit. Henry set himself up behind a short, bricked flower bed where he had once helped his grandmother water her daisies. Now, it would make a suitable shield for dodging bullets.

***

Kaiser, whose left calf was struck and bleeding from one of Henry's last shots, limped down the stairs and felt around for a light switch. He found it, but nothing happened. The fire had already destroyed the electrical systems of the house. The cool and relatively clear air of the basement was an instant relief, and Kaiser took a few seconds to breathe it in before moving on.

Moving into an unfinished portion, Kaiser finally saw a faint light shining through the glass on a wooden door a few feet away. He staggered over and tried the knob, but found it locked. There was no time to search for a key, especially in the dark. He stepped back and fired a shot, peppering the door with holes and weakening the old lock. With one kick below the knob, the door swung open and revealed the peaceful darkness of the side yard and the forest beyond.

***

Henry watched from a few feet away, crouched behind the flower bed in perfect firing position. He held the pistol with both hands after realizing the power of the weapon in his first attempts at firing it. He heard the impact of Kaiser's shot to the door, then saw Kaiser kicking it open and emerging in the doorway. Henry stood up, keeping the gun trained on Kaiser's chest.

"It's over, Phillip. Put the gun down. I'm willing to kill you, you know that. But I don't want to. You make the choice."

The house burned brightly above their heads, and that light was now joined by the red and blue flashes of police cars and firetrucks that were flooding the scene. Now he really could turn the situation over to the police, but Henry didn't want to.

Still holding the shotgun, Kaiser turned his body to face his nemesis for the last time.

"Perhaps I should have known better than to attempt to best you on such familiar turf. Again, bravo. We both know how this must end. One of us, if not both, must die. I am prepared for such an eventuality. The question is, are you? Are you prepared to die, Henry?"

With a blitzkrieg movement, Kaiser lifted the shotgun and fired at Henry in a fraction of a second. But there was no overwhelming blast of sound. No spray of metal that would rip Henry's flesh along with the brittle brick of the flower bed. There was only a click.

Kaiser looked down at his useless weapon and smiled. Henry blinked and numbly acknowledged to himself how close he had just come to death. He began to walk forward toward Kaiser, who dropped the shotgun and put his hands in the air.

"What was the mythical phrase from Ferguson? Ah, yes. Hands up, don't shoot! Well, Henry, what are you waiting for?"

Henry's finger squeezed ever tighter on the trigger, ready to end Kaiser's life and this ordeal for good. Still, something held him back. He had never taken a life, though he almost had in an episode at the Ravens' lair that felt like months ago. He remembered how it felt sticking that knife into his ribs, seeing the pain and fear well up in his victim's face. He remembered how much he liked it, though he didn't want to admit it. Kaiser had done that to him. If he killed Kaiser now, would there be a way back to a normal life? Was it already too late?

Kaiser bent down to pick up the shotgun. With his right hand, he calmly reached into his jacket pocket and found his last two shells. He cracked open the weapon and prepared to load them.

"No, Henry. There's no running away from this. No letting the police finish your work for you. This is your business, and yours alone. You must kill me, Henry. Consider this our Colosseum, and we are gladiators. You have me pinned to the dirt, your sword's blade at my throat. If you allow me to recover, I won't hesitate" He loaded one shell into the chamber.

"I thought you were special. Together, I believed we would create real and lasting change in this country. Tonight was only a sample of what we could have accomplished. Perhaps I was wrong. Maybe you're just one of the billions who don't matter and won't ever make a difference," Kaiser continued, then loaded the second shell.

"I won't ever stop, Henry. I may not survive this, but we both know my cause lives on. Someone, some brave and intrepid spirit, will pick up where The Ravens left off. The hate and resentment in America is a tangible, pliable material. It can be molded. I have proven that tonight. But, enough of that. Time to discover what lies inside of you." Kaiser snapped the shotgun closed.

Four blistering cracks rang out, muffled by the sound of the raging fire above them. Kaiser drifted backward, his back striking the door frame. Henry stood motionless, holding the pose and watching the enemy struggle. Kaiser wriggled on the ground. All four bullets had found their mark.

In only a few seconds, Kaiser's movements ceased. Moments later, numerous police officers appeared from both the front and back of the house. They streamed down the hill with weapons drawn.

Henry threw down the pistol and instinctively raised his hands into the air. He was convinced they would throw cuffs on him and charge him with murder. Instead, one of the officers, a Posey County sheriff, approached him and explained they were there to help. Thankfully, they had been apprised of the situation and knew who he was.

Henry nodded understanding, then stumbled to the front of the house and began to ascend the steep hill. His legs refused to cooperate and left him on his knees in the yard. Carrie and the others ran toward him, crying and shouting. Carrie embraced him and kissed him hard, leaving Henry breathless and giddy with release.

The nightmare was over.

Chapter Twenty-Seven

Wednesday, June 1; Deaconess Hospital; Evansville, Indiana

"What's up, family?" Ty asked in his high-pitched joking voice. He entered Henry's hospital room, followed by Deja. They found Henry wearing a fresh pair of khaki cargo shorts and a Cardinals T-shirt, packing up a plastic Personal Items bag provided by the hospital.

"Nuttin' much, pal. Just trying to make sure I can leave as soon as they bring the papers. It's been over two hours since they gave me the green light."

Ty, Deja, Carrie, David, and Henry had all spent at least one night as patients in the last three days. Incredibly, Deja was treated only for a sprained ankle. Carrie had minor lacerations on her wrists and ankles from the zip-ties The Ravens had used on them. David required a bit more care because of dehydration and a busted ear drum from the explosion. However, they all considered it a miracle their injuries were what you might suffer during a raucous outdoor concert.

Ty sported a variety of cuts, bruises, lumps, and scrapes from his wild night of roof jumping and yard wrestling. His right knee was in a brace, thanks to a sprained ACL. Regardless, Ty was in an exceptionally bright mood.

"So, where we headed, big dog? We doing some KFC? Maybe a little Cracker Barrel? What are you thinking, Hankster?"

"I was thinking home, to sleep for a few days. They wake you up every damn hour to check this and that, not to mention all the friggin' cops who have been in and out of here."

"Sleep later, food now! We haven't had a chance to celebrate yet, my man." He slipped behind Henry and began massaging his shoulders like a boxing trainer.

"All right, all right. You got it. But I'm feeling Mexican."

"Nice! That's my boy. I see a beautiful golden beef chimichanga in my future. What about you, Dee?"

She grinned and looked up from her Samsung Galaxy phone. "Black bean quesadilla for me. But who's buying?"

Henry and Ty looked at one another and broke into laughter. Henry responded, "It's on me. And every meal is on me. For life. You two. I can't . . . there's no way to express how thankful I am. I owe you two everything. I'm serious. You need anything ever, you call me."

Henry began to choke up as he put a hand on Ty's shoulder. Ty broke the seriousness of the moment by doing his version of Eddie Murphy's *Beverly Hills Cop* laugh. Henry shook his head.

Deja gasped as she looked at her phone. "Oh my God, guys. Kessler . . ." She jumped up and turned on the TV. "It's over! They got him."

Evansville's Channel 14 News was reporting the story live not far from the scene. Kessler had managed to evade the police on the night of Kaiser's death, but had been located hiding out in an old farm house only five miles from Herman's property and had died in a shootout with police.

It was official: all four Ravens were dead. Ty and Henry exchanged a forceful high-five as they listened for more details. It seemed surreal to be at the end, with their mission complete and with everyone still alive. Henry sat down on the bed, thinking of all the different ways he and his family could have died over the last days and weeks. He had taken so many risks. He knew then it was going to take years to fully decompress.

A minute later, with the breaking news brief done, Henry looked at Deja. "You know, I never got to hear how you managed to get free from the garage. Ty said you were cool under pressure. I wish I could have seen it."

Deja blushed slightly at the compliment. "Oh, I have my methods. Actually it wasn't all that Houdini-esque. They left us in there with no supervision, so I scooted around until I found an old drill bit lying in a corner. It took a while, but I was able to saw through the plastic tie with it and get myself free. Once I had Carrie and David untied, I pulled the cord on the garage door opener to trigger a manual opening. I pulled up the door just far enough for us to squeeze under, then closed it. Simple as that."

"But where did you get that gun?" Ty asked.

"I took it off that dead Raven with his eye knocked out."

Henry slowly shook his head. "That's amazing. Again, I'm so glad I had you two there. I want you to know, if it had been the other way around and it was your relatives in danger, I would be there. Count on it."

"We know, brother. We know. Hopefully we'll never need you to return that favor. You and me, you know we just clicked from the very beginning. I had a feeling about you. I knew you were a solid dude when you faced up and told me about what Herman had done to my grandfather. That took some stones," Ty said.

"Trust me, I was shivering on the inside. Talk about awkward. So glad I did, though. You seriously are my brother from another mother."

"Right! We're like Mel Gibson and Danny Glover. Like Bruce Willis and the dude from *Family Matters*."

"Like Dan Aykroyd and Eddie Murphy in *Trading Places*," Henry chimed in.

"Sure, that too."

Deja rolled her eyes at both of them and returned to checking her emails.

***

That night, Henry and Carrie had eighty-six messages waiting on their landline answering machine. A few of them were calls from neighbors with congrats and well wishes. Several others were from law enforcement agencies needing to clarify a few details from the statements they gave during their hospital stay. The majority of the messages were from media outlets of every variety from NBC's *Today Show* to NPR to *Time Magazine*. They all wanted Henry's story.

There were also five messages from publishers offering him advances larger than his yearly teacher salary to tell his story in detail. Henry was overwhelmed listening to the voices representing America's largest and best known media outlets, all begging him to fill up their air waves and empty pages.

There would be time for all of that later. Henry pulled the plug on their landline, turned his and Carrie's cellphones off, and curled up in bed with his beautiful wife and son. He thought he might never leave the bedroom again, as long as they were there with him.

As David slept between them, Carrie and Henry lay facing each other, staring into each other's eyes and thanking God they were together again.

It would be a long road ahead to normalcy. David's hearing might never fully recover. Henry would need counseling for post-traumatic stress. He knew he would still be seeing that man's face, the one he had narrowly avoided murdering, for the rest of his life. He would hear Kaiser's voice as well.

But there was also the voice of Herman Bowersox, the sage, to balance him when he needed it. That voice would be welcomed once again, now that the circle was closed. Henry had set out first to discover the truth, then to stop it from destroying him, his family, and countless others across the nation.

He had achieved that. No matter what phantoms would appear in his nightmares, Henry could rest knowing his family's legacy was secure.

Epilogue

Friday, July 8; Bowersox residence

Henry sat in his recliner as he watched the news coverage from Dallas unfold. Five police officers had been murdered in the street yesterday, with nine more injured. An African-American sniper, with a military background, appeared to be the culprit.

The nation was stunned, but not surprised, by the vicious attack. Racial violence had been on the upswing even before The Ravens pulled their antics and nearly launched a national race war. Kaiser had been correct on at least one point: the war would carry on long after his death. Perhaps it would never end.

Henry, who was in the midst of writing a memoir about his ordeal, called Ty and talked with his friend about yet another heartbreaking event. Their relationship had blossomed even more since their exit from the hospital. Each took turns driving to see the other on available weekends. David had even taken to calling him "Uncle Ty."

Their friendship was born from an act of hate that took place many years before either of them were born. On this day, when another act of hate was being broadcast to the world, Henry hoped that new friendships like theirs would spring up and eventually overshadow the evil. That could take years or even decades, but it was all they had to hold onto in that grim moment.

Since the media had first reported Henry's story, he had received thousands of Facebook messages and tweets from strangers all over the world. He estimated around five percent of them were hateful messages sent by racists who sympathized with Kaiser and his men. The other ninety-five were positive notes of thanks, congrats, and "atta-boys." His Twitter following had grown from around a hundred and fifty, many of those being former students, to over half a million. Their words of encouragement, and their stories of how they had been inspired by him to become more active in uniting their communities, were daily reminders of the good work that he and his friends had accomplished.

Henry didn't hate the attention, especially considering he was hoping to make enough money from his book to quit teaching, but it was a strange new reality for an average guy, in an average city, with an average career. In another month, he along with Ty and Deja were even going to Washington, D.C. for a meeting with President Obama.

He enjoyed being known, but the attention was beginning to wear on his family. A few death threats were enough to make him put their house up for sale and hire a small security firm to add some peace of mind.

While Deja shunned the new attention she was receiving, Ty soaked it in. Bored with his old existence, Ty used the spike in recognition to launch a new career: investigating race-based violent crimes. He was already in the process of obtaining his private investigator's license, as well as renting office space in downtown Nashville. He offered Henry a partnership, but Henry had seen enough violence to fill a lifetime.

Three days after the Dallas shootings, Henry awoke to find hundreds of comments on his Facebook and Twitter pages about the incident. Scrolling through, one Facebook post caught his attention.

Her name was Janet Mattingly.

"Hello, Henry. My daughter, Aleah, has been missing for months. We live in Vicarstown, so when I saw all of the coverage about you and those Ravens, I knew it had to be them. They took my little girl away from me. I'll never know for sure, but in my heart I'm convinced. Anyway, I wanted to thank you for what you did. You saved so many others from the heartache that I've had to go through. You're incredibly brave, and I hope you and your family are blessed by what you've done. God bless."

Henry sat in silence for a long time, reading and re-reading the comment. He vividly remembered seeing her face on the news and somehow knowing at the time it was the work of Kaiser.

Finally, after typing and re-typing his response, he sent his reply: "You'll see her again, Janet. And she'll be more beautiful than you remembered. Thank you for reaching out to me. Your words will stay with me forever. I will pray for healing for you and your family."

And he did pray. He prayed for Janet and the Mattingly family. He prayed for the loved ones of the slain Dallas police officers. And he prayed for his nation . . . for a way to mend the festering wounds from centuries of hate and distrust.

He said "Amen," then wiped the tears from his face.

The End

About Chad A. Cain

Chad A. Cain is a novelist and high school history teacher who resides in Mount Vernon, Indiana with his wife Heather. His first novel, One Night In October, was released by Solstice Publishing in April of 2015.

Social Media

Website: http://www.chadacain.com/

Twitter: https://twitter.com/ChadACain @chadacain

Facebook: https://www.facebook.com/chad.cain.771

Acknowledgements

I would like to thank John DeBoer for all of his wonderful work in the editing of this book. I couldn't have hand-picked a more thorough and professional editor to work with me. Your ideas and suggestions helped this story immeasurably, and pushed me to be a better writer. That's all an author can ask for. As you are fond of saying: cheers!

If you enjoyed this story, check out these other Solstice Publishing books by Chad A. Cain:

One Night in October

Fifteen years. That's how long Paul Gibson stayed away from his father, Johnny Ray, after he tried to wreck his son's wedding in an alcoholic stupor. But on this crisp late October night, Paul is coming back to his childhood home. He's got one final chance to reconcile with a dying father who devoted his life to whiskey and horse betting instead of his family.

Paul has chosen the night of game six of the 2011 World Series to face the man he has never understood or connected with. Their one chance at reuniting as a family is linked to their only shared memory: a love of St. Louis Cardinals baseball.

As they watch the Cardinals attempt to save their season against the Texas Rangers, Paul and Johnny Ray will rip open the wounds of the past and struggle to find a way beyond them. The grudges and fears of their past will resurface, but so will the forgotten need to accept and forgive.

One Night In October is a touching story of a father and son spending one final evening searching for a way to bridge a chasm built on years of anger and bitterness. The outcome for both their beloved Cardinals and their relationship will hang by a thread until the very end.

https://bookgoodies.com/a/B00VQSHN3M

www.ingramcontent.com/pod-product-compliance
Lightning Source LLC
Chambersburg PA
CBHW070443030726
47503CB00004B/867